Our Friend Jimmie

To order additional copies, please contact us.
BookSurge, LLC
www.booksurge.com
1-866-308-6235
orders@booksurge.com

Our Friend Jimmie

James D. Sweat

2006

Our Friend Jimmie

There were many people who helped during the writing of my book. First and foremost, I'd like to thank my best friend and wife Terri for chaining me to the computer and cajoling me (never once used the word nag) to work on the book on days when I came up with a ton of other interesting and fun things to do (Braves games, happy hour, like that).

I owe a great deal of gratitude to my brother Lynn and sister-in-law Cindi, who were my biggest cheerleaders in the early days. Also helping tremendously were: my editor Rebecca (now in therapy); Lindsay the drill instructor who kept everything moving; Julie who worked endlessly on the cool cover design; Jorge, John and Charlie who encouraged me at FPC-Jesup; Billy who discovered I really am a writer.

Last, but certainly not least, my thanks to bartenders around the world who allowed me to do forty years worth of research for this book.

FORWARD

The flight was long and he was tired. He shook his head, thinking it didn't take much to wear him out anymore. Once your body failed you and the process started, endurance was a thing of the past.

"Could be worse," he grunted, shaking his head. At least there wasn't a lot of joking around, passengers playing grab-ass this early in the morning. The flight attendants hadn't started the cheerleader crap, fake smiles, repeating the same drivel over and over again. It suited him; once a garrulous man, he now preferred the quiet. He lay back and took a nap.

***

Landing in Fort Lauderdale and not wanting to stand unnecessarily, he waited until most of his fellow passengers had deplaned and pulled his cancer-wasted body out into the aisle, slowly walking through the plane and cabin door and down the ramp into the terminal.

He spotted his friend, who waved him over. His friend, a short, fat man, was sweating in the South Florida heat. The friend asked, "Good flight?"

"A flight's a flight," the thin man said. "You get on a tube and sit next to some other asshole for a couple hours. If you land, it's a good flight." He looked at the fat man and asked, "What's with the small talk? You a talk show host now?"

The fat man frowned as they walked through the terminal. "I'll let it go. You aren't feeling well. Lost some more weight, didn't ya'?"

"You didn't." The reference to his friend's obesity wasn't called for and the thin man felt bad about it. "I'm sorry." The fat man nodded acceptance and he continued, "Yeah, lost some more weight. It's what happens when you're dyin'. Ya' lose weight." He noticed the look on his friend's face and said, "Listen, I got a bunch of things to do and not much time."

Outside the airport the fat man said, "Lemme' get the car. We'll meet Don and get you all set up for seeing Betty and Dotty. I'll tell Don to rush it. Get everything ready to sign and we'll get it over with quick." The fat man was dialing on his cell as he walked away.

The dying man stood on the curb at passenger pickup, waiting on the fat man. Twice he had to go into his pocket for a handkerchief. Florida was hot. Nice clear day, but the humidity was high. His shirt was already sticking to his back.

In minutes his friend was back with the car and the thin man asked, "This guy far?"

The fat man said, "Twenty minutes or so." He noticed the frown on his friend's face. "Ain't New York. Got to drive to get around here, spread out like it is. Told him we'd meet him at his house and do the paperwork."

"He lives here? Florida?"

The fat man said, "Part time. Lives in the city mostly. Not far from your place in Battery Park. Got an office in the Towers."

It was silent in the car as they drove on the busy expressway to Davie, Florida. The air-conditioning was on full to combat the midday Florida heat. Its humming was the only sound as they passed pine trees and billboards. It was obvious his friend didn't feel like talking and the fat man didn't push it.

As they got off the expressway at the Davie exit, the thin man said, "Good! The lawyer lives in Davie. That's where the home is. Crestwood Adult Community."

"Yeah," said the fat man. "I thought you'd like that. Makes it easy, no?"

"Can this guy be trusted?"

The fat man said, "As much as any fuckin' lawyer. Besides, you got me lookin' out for 'em. Ain't gonna be no problems."

They pulled into the drive of a large home in a fashionable, tree-lined neighborhood. All the lawns were well manicured and professionally landscaped.

The fat man said, "This is it. Guy has a little money, no?"

"Hope it ain't from stealin'." The fat man frowned and the thin man added, "Always hated the burgs." He got out of the car and took in the surroundings. It was actually pleasant, but his mood wouldn't let him comment on it. Reminded him of the neighborhood in "Leave it to Beaver."

"Gotta' admit," said the fat man, "Nice and quiet."

"Suburbia! Whoop-ti-do! How can people live like this, all wide open? Give me the city anytime."

They walked a gravel pathway up to the front door and the door opened.

"Nice seeing you guys," said a six-footer with jet-black hair. His hair was too dark to be natural. With a big, white toothy smile, the man said, "I'm Don Greer." Shaking hands with the thin man, he asked, "Did you have a nice flight?" Greer was lean, wearing Dockers with a pullover shirt, shoes and no socks.

The fat man winced at the question, but the thin man answered less gruffly than earlier. "Yeah, it was fine." He stared, sizing Greer up. Looked like a guy in a catalogue.

Greer rubbed his hands together, smiling even brighter. "Who's ready for a tour of my hacienda?" Neither man spoke and, still smiling, Greer said, "Perhaps later. Let's go in my office." He motioned for them to follow him.

They walked into a spacious, indirectly lit office and Greer sat behind an antique desk. He motioned for them to take the two large, over-stuffed leather chairs across from him. "Anyone for coffee, perhaps a cold drink?" Taking their orders, he spoke into an intercom.

The drinks were delivered and after the maid left the thin man said, "I'm told you're the guy that can help me. Has everything been explained to you?" Greer nodded and he added, "You know about the money out of the country? The three mill?"

Greer answered, "Yes. It causes a little problem, nothing insurmountable." He waved it off as if it were a fly. "You also have funds in the country I'm told?"

"Some, a couple hundred thou' in the bank. Sell my bar and apartment there will be more. Made a little in the market. Put it in CDs at MBNA."

"Guy's a genius in the market, Don," said the fat man, gesturing toward his friend. "Maybe we can get some tips?"

Greer brightened and started to speak, but the thin man cut him off and said, "Fellas', if you don't mind, let's dispense with the smoke blowin'." He looked at both of them to show he meant it. "Mr. Greer, I heard you had everything ready for me to sign?"

"It's Don, please." He hesitated, but his visitor said nothing. "All set. Need your signature and account number and name of the bank for the overseas account." Greer pushed a folder across the desk. "The documents are fairly straightforward. Standard Power of Attorney for each separate account here in the U.S. Next to last is the inclusion of myself on your overseas account."

The thin man cut him off and said, "I'll read 'em." He went through each set of documents, reading them slowly as Greer and the fat man made nervous conversation. On the last document, he looked up, a scowl on his face. "The fuck is this? A blank page? You want me to sign a blank page?"

"It's nothing." Greer coughed and continued, "I find that even with care, there is always something forgotten. Purely a contingency. People always forget something." His visitor did not speak and Greer decided not to push it. "If you'd prefer, don't sign it."

"Jesus, but you're a hard-on," said the fat man, staring at the thin man. "You're embarassin' me here." He talked with his hands, the Italian gene pool at work. "Fuck you tryin' to say? I'm gonna' rob you. Jesus Christ! Bustin' my balls all day and I'm helpin' him," the fat man said, looking at Greer and gesturing to his friend.

The thin man gazed intently at Greer, ignoring the fat man's bluster. He said, pointing toward the fat man, "Guy's a fuckin' bookie and comin' across like St. Theresa." The room was silent. Rubbing his head, he said, "I'll sign it, but don't even think about fuckin' me." For emphasis he added, "Understand?" Greer didn't say anything, choosing to stare at the floor. "Look at me." Greer returned his gaze. "Understand?" Greer nodded. The thin man turned slowly from Greer to the fat man, "Understand?" The office was silent as the fat man nodded.

***

The ride back to the airport was quiet. At the passenger drop-off point, the thin man said, "Listen, you're tryin' to help and I know it. Maybe I was a bit harsh back there."

The fat man guffawed, "A bit. You fuckin' talk to me like I'm robbin' ya' or somethin'. Tryin' to help, goin' out of my way and that's the thanks I get. Who fuckin' needs it?" A horn sounded behind their double parked car and the fat man stuck his head out of the window and yelled, "Do it again and it's goin' up yer' ass." Turning back to the thin man he said, "And ya' made me look bad, like a fuckin' kid, in front of the friggin' lawyer. Jesus!"

"Hey, I said I'm sorry. You want blood?" The fat man didn't respond and the thin man asked, "When you comin' back to the city?"

"Got some kind a' deal in Jacksonville with my nephew."

The thin man choked back a laugh. "Your nephew is an idiot. Don't let him get ya' in trouble." The fat man smiled. "When ya' get back we'll have dinner."

Smiling, the fat man sad, "You're on. Go catch your flight."

After his passenger left, the fat man called the attorney and said, "The fuck you tryin' to do? Blank page?"

"It's normal," explained the attorney.

"Ya' almost fucked up the deal with this 'normal' bullshit. Acted like you was gonna' piss your pants."

The attorney said, "Guy scares me."

The fat man laughed, "Ya' scared of a dead man? Maybe I got the wrong partner. Can't be no easier. He fuckin' dies and we dole out some money to his wife and the retard. No fuckin' way they can use it all. We steal the rest of his money. Capice?" Point made, he hung up his cell.

CHAPTER ONE

Jimmie poured the coffee carefully, then put the pot on the tray with the cups. He looked around the large kitchen making sure he hadn't forgotten anything. He picked up the tray, took two steps toward the door and stopped. "Forgot the friggin' sweetener." He put the tray down and searched the kitchen for the bowl of packaged sweetener. He couldn't find it and settled for the box. He carefully placed it on the tray next to the rose in a vase. He'd picked up the rose from a florist last night.

He shrugged. The box didn't help his presentation. Frowning, he said, "It'll have to do. What the hell? I ain't Martha Stewart." He took a final look around the kitchen. He knew something was still missing.

"Fuckin' spoon," he said, grabbing one out of the drawer. It was a soup spoon, not a teaspoon, but he was just going to stir with it.

Jimmie was first generation Irish with the standard ruddy complexion. He was well over six feet tall and a big-boned two hundred thirty pounds. At fifty-four, Jimmie still had great hair; thick, white and combed straight back in one of those 'I don't have to do much to it' styles. He worked out regularly and always had a tan, at least a tan for an Irishman. A machine job for the most part but it looked real.

Now, his arms fully loaded, he walked carefully from the kitchen and up the stairs of his townhouse, heading toward the bedroom. He narrowly missed the chair trolley he'd recently installed on the stairs for his wife. His close call caused him to spill a little of the coffee in the tray.

"Damn it," he said out loud. He went back to the kitchen to get something to wipe the coffee. Mopping it up with a drying towel, he threw the towel back on the counter.

The second time up he was careful and made it to the bedroom without further incident. He pushed the door open with his foot and entered the room, saying, "Happy Anniversary, Betty."

His wife, awakened, smiled up at him. "Happy Anniversary to you too, darling. I can't believe you still remember after all these years."

He put the tray down and sat on the bed. "Only thirty-seven! Who wouldn't remember? Think I'm that fat guy married to the blue-haired woman on the TV cartoon, friggin' Homer what's his name?"

She laughed. "No, I didn't mean to imply you were Homer Simpson. Would've been a half-eaten donut on the tray if you were."

Thinking she was hinting about donuts, he said, "Is that a trick question?" She laughed. "Kind a' like 'do you think I'm gaining weight?'"

She said, "You are losin' weight, Jimmie."

"It's that diet Lou and I are on. One where you jus' eat meat and piss on these little strips they give you."

She laughed. "How does eating meat and peeing on strips make you lose weight?"

He smiled. "Supposed to put your metabolism in some kind of mystical state. If the strips change color, the diets workin'. Hard to hit the wee things."

She laughed again, then frowned, the wrinkles gathering around her eyes. "The last years have been tough for you, haven't they?"

He took her hand. "Wouldn't trade for anything. I'd do it all over again, no changes."

"You're a liar and I love you for it." She squeezed his hand.

He laughed. "Remember when we met? So long ago? Me a kid, a stupid Mick, sneaking in from Canada, workin' at your Pa's store? You a teasin', young, sexy thing of sixteen?"

"I wouldn't call you a kid. Taught me a thing or two, sneaking off at night," she laughed, then turned serious. "James Collins, you know what I'm talking about. Don't change the subject. Getting near the end, darling." His wife had been diagnosed five years ago with multiple sclerosis and it was progressing quickly. She used a walker to get around from room to room and needed the chair lift to go floor to floor. "I worry about you and Dotty. What will happen to the both of you?"

He looked at her. What made her disability hard to take was the fact that her features hadn't changed much. She just didn't look sick. Her once lustrous blonde hair was gray-streaked, sure. If anything, her lack of movement had caused her to gain some weight. It would be easier to take if she looked sick. Betty didn't. She still had those piercing blue eyes. The eyes that never let him get away with much, and always caught him in a lie. Still had that beautiful smile that won his heart so many years ago. She just could not will her limbs to cooperate. Her doctor explained it to him, MS, but it was beyond his comprehension.

"Betty, I mean it. I wouldn't trade the years with you and Dotty for anything." He felt a familiar stirring in his loins and blushed. Damn, even sick she still had that affect on him. "Dotty and I will be just fine. And you aren't goin' anywhere for a long time."

Betty said, "You work so hard. I'd like to see you enjoy life." He started to speak and she waved his comment away. "Jimmie, it's been tough on you. With Dotty, now me! You work hard. You're a good man. You deserved better."

Dotty, thirty-seven years old, was their only child. Betty was pregnant with her when they married. Dotty was born retarded and had the mind of an eight year old. Betty, a staunch Catholic, blamed it on their premarital sex. But they both loved Dotty and had always taken care of her, and had not sent her off to an institution as some had suggested. Dotty would remain in their care until the day she, or they, died.

He leaned over and kissed her forehead. "Shush! I'm happy." He nuzzled her and said, "I think it's time we brought in someone." He saw her expression and said, "Not that you aren't still keepin' up. I'd rather you spend your time with Dotty and me. You've earned it. Let someone else clean the damned house."

She smiled. "You always know how to put things in a nice way. Full of the blarney, you are," she laughed. "Hire a maid. Life of leisure for me." She grabbed his hand and said, "I have literature on some places. You remember, the assisted living places. When are we going to sit down and discuss them?" He started to speak and she said, "Shush! Can't dodge it forever." She saw the hurt in his eyes and said, "Soon, Jimmie?" He nodded and she looked at the clock. "And where are you off to so early, Mr. Collins?"

"Got to meet a truck at the warehouse. Some of the boys got a load for the drive."

"See, that's another good thing about you, your toy drive. And don't think I don't know that they bring you more than toys sometimes." She smiled. "Be off, Mr. Collins. Say hello to Sal for me. It'd be nice if he weren't on TV so much. One hearing after another."

Jimmie said, "That's what he gets, hangin' around the 'Teflon Don.' Maybe his TV appearances will be fewer now that the public is startin' to forget Gotti." He laughed and kissed her. "I'll put in a couple of hours and open up the bar." They finished their coffee and he left for his warehouse on Canal Street.

***

Coming from Ireland and born poor, it only seemed natural to Jimmie that he should share his newfound wealth. Twenty years ago he'd started his 'Toys for the Wee Ones' campaign in New York. That it actually grew out of some of his shadier activities didn't bother Jimmie in the least.

Early on, after making his way to New York, he supplemented his legitimate income with small time robberies and truck hijackings. He had to. Medical costs for Dotty ate away his legitimate salary.

A friendly guy, he didn't confine his activities to any one particular group. He became acquainted with a wide assortment of young and up and coming Mafia members. Now some of the more ambitious of his friends were at or near the top. Jimmie knew them all.

One day Jimmie and his friends stumbled on the heist of their careers. They stole a load of bearer bonds from a Wall Street company specializing in courier deliveries. They netted, after fencing, a little over two million dollars each.

Jimmie took his share and bought a bar. He now had a legitimate and profitable occupation. Still, he kept his hand in with the Mafia. He helped other small-time crooks fence the merchandise they'd stolen. He specialized in goods he could sell at the bar, specifically booze and cigarettes. Occasionally he'd sell jewelry, furs and suits that came his way.

One day, two guys he knew well hijacked what they thought was a load of TVs. It turned out they'd taken the wrong truck and ended up with a shipment going to FAO Schwartz. Being the Christmas season, Jimmie took the load off their hands for a couple hundred dollars.

He then went to the Washington Heights section of New York dressed as Santa Claus and gave the toys out to kids on the street. His best friend, Sal Russo, went with him to help. They both enjoyed themselves.

Sal, a Capo in the Gambrelli family, put the word out to the other Mafia families the next year. Now the operation was so big that Jimmie accepted toys year round. Jimmie's warehouse covered half a block and was always jammed to the rafters with every toy imaginable. Of course, hidden well amongst the toys was an assortment of stolen merchandise waiting to be moved.

CHAPTER TWO

Jimmie caught a taxi from his Battery Park townhouse to Canal Street. It was already a beautiful day outside. He loved the early mornings. New York was coming to life, fresh and clean, to start another hard-fought day. His mood was excellent and he was whistling as he got out of the taxi and went into the warehouse.

"Good," he said, reaching the door and finding it unlocked. "Sal," he yelled, coming through the entrance.

"Yeah, Jimmie. Coffee's ready. Bring me one too."

Jimmie walked into the small, bare office with two beat up, government-issue metal desks and broken swivel chairs. The only thing that worked in the room was the Braun coffee maker. He got two cups out of the cabinet and filled both. In Sal's cup, he dumped four spoons of sugar and shook his head. His buddy had been shot several times in his Mafia career. Fucking sugar isn't going to kill him, Jimmie thought.

He carried their coffee back into the warehouse and found Sal sitting on a milk carton. He was sorting through the toys, separating them. His several piles represented the likely age groups of the kids that would be interested in them.

"How ya' doin', Sal?"

"Look what the cat drug in. Good afternoon, Mr. Collins." Sal was Jimmie's age, thin, six feet tall with dark, nicely cut hair and olive-tinted skin. "Nice of ya' to join us this afternoon."

Jimmie laughed, "The fuck you mean 'afternoon?' Told you I'd be here by eight. Ten till buddy."

"Fuck, I just about finished the load the fellas' brought in. Barbie dolls mostly. Don't nobody make trucks and shit anymore?" Sal was wearing a five-hundred-dollar Italian knit shirt, silk slacks probably running more than the shirt, no socks and expensive Italian loafers.

"You know, you gotta' give Gotti one thing, Sal. Fuckin' 'Goodfellas' dress much better now. Why don't you put on overalls or somethin' to do that shit? You're ruinin' your slacks." Jimmie knew how to piss Sal off. Just mention John Gotti. A lot of the old timers like Sal blamed Gotti for screwing up the Mafia with his 'Hollywood ways.'

"Don't get me started, Jimmie." Jimmie was laughing and Sal added, "Fuckin' Mick." He stood and they shadow-boxed a quick fifteen-second round. Then Sal hugged him and said, "How's Betty?"

"Getting worse." Jimmie was breathing hard after the short exertion.

Sal noticed and asked, "You okay?" Jimmie nodded and Sal said, "Getting' old, you fuckin' prick."

"Younger than you, ya' Guinea bastard."

Sal wasn't giving up easily. "A fuckin' month. Jesus, won't you ever let me forget it," he wailed. Pleading his case toward divinity, he looked up toward the roof.

Looking back at Jimmie he grew serious, "Thought about a home?" Sal sat back on the milk crate to take a break. "Fast Eddie's gotta' piece of one in Wayne." Noticing the sour look on Jimmie's face he said, "It's Jersey, but it ain't like Newark. They got flowers and shit. Fast Eddie has a couple of medical directors on the hook who write prescriptions for these heart monitors. Medicare lets the patients have heart monitors twice a year so you got all these patients walkin' around with broke cell phones taped to 'em s'posed to be heart monitors. Shit, he gets $70 a day for a week every six months." Jimmie had a pained expression on his face so Sal said, "Course Betty wouldn't have to wear one."

"It's not Jersey. Just that while I can take care of her, I want to keep her home."

"Bad fuckin' break Jimmie."

"That it is, Sal. Woman never harmed a fly, now this. She's on me to make a decision on a home. Says it ain't long now. Thinkin' this mornin' when I brought her coffee in bed…it's our anniversary, ya' know." Sal nodded. "She don't even look sick." A tear rolled down Jimmie's cheek and he turned away from Sal. Sal pretended not to notice, fighting one back himself.

He'd known Betty before he met Jimmie. He'd had a crush on her himself until Jimmie showed up.

They were interrupted by the front warehouse door opening with a bang. A large, red and white van with a moving company logo on it backed into the warehouse.

Sal said, "Louie Carmelotta, Jimmie. I told him you'd probably want to look at some stuff. Peter's with him, brought him over. Joey looked at the stuff. Good quality. Says the coats range from $2,500 to $10,000 retail, about half wholesale."

Joey Russo, Sal's brother, was considered the last word on the value of stolen property. Joey had connections in art, and with furriers and jewelers that he tapped into. A nod from Joey meant you could depend on authenticity. Joey, a childhood victim of polio, made up for his handicap by using his head. He was called 'the brain' on the street.

Sal asked, "Want to do it?"

"Fuck yeah," said Jimmie. "Change the labels."

Sal nodded as two men emerged from the van. An obese man with an open-necked shirt, chest hair spilling out the front, and the obligatory medallions and chains, yelled out, "S'up, Jimmie?" He danced around and threw a mock punch.

"It's all good, Petey. How ya' been?"

"Good bro'. Look at you slimmin' down. Gotta' write me down that strip pissin' diet." Pete Giotto, with his early morning garlic breath, hugged Jimmie. At six-and-a-half-feet tall and close to four hundred pounds, Pete's hugs were known to crack ribs. An enforcer for Sal and a regular at the bar, Jimmie loved the guy. At fifty-four, Petey was the same age as Jimmie and Sal. They'd grown up together. Petey had been Jimmie's first partner in his small-time crime group.

Petey, always smiling and laughing, said, "Man, look at all this shit," motioning toward the toys. "Gonna' be a good Christmas this year. Need some help?"

Sal took a sip of his coffee and said, "Petey start puttin' 'em on the shelves where it's marked. First stack is the under six year's old. Second is six to ten and that last stack, who the fuck knows?" Sal picked up a box, looked at it and turned to Jimmie, "What's an action figure doll, Jimmie?"

"An action figure doll?"

Sal turned the box toward Jimmie. "What it says."

"Maybe it's like a doll for boys," said Jimmie.

Pete asked, "You mean like for fag kids?"

"No," said Sal. "Fag kids play wid' girl dolls."

"Wouldn't jus' regular boys play wid' girl dolls? I used to undress my sisters' dolls all a' time. See if they had tits and a pussy."

"Jesus, Petey," yelled Sal. "Undressin' fuckin' dolls?"

Jimmie saw the hurt look on Petey's face and said, "Petey, you ain't gotta' take this shit. Come in with me at the bar. Twenty percent, no... make it twenty-five percent and no stealin' from the register. You ain't even got to take no blood oath or whatever it is you guys do now."

"Ten percent and I steal from the register." Seeing Jimmie's look, he modified it. "Only during Happy Hour, Jimmie."

Jimmie gave him the finger and said, "Probably right, Petey, about fag boys."

Petey nodded and said, "Makes sense they'd play with fuckin' boy dolls. What you think, Sal?"

"I don't fuckin' know, Petey," said Sal. "I don't make the toy rules and I ain't a fag. Where you want 'em Jimmie?"

Jimmie thought for a second. "Shit, just mix 'em in with the rest. I don't know shit about it either. Action fuckin' figures could be anything. Don't want to get no kid started in the wrong direction. When we give 'em out and a kid looks unhappy, give 'em somethin' else. No questions asked."

"Hey Sal, what kind a' dolls does a little lesbian girl play with?" asked Pete, laughing.

"Fuck you, Petey," said Sal, trying to be stern, then laughing. Pete was a guy you couldn't be mad at. Not for long, anyway. He was like a big kid unless he was after your ass. There was nothing funny about Petey then.

The other man with Petey stepped forward and introduced himself. "Eddie Silvano. Nice to meet ya', Jimmie. Sal said you might be interested in some furs. Got a good collection."

Jimmie asked, "Shit ain't gonna' hurt my hands, is it?"

"Naw, ain't that hot. Not around here, anyway. Came from somewhere in Virginia, like Richmond or Atlanta."

"Guy okay, Sal?" Sal nodded, the nod meaning he was fully responsible for Eddie. "Let's go look at 'em."

The way Sal and Jimmie played it, Sal would bring him stuff, telling whoever had stole it that he'd get top dollar from Jimmie. Sal would tell them he'd get them between fifteen and twenty percent wholesale. Jimmie would offer ten and Sal would help the guy out by getting Jimmie to up his offer to twelve.

Sal had a sweatshop where the labels were changed on the garments. Sammie Yan, also a childhood friend of both of them, ran it for Sal.

Jimmie saw the little side business as a perk for his bar patrons. He'd unload the coats for half of what the retail price was. He'd then split a tidy profit with Sal. Both would throw a percentage in the kitty to cover the Christmas costs.

Jimmie would drive a psychiatrist crazy trying to buttonhole him. He'd shrug, if asked, and say nobody is completely good or bad. Financing his charity event with ill-gotten gains seemed logical to him. A religious man, Jimmie saw it as a hedge. Maybe the charity erased some of the bad stuff he'd done. He figured at least the decision between heaven or hell would go to arbitration. Being Irish, and having the gift of gab, Jimmie knew he could plead his case. If he got a chance to talk, he figured his odds were far better than fifty-fifty.

CHAPTER THREE

Nathan Melton was a big man. At just a tick under six-feet, four-inches tall, he was close to his old NFL playing weight at two—hundred—forty-five pounds. His waist, however, at fifty-years old, was six inches larger than when he played. He figured it gave him character. It was easier than dieting, the character thing. He often explained his weight, to anyone who would listen, as a product of his Germanic/Irish heritage: beer, potatoes, whatever dumplings were made from and creamy gravies.

Recruited away from his post as a senior retail executive by a large venture capital group, Nathan relocated to New York from Atlanta. His job was to build a startup retail site on the Internet.

He bought an apartment on West 57th Street, close to his office on East 53rd. He loved the area and his new home and spent time having it decorated. Even bought a big screen TV. He subscribed to Direct TV and bought every sports package available. He called his brother and had him fly his dog to New York, now that he was out of the hotel and had his own place.

Chucky, his indeterminate-aged Chihuahua, was not the best of company. Nathan came across Chucky one night in Atlanta. The dog was begging outside a convenience store, and when asked, the clerk told him he was a stray. Nathan took pity on him. He picked him up, took him to the vet and paid just under three hundred dollars for shots.

He discovered quickly that Chucky wasn't a good New York dog. The beast had the nasty habit of wagging his tail at strangers. When they tried to pet him, Chucky would bite the hell out of them. Chucky was cunning, and not friendly in the least.

Working sixteen to eighteen hour days wasn't conducive to a social life, but Nathan didn't really know where to go in New York. He'd talked about his dilemma with the two guys who financed the operation through venture capitalists. They were nice guys and suggested places they'd heard of or read about in the New Yorker. To be fair, one was married with a large family. The other was gay. So their selections were a bit clouded. Somewhere between Fire Island and Chuck E. Cheese. None of them were for Nathan.

He'd tried some places on his own, supposedly trendy fern bars, a meaningless New York term. They weren't for him, but he'd discovered some really interesting uses for leather.

He ran an ad in the personals section of the New Yorker and that didn't go well either. The responses ran the gamut of severely eccentric to mass amounts of excess baggage. A few never returned his email of interest. A few were prostitutes. Most used pictures other than their own, or lied in their ads. So did he, of course, but that was beside the point.

There were a few good ones, but they were equally divided. The women he liked, didn't like him. The ones that liked him, he didn't like. It was a vicious circle. His efforts so far had disproved the old saying 'Beauty is only a light switch away.'

He discovered in New York that doormen know everything. Not nearly everything, everything! So, coming home from work one day, he asked his doorman. "Whitey, I'm interested in female companionship. Where do I go to find professional women? Around here?" It was important for Nathan to discover a spot close to home or work, as he was known to get lost easily.

"Fuck, 11B, should'a said somethin'," said Whitey, a short, thin white man with a three-day beard growth. "What kind ya' like? Gimme' an hour and I'll send somethin' up." He had his hand out, so Nathan gave him a ten. Everything the doormen did in New York was a ten. Get a FedEx, ten. Let the phone man in, ten. Deliveries, ten. Everything was a ten except Christmas. Then it was based on how high up your floor was, a hundred a floor. It was like a union in New York.

"No. I mean a place to go. Meet some women. Real women." Whitey was staring so he threw that in. He'd discovered that in New York, everything wasn't as it seemed. "Somebody nice, wearing a business suit." Nathan loved professional women.

"Fuck, 11B, they'll dress however you want 'em to. Just tell me what kind a' costume you want. Girl scout, nurse, squaw, astronaut, how old, like that?"

A voice came from the front entrance, "Yo man, I can take care a' all yo' problems. Jus' tell Uncle Rodney."

Rodney was the nighttime doorman. He was a young black man in his twenties. Sometimes a little too helpful, Rodney had his moments. He had found Nathan a Korean grocer that sold and delivered Michelob.

Nathan, getting a little exasperated, said, "I want a nice bar where I can pick up straight women. You know, coming home from work, stopping for a drink, stuff like that? Just regular women."

Whitey said, "Should a' said somethin'."

"I did," said Nathan. "Been tryin' to tell you."

"Damn, 11B, you lookin' ta' get married?" Whitey said, "Remember one thing, 11B, no matter how good they look, some other guy is sick and tired a' puttin' up with their shit. Go to Hooters on 7th. Be better off."

Nathan said, "Nothing against waitresses, but I'm looking for a bit more upstairs."

Whitey harrumphed. "They got big-tit waitresses in Hooters. Why they call it Hooters. 11B, you ain't in Podunk no more. In the apple now, brother."

"That ain't what he means, Whitey," said Rodney. "Man talkin' bout like a secretary and shit. You know, like clerks and stuff. Stockbrokers, brief cases, lawyers. Got clean gigs. Office workin' types!"

Rodney had his hand out and Nathan gave him a five. Fuck him, thought Nathan. Let him earn it. "Tell ya' what, go to Mindy's, 54th and 6th. Nice place. Hit Julian's on 55th, nice after work crowd." Nathan gave him another five and started for the door. "Yo man, you in da' big city now. Get shot down at one place, get the hell out. Women like animals. They can smell blood." He could see Nathan did not understand. "Don't try anybody else in a place where ya' been shot down. Women don't want nobody else's hand me downs, dig?" Nathan still didn't understand and Rodney said, "You ain't good enough for the bitch across the room, you ain't good enough for dey ass. Know what I mean?" Nathan still looked confused so he added, "Damn, 11B, try harder to follow. Dis' ain't no foreign language or nuttin'." He looked at Whitey, shaking his head. "Nigga', puh-lease!"

As Nathan was leaving, Whitey said to Rodney, "Motherfuckah should have a sign over his mirror says 'No wonder you always go home alone.'" They laughed, high-fiving.

***

Nathan walked the couple of blocks to 54th and entered Mindy's. It was furthest from his home and he operated on the 'work back' theory. The bar was almost completely dark and country music was blaring. He grimaced and walked in. He hated country music—that twang, the depressing stories, fuck. It always reminded him of the Jerry Springer Show.

He ordered a Michelob but the bartender didn't have any. No Coors either! He ordered a Bud for the hell of it and the bartender suggested a Sapporo. He nodded and looked around as his eyes adjusted. Hanging plants were all over the place. "So this is a regular New York bar," he muttered. "Fuck! I'm goin' to have to make a road trip."

Most of the patrons were dressed in western garb and he wondered where in the hell they bought it. When they started line dancing, he headed for the door, throwing a twenty on the bar for that lovely, refreshing Sapporo. He mumbled, "Jap beer in a friggin' country and western bar. Only in New York."

"Julian's can't be this bad," he said, walking the block to Julian's. He reached in his pocket for his breath freshener to take the Sapporo taste out of his mouth.

Some great-looking women were walking down the sidewalk and he enjoyed the eye candy before entering. You see great looking women on the sidewalks, where do they go? Damn sure not where he'd been.

Julian's was also very dark, but the choice of music was much better. Straight top forty and a little elevator mixed in. He sat at the bar and went through a litany of American beer they didn't have.

Finally, the bartender said, "Micro brewery man. I can give you something close to a Mick?" Nathan nodded and the bartender gave him something called a 'Midtown Moonie' He tasted it and it was okay.

"Not from around here?" the bartender asked.

"Just moved from Atlanta. Live a couple of blocks over." He had to yell over the crowd noise. "Let me ask you a question. There any regular bars around here?"

"Man, you upscale. Got to go across water, like Brooklyn, or Queens where I'm from, to find a regular bar. Even Jersey, though they're a little weird." He noticed Nathan's puzzled look, "Inbreeding!"

Nathan nodded, understanding. "So no regular people around here?"

"These people," he said, motioning toward the crowd, "are irregular."

"I noticed. They like these places, huh?"

"Read about 'em in magazines. Think they're 'in.' Least that's what the magazine says. Follow the crowd like the Eveready Bunny. You lookin' to get laid or drink? Places like this are good for gettin' laid. Ain't worth a shit for drinkin'. Too fu fu."

"Laid would be nice."

"Man or woman?" He noticed Nathan's look and said, "Sorry. Around here, you got to ask. For women you got to put up with this shit."

"Jackin' off ain't that bad."

The bartender laughed and said, "You a golfer?"

"Hate the game. Terminology is too goofy."

The bartender asks, "What do ya' mean?"

Nathan said, "TV commentators are sayin' look at the size of his putter, shaft's all bent, lift your head and spread your legs, nice stroke, he needs to wash his balls. I end up laughin'. I like the shirts. Pants make me look fat."

The bartender laughed and said, "Got a joke for you, a golf joke. Two older folks got married. They are lying in bed in the honeymoon suite staring at the ceiling after making love. Guy leans over and says, "I got a confession. I think the world of you, but golf is my passion, my first love." They stare at the ceiling for a bit and the woman says, "While we are baring our souls, I also have a confession. I've been a hooker all my life." The guy jumps out of bed, looks at her a moment and says, "Have you tried widening your stance and adjusting your grip?"

Someone yelled from across the bar, "You serving drinks or trying to pick somebody up?"

The bartender left after rolling his eyes in a "see what I mean" gesture and Nathan eyed the crowd. Instead of western garb, everyone here was in black, some going as far as wearing trench coats in summer to accentuate their black outfits. Nathan laughed and the bartender, back from delivering an order, looked at him questioningly. Nathan shook his head.

A couple of minutes into his beer, the bartender set another in front of him, saying it was from a woman across the bar.

He asked who and the busy bartender told him, "Lady in black."

Nathan smiled across the room at the sea of black and a lady waved him over. "Much better," he muttered as he picked up his beer and went to the other side of the bar to meet her.

He thanked a mid-forties, medium height woman named Lucinda and introduced himself. He noticed she had black lipstick and nails to match. "Like your outfit."

"Thank you," she said. "Why are you dressed so straight?"

"Just came from work," he answered, like he didn't have the time to stop and put on a Halloween costume.

"You're cute. Come here a lot? First time I've seen you."

"First time I've been in," said Nathan. He was horny and black was starting to look good.

"Oh shit, there's Don," she said. Nathan was looking toward the entrance when she gave him a business card with her home number on it.

"Who's Don?"

"My fucking husband. Call me," she said, as she walked across the bar, hugging a guy in all black.

"Fuck me runnin'," he said, pissed, going out the door as couples stared at him.

Sitting a couple of tables away, a group of women were winding down after work. A tall blonde look-a-like for the girl from Friends eyed the blonde next to her. "Jeez, Terri, you using your x-ray vision on that guy?"

"What? Jus' lookin' at the guy. Shame he left."

Laughing, she said, "Terri, friends don't let friends take home ugly men."

"I thought he was kind of cute."

"He's a hick," she laughed. "You 'bout ready to mount up again?" She was referring to Terri's break-up six months ago.

"Are you crazy, Gail?" Terri asked. "Now that food has replaced sex in my life, I can't even get into my own pants."

Gail laughed. "Being miserable because of a bad relationship means the other person was right. Roger was handy to have around, right? I mean, things break, bugs appear."

"Roger? Guy had two tools, WD 40 and duct tape. His motto was if it was supposed to move and didn't, WD 40 it. If it wasn't supposed to move and did, duct tape it. Rule of thumb, Gail, if it has tires or testicles, I'll have trouble with it." Shaking her head, she said, "Don't get me started."

"It was a relationship. They're hard to come by."

"You kiddin'? You can make any relationship last with just five words. 'I apologize' and 'You are right'," said Terri. "Men are like wine. They start out as grapes. It's up to women to stomp the shit out of them until they turn into something acceptable to have dinner with." Shrugging, "Just like to meet a normal guy. Tired of New York hustle. Hick might be good."

Gail laughed and said, "My mother used to say they are all normal. Till you get to know them."

"Only advice my mother gave was 'Go, you might meet somebody.' Order us another if you see the waitress." Terri excused herself, walked outside and looked up and down the sidewalk, not seeing him. "Damn," she muttered. "Oh well, never pass up an opportunity to pee." She walked toward the Ladies' Room.

CHAPTER FOUR

Stuart was a tall man, all knees and elbows, thin and raw boned. He pictured himself as the guy that used to do all those cigarette commercials. Cowboy riding the range. Kind of a Marlboro Man or Clint Eastwood in *Rawhide*.

His range was Midtown Manhattan, but he loved the analogy. What he did was kind of riding the range. He often thought he was born too late for his time. Stuart was a cop, but could see himself in the old west, taming some town. Maybe fucking some good-looking school "Marm" like they always had in the movies. Maybe like Roz, the girl from "Frazier", or Gloria Estafan if the schoolteacher was Mexican. He wasn't sure they had Cubans in the old west. Never saw one in a movie, but surely they'd make an exception for Gloria. He could see it.

He had his legs propped on the seat across from him and sat rubbing his elbows. He wasn't sure he liked the patches on his sport coat. Supposed to be the latest fashion, according to his girlfriend, but he hadn't seen anybody else with them. She wasn't that far out in front of fashion trends, he thought. He looked under the booth's counter top and Stuart eyed his shoes.

"Friggin Hush Puppies," he muttered. With corns on both feet, he had to wear comfortable shoes. No more NYPD Oxfords for him. He'd gone to a cop funeral recently and worn his full dress uniform. Towards the end of the funeral, his feet hurt so bad, he'd have gladly traded places with the guy from Manhattan South being buried.

"Think it's gonna' happen?" Ken, his long time partner asked, sitting across the booth from him.

"Fucker's late, but it'll happen. I can't stand much more a' this stakeout. Sittin' in this booth drinkin' coke is turning into a sentence," said Stuart, still rubbing his elbows. "What do you think about patches?"

"Hell of a song. Don't remember who did it. Do you?"

"Not the song, Ken. Patches! Like on my jacket?"

Ken looked around the luncheonette. "Looks fruity, les' you're a professor or somethin'." He thought for a second. "Still looks fruity, even if you are." He looked up at the ceiling and said, "Course those dudes get all that young stuff."

Ken was also a tall man, but that was where the similarities between them ended. Where Stuart was bony and angular, Ken was broad and muscular.

Ken asked, "When we gonna' get out and hit some of them little white ones again? Only fuckin' thing this night shift is good for, golf during the day." His partner didn't answer him. "Played two times this week already." He looked to see if Stuart was paying attention. Satisfied, he said, "You're getting much better." Since his recent marriage to a public relations executive, he'd changed a lot of things. Like taking up golf. Used to make fun of it and now he had to act like he enjoyed it just because his wife thought he should. He really hated it now.

Stuart said, "Shit." He had yet to break a hundred, or even come close, in his five years at the game.

Both divorced three times, Ken was on his fourth, a marriage doomed because his new wife was trying to make Ken over. The project was starting to hit snags as Ken was getting tired of being made over. But misery does love company. "I love being married. 'Bout time for you to try it again, partner."

"Yeah, guess so," said Stuart. "Can't wait to find that special person to annoy for the rest of her life."

"Bad attitude, partner. Always two sides to every divorce," said Ken.

"Yep," said Stuart. "Mine and shithead's."

Ken and Stuart had been partners since making detective five years ago. Both had made second grade, but neither was on the "up and comers" career path in the NYPD. They tried hard. Just had bad luck. Like the reason they drew this ATM robbery stakeout. They arrested the Deputy to the Brazilian Embassy while investigating a robbery case blocks from the UN.

They could have sworn the guy was a Puerto Rican trying to run a game on them. Both had told him so while giving him the "wild ride" in the back of their car before booking him. The "wild ride" was a cop favorite. Cuff an individual, place him in the back seat and see how many times you can sling him from one side of the car to the other while driving wildly through the streets of Manhattan. You got extra points for blood and large bruises. Ken came close to setting the new record that night. Two points short.

It was after booking the man that they discovered the guy was actually telling the truth, and had diplomatic immunity. Then the shit hit the fan! They had their asses chewed by the sergeant, the lieutenant and then the captain. Hence their bullshit ATM robbery stakeout.

They had been sitting in the luncheonette ever since. Seven nights in a row now, just staring across the street at the Chase Bank on the corner of 55th and Sixth Avenue. Waiting for a slim black male, mid-twenties stick-up artist to rob someone going to the ATM.

Stuart asked, "Think this fucker will show?"

"I don't know," said Ken, pushing his red hair out of his eyes and back where it belonged. "Fucker hits two a night for six nights straight then takes a week off. Maybe he got enough money to start a business." Ken hated his hair. He now wore it long and styled versus a brush cut like his partner.

Stuart said, "What kind a business is a guy going to start with $3,600? Bought some crack and hittin' somethin' else now." He ran a hand through his military-style, short blond hair. "Workin' another location. Wore this one out."

Ken said, "What I told the Loo! Says the mutt started on a Wednesday. He'll be back. Here we sit, brother." He motioned to the waitress and ordered another coke.

She walked off after saying, "My favorite customers. Huey and Dewey. Another free coke coming right up! No need to tip. Haven't all week."

They both watched her walk away. Stuart said, "You know, for an ugly girl she's got some mouth on her."

Ken said, looking around, "Got a big ass too, but don't say nothin'. We'll be swappin' spit with her in every coke she brings the rest of the week. Let it go."

"Her attitude, I can see her layin' a loogie," said Stuart. "Probably sneaky enough to give you one had no bubbles so you wouldn't even suspect. Smart mouth she's got on her."

Ken laughed, "You started it. That first night. Remember? She was wearing that Guess T-shirt. You said implants. Downhill after that."

Stakeouts were like that. Interplay with your partner. Nothing sacred or out of bounds, a series of 'top this.' Ken and Stuart, both in their forties, were past that in their partnership. They could spend long hours talking or not saying anything.

"Gettin' a little action," said Ken, facing 56th Street. "If you turn and look over your shoulder you'll see a young black man, slim, crossing the street right now."

"Got him," said Stuart. "Looks more like a pimp than a holdup man." The young black man was dressed in a pearl gray three-piece suit, dark gray silk shirt, no tie and a snappy matching fedora. "Headin' to the news- stand."

"Maybe he's got taste," remarked Ken. "Newsstand's just five feet from the ATM door. Best we've had in three days. Luck's changing, partner."

"I say he's a well-read pimp," said Stuart. "I can see you wearing his outfit."

"You're one to talk, Patches." Ken scanned the guy again and said, "Be a little more positive. I got Formica growing outta' my ass from this booth. Look, got a big dude in green headin' toward the ATM."

"If it's the perp, he ain't gonna' mess with that big dufus. Guy looks like he could lift a fuckin' house."

Ken said, "Told you to be positive. Besides, he's got that 'I'm from outta' town' look."

***

The only thing saving Whitey and Rodney from a thrashing was the thirst Nathan built up from walking. He was heading home and spotted a bar mid-block between 55th and Sixth Avenue. He had passed it a couple of times going to the grocery down Sixth. Short on cash, he decided to cut across the street and hit the ATM on the corner. He could throw cash on the bar and get out quick if it was a bust. He always had beer at home.

As he went into the ATM kiosk, he was grabbed from behind and pushed into the wall, butting his head.

"Damn," he said, "end of a perfectly bad night."

The attacker turned him around and hit him in the mouth, knocking Nathan's glasses off. Nathan's first reaction was to hit him back. He was lucky and caught him square. He rushed him and hit him several more times, pinning him against the wall, then backed off and let him fall.

It was then he noticed the man had a knife. Being legally blind without his glasses, he hadn't seen it when hitting him. "Jesus," he yelled, jumping back as two men rushed into the kiosk. Nathan backed up, thinking they were with his attacker.

The first through the door knelt by the guy with the knife. The assailant was yelling, "Motherfucker crazy. Get him away from me."

The second man rushed up to Nathan and Nathan swung, catching him solidly in the forehead. He went down like a stone.

The thin man, kneeling by the guy with the knife, pulled a gun and yelled, "Police." Nathan's first thought was the police were coming and the attackers would leave. Then the thin man yelled, "Against the wall, asshole," while cuffing the mugger.

Nathan moved against the wall, resigned to the fact he was being robbed. The guy he'd hit got off the floor and he noticed then the guy was big. The guy rushed him, hitting him in the mouth again and in the nose. His mouth was already bleeding, this being his second hit of the night. Now he could feel blood coming from his nose. The big guy could punch a lot harder than the original attacker, he thought as he went down.

On the ground, Nathan was turning to protect his head from the kicking he was sure would follow. The guy with the gun yelled at the big guy, "What the fuck's wrong with you, Ken? You're a fuckin' cop."

"He hit me."

"Guy's hurt. He doesn't know we're the cops. Dumb ass," said Stuart. "We ain't said nothin'."

"Yeah," said the big guy staring at Nathan. "It wasn't you he hit. Damn near cracked my skull."

He leaned over and grabbed Nathan, yanking him to his feet. Nathan had been hit three times and nothing was making sense. He kneed the big guy in the crotch and the guy went down again.

The other guy yelled for him to get against the wall. It finally registered with Nathan that they were cops and he was in trouble. Deep trouble, if New York cops were anything like they were down South.

CHAPTER FIVE

"Nathan Melton," he said, introducing himself.

"Sorry about hittin' you."

"Me too," said Ken, still rubbing his crotch. "What the fuck's wrong with you?" He gestured toward the mugger. "He could have cut your heart out."

Nathan said, "Never saw the knife. He knocked my glasses off." He pointed at the black guy for emphasis. "He screwed it up. He should've said, 'This is a stick-up.' I'd of given him my wallet."

They all looked at the assailant and Stuart said, "He's right. You screwed it up. Don't they teach you guys nothin' in muggin' school?"

The black guy, still on the floor bleeding, said, "Crazy white people. Should a' stuck with my own kind."

***

Before the squad car arrived, they settled on a story. Nathan agreed he wouldn't say anything about being hit and they wouldn't arrest him for striking an officer.

Ken said to the assailant, "You go along with the story and we'll forget about the weapon. If not, it's your ass." The guy nodded. This wasn't his first trip down robbery lane. The weapon would have added years to his sentence.

The sergeant arrived first. "Jesus, this little guy kicked both your asses? Big guys like you?" It did seem absurd. The assailant was a short skinny guy.

"He's pretty feisty," Nathan said, looking from the sergeant to his attacker. The attacker nodded, going with the story.

"Damn feisty," said Ken, nodding toward Nathan. Both of them nodded to the assailant, who nodded again.

"Guy's like a rabid dog," said Stuart. "Fast. Probably on PCP or somethin'. You know how strong it makes 'em."

The sergeant gave them a dubious look as another squad car arrived, followed shortly by the EMTs. The bad guy was loaded into an ambulance and taken away to a nearby hospital for evaluation. The EMTs started working on Ken and Nathan.

The sergeant looked at Nathan and said, "Where you from?"

Nathan said, "Originally Florida."

The sergeant said, "You guys sure fucked up Gore." Everybody was a political pundit in New York.

Nathan laughed, "Clinton got him before we did."

"Was a shame what we had to choose from," the sergeant said, "Makes no sense. Two for President and fifty to choose from for Miss America?"

One of the EMTs said, "I like that. Did you hear that Arkansas is very proud of Bill? All those women came forward and not one's his sister."

Ken said, "I hate political jokes. Seen too many of 'em get elected."

Stuart said, "Ken, did you hear about Hilary going to a fortune teller? She was told, 'Prepare to become a widow.' Hilary took a deep breath and asked, "Will I be acquitted?"

"Enough with the Clinton jokes," Ken screamed.

Nathan said, "Guys, I was heading for a beer. Need to get something cold on my lip. Like a frosty mug." By then the EMTs had stopped the bleeding from his nose and mouth. "Can I buy you guys one?"

"Place right here is good," Ken said, pointing to the bar on the corner across the street. "Jimmie's."

Nathan, prepared to have to argue about them being on duty and all, was amazed. No reticence on their part at all. Yay, Big Apple!

They went in, followed by most of the patrons who'd been out on the sidewalk watching the action. Nathan waited for the bartender to start naming a bunch of beers he'd never heard of like in the other places.

He didn't, though. Brought Nathan a Coors without asking. Actually, he brought a Coors Light. Nathan toyed with the idea the guy might be taking a shot at his weight, but dropped it. Also brought Ken and Stuart shots without asking. They were obviously no strangers here, witnessed by the fact they were greeted on a first-name basis by several patrons and two of the bartenders. Nathan drank his beer and motioned for another. Wasn't his brand, but he was paying the bartender homage out of respect for not offering something trendy and fruity.

Three beers later, the bartender came to his end of the bar just as Ken and Stuart were leaving.

"Got to get back on duty, Nathan. You take care," Ken, his new friend, said.

"Probably see you back in here," said Stuart to a wave from Nathan. "Take care of him, Jimmie."

Nathan was catching the scores on ESPN on the TV behind the bar and didn't notice the bartender at first. During a commercial, he saw him staring.

"You still pissed or ya' over it?" the bartender asked, waiting for an answer.

"Over it." Fuck, the guy's going to hit on me now, he thought. Just when he found a reasonable bar, this guy's going to ruin it. Just order out. Get to know Chucky better. Give up. Can't win. Those smiley faces in the 'I heart NY' bumper stickers were upside down.

The bartender came over and held his hand out to shake. "I'm Jimmie."

Here it comes, thought Nathan. Want to go steady? Got a date for the prom? "Nathan," he said. "Good crowd. Work you hard, huh?" Get your mind off my ass, he thought.

"Yeah. Pretty good. I own the place so I ain't bitchin'. You live in the area or just getting' off work?"

Nathan said, "Live a block away. Just moved in." And if you're gay I don't need walking home, he thought.

"Good. In that case, it's on the house. Got your lip fucked up pretty good. Ken hit you a good one, huh?"

"What do you mean, on the house?" He decided to ignore the mention of his split lip.

"I do this you'll keep comin' back. Costs me a couple of bucks tonight. You'll probably drink here for twenty years. I'll get it back a thousand times over. I'm a marketing genius." Jimmie grinned ear to ear.

"If I come back?" There is a flaw in everything if you looked hard enough, he thought. "Kind of like the Video Professor on cable giving computer lessons away?" Jimmie nodded recognition. "What if I don't?"

The expression on Jimmie's face went from genius to simple. "That would fuck up my system. You don't come back."

Nathan laughed. He liked the guy. Maybe he wasn't hitting on him and was straight. Then his over-active mind suggested that maybe Jimmie didn't find him attractive. Depressing, but he wasn't going to let it bother him. "Place always have this many women in it?" Nathan was checking out the room and sending Jimmie a signal if he was wrong.

There was a fair amount of women. Straight from work, it appeared, still dressed for the office. Nice conservative dresses and business suits.

For some odd reason, business suits on a woman always turned him on. Of course, nothing on a woman also turned him on.

"Yeah it's always good for women. But it ain't a pick-up spot. It happens, but most of 'em are in here to unwind from work and then head home. Some of 'em live in the area. Some unwind while the subway crowds are thinning. In here, it's kind of an unwritten rule that you don't bother somebody who doesn't want it. Want my customers to feel comfortable. There's enough of them other kind 'a places." He paused and studied Nathan. "See somethin' you like, ask me first. Might save ya' some time." He handed him some napkins and motioned that his lip was bleeding. "If I was you, I'd wait for my lip to heal before doing some kind of Romeo routine. Look like a beefed-up Mick Jagger with that puffed-up lip."

"That's reasonable. I mean, without the lip I'm not an ax-murderer or somethin'."

Jimmie said, "Could tell. You ain't gotta' ax."

Nathan watched him wait on another customer. The guy was up-front. Just being friendly, which is always questionable in New York.

The bar itself wasn't impressive. It was in a horseshoe shape in the middle of a large room. It sat twenty-five comfortably around the bar and another fifty or so at small, two-person tables.

Jimmie came back down the bar to stand in front of Nathan. "So, ax man, you comin' back?"

Nathan smiled, "I'm coming back, Video Professor."

CHAPTER SIX

Terri McCumber sat at the bar in Jimmie's having a self-declared 'pity party.' Nothing was going right in her life. She'd put in almost thirteen hours a day, two days straight, on month-end reports and nobody seemed to appreciate it. She'd radically cut her hair, and changed the color frequently, and nobody noticed. It was almost like she was invisible.

She hadn't had a date in six months. She frankly hadn't been interested in anyone for a longer period than that. Her friends were all married and seldom called her anymore. The girls at work were all much younger. The only time they wanted to hang out was if they were having problems with their boyfriends and needed her as a sounding board.

All she had going for her was her little group at the bar. But they were becoming boring. She needed something in her life, but wasn't sure what. Lately her best, and only real friend, was Jimmie.

"Give me another, Jimmie," she said as he was passing.

"You sure, Terri? Been here a while. Maybe you should just go home. Call it a night."

"Why? Nothin' there." He took off his apron, which usually meant he was going to lecture her. Before he could start she asked, "Jimmie, am I invisible?"

"What?"

Terri complained, "Nobody sees me anymore. I'm like fuckin' furniture."

Jimmie said, sternly, "That's enough of that vulgar talk out of you, young lady. You'll only be noticed by the wrong sort with that gutter mouth."

She said, "Men do it. You do it."

Changing the subject, Jimmie said, "You've been in the dumps too long, Terri. Is it because you think your clock's ticking?"

"Jimmie, I'm forty-eight years old. Battery ran out on the clock a long time ago. Kids are overrated anyway."

Jimmie said, "You'll make a comeback."

Terri said, "Hard to make a comeback if you haven't been anywhere."

"You need to meet a guy. I'll start lookin' today. That'll fix you up. A nice fella'." Scratching his head, Jimmie asked, "What kind of guy would you like? You know, looks and all."

Terri said, "I don't know anymore, Jimmie. Something different. Nothing special, just somebody that won't embarrass me at a Christmas party. A guy that doesn't have an ashtray on his treadmill. Know what I mean?"

Jimmie answered, "Maybe."

"Jimmie, what I'm saying is a guy that won't pick his nose in front of the punch bowl at a party." She said, disgusted, "It's impossible, Jimmie. There isn't anybody out there. I've looked. Don't waste your time! Now, how about my drink?"

Jimmie turned and motioned to another bartender. As the man approached, Jimmie said, "Watch this end a minute, Lou. Got to take Terri home." He turned toward Terri and said, "Let's go, young lady. Slurring your words, making damn little sense, time for you to go home."

***

Nathan quickly established himself as a regular. All it took was true grit, dogged determination and visiting three to four nights a week and most weekends. Hundred-dollar bar tabs didn't hurt his cause either. Good tips always guaranteed a Michelob Light would be waiting for him as he came in the door.

Nathan became friendly with some of the other regulars. Stuart and Ken were instrumental in introducing him to a good many of the patrons. Mostly guys, he became close enough that some of them started doing the blind date thing. Hard to turn those things down because you don't want to hurt feelings.

Not a candidate for 'best looking,' he still did okay. In a short period of time he went out with everyone's sister, aunt, cousin and ex-wife. A good many of the guys that set him up were Italian and he'd discovered some unique styles of female facial hair. Against the law of averages, there wasn't a winner in the bunch.

One day Petey and Jimmie were having a beer with Nathan and Jimmie asked, "How's it goin'? The datin' thing?"

"Rough."

Petey said, "Thought you were gettin' plenty a' pussy."

"Sex is plentiful, but quality is lackin', Petey. I swear, people approaching me with 'she's got a great personality.' Jesus! You know what that means, don't you? Great personality?"

Petey asked, "They're nice?"

"Wrong," said Nathan. "Means I'm the good lookin' one of the two."

"That is bad," Jimmie said.

Petey said, "Guys are just trying to help. You sit around here every night bitchin' about meetin' women. Whine, whine, whine, Nathan, all you do."

Nathan said, "Don't get me wrong, I appreciate it. Just wish they knew better-looking women. I got a sweater for Christmas last year. I really wanted a screamer or a moaner. Somebody excitin'."

Jimmie waited on another customer and yelled over his shoulder to Nathan, "I saw Ken's sister. Should only be allowed out at night. Woof!"

Nathan laughed. "Don't get me wrong. I appreciate the good intentions."

Jimmie asked, "So I guess you don't wanna' go out with my sister?"

"What?"

Jimmie laughed, "Just kiddin', Nathan. Get a grip. I don't have a sister. If I did, she wouldn't go out with the likes of you. My family's got standards."

"Sounds too smart for me anyway."

"Hey, you're a pretty smart guy, Nathan," said Petey. "I'm reading that 'Scopes' book. You know, the one about evolution. It's confusin'."

Nathan said, "Pretty deep, Petey."

Petey said, "Got that right."

Nathan said, "Maybe I can help. What's the problem?"

Petey said, "Something's been botherin' me. If we evolved from the monkeys, how come there are still monkeys?"

Nathan said, "It'll give you a headache, Petey. Way too deep! Go back to the comics. Better for ya'."

Petey scratched his head, "Another thing. How come Tarzan doesn't have a beard?"

Nathan went to the bathroom to get away from Petey and ran into Ken. He had some new bruises on his face. Nathan asked, "What the hell happened to you?"

"Had a fight with the little woman."

Nathan looked at his face. "How'd it end?"

"When it was over I had her on her hands and knees."

Looking at his face Nathan said, "Really?"

"Yeah. She was screaming, 'come out from under that bed, you weasel.'"

He left knowing he'd been had. Back in the bar area, Petey said, "Jimmie, why don't you introduce Nathan to some of the women who come in here?"

Jimmie said, "Just thinkin' about that. Couple a' women come in are pretty nice, one in particular. Not gonna' drive away my customers, are you?"

Smiling, Nathan said, "Shit no. Never do that."

Petey asked, "What kind you like, Nathan? Other than six to sixty, blind, crippled and crazy?"

"Fuckin' comedian, Petey! I like regular women.

Nice lookin', forty and up, maybe up to fifty-five if they take care of themselves. Oh yeah, got to have something up top."

Petey said, "I know what ya' mean. I'm a tit man myself."

Nathan said, "No, I meant they got to be smart. Good legs, regular tits 'cause I have that reflex thing." Both looked at him with blank stares. "I choke easily."

They laughed and Jimmie said, "Good thing you aren't gay!"

Nathan laughed, "Big thing is they have to be intelligent."

Petey said, "Fucked yourself there, buddy. If they're smart, won't have anything to do with you."

Jimmie said, "Got a couple in mind. We'll just do 'em one at a time, keep you from breakin' all my customer's hearts. The one I'm thinking of is like a daughter to me. You don't like her, just tell me. You hurt her, I'll hurt you. Understand?"

***

Terri McCumber was the first woman Jimmie introduced to Nathan. Her office was in the same building as his. He'd actually seen her at the office before seeing her at the bar. She was the Chief Financial Officer for a small insurance company.

An attractive, petite woman in her late forties, she had radically short blonde hair and sparkling blue eyes. Very outspoken and assertive, she was witty and always surrounded by people in the bar.

Jimmie pointed her out and Nathan nodded yes and asked, "She's not datin' anyone, Jimmie?"

"Nathan, she isn't dating anyone."

"What about her chemo treatments? How long does she have?"

Jimmie was aghast. "What?"

"Her hair, Jimmie."

Jimmie laughed. "She just wears her hair short. I knew her when it was waist-length and brown. Just tryin' to look younger and chic or somethin'."

"Jimmie, is she, you know, into men?"

"You mean lesbian?" He started laughing hard.

Nathan argued, "I never see her with men." Jimmie laughed, but Nathan didn't think it was stupid question. In today's society, it wouldn't be that outrageous. Sure wasn't in Atlanta.

Jimmie was still laughing. "She's nice, talk to her. You don't like her we'll find somebody else. Or you can go back to Ken's sister." Nathan had a worried look on his face and Jimmie said, "You're just chicken shit, Nathan. I've learned in life that you don't sweat the petty things. Or pet the sweaty things."

"Okay. I'm willing to overlook the hair."

Jimmie said, "I'll point you out to her and see if she's interested."

"Tell me when so I can hold my stomach in."

"Suck it in 'cause I'm goin' over now," said Jimmie.

Nathan said, "I'm ready."

Jimmie laughed, "You sure?"

Alarmed, Nathan asked, "I got somethin' between my teeth?" He frantically looked in the bar mirror.

Jimmie teased, "Don't look like you're holdin' your gut in."

CHAPTER SEVEN

Nathan watched as Jimmie approached her and tapped her on the shoulder. "Terri, got a second?" She nodded. "See the guy over at the bar? The big guy?" and pointed his way.

"Yeah."

"Would you like to meet him?" There was a look of recognition in her eyes and she nodded.

Nathan, watching the whole thing in the mirror, grinned.

Jimmie introduced him and he enjoyed talking to her but hesitated to ask her out, as Jimmie suggested. Jimmie could have been wrong and she might have a contagious disease. Jimmie didn't strike Nathan as any kind of healthcare expert.

"I've seen you before," she said. "At Julian's I think."

"Go in there much?" he asked.

"Hate the place. Look bad in black," she said.

Good, he thought. "Wait a minute. You're the guy with all those weird people in the building. You guys have totally no dress code. People always wandering around drunk in the building."

He resented the 'always drunk' thing. Sometimes they were high. "We're an Internet site. E-tail."

Terri said, "Oh," and laughed.

Nathan said in defense, "My group is as normal as any e-tailer on the right coast."

"Don't get defensive. Just a casual observation."

She turned to the people next to her before he could make an observation about the tight-assed insurance industry.

Over the course of several days, they kept up a running conversation at the bar. By the time he sorted out that she had nothing contagious, and indeed liked men, he'd built up his courage and finally asked her out. "Would you like to have dinner sometime?"

She smiled. "Why?"

He was stumped. "You know. Get to know each other better."

Terri said, "We know each other pretty well now."

"Could be better."

Terri again asked, "Why?"

She was making this tough and he was sorry he'd asked now. Mad, he said, "Listen, I just asked you out on a date. Not to do things you could go to jail for doin' to farm animals. Don't wanna' go, just say so."

"Why not? Doing those things could be fun."

Did she just say what he thought she said? Yab-a- dab-a-doo! "Especially with an older, experienced man," he said.

"Been with a lot of farm animals, have you?" She noticed his face had reddened and said, "Just givin' you a hard time, Nathan. Thought you'd never ask."

***

They had the obligatory first date where he had to be on his best behavior. He took her to a nice dinner and to a show, *Chicago,* as a matter of fact. It was one of his all-time favorites. He dressed up and smelled nice. He was polite and politically correct when the Pakistani cabbie was an asshole. He acted interested in what she had to say, didn't burp even when he had to. He laughed when she was funny, which was easy. She was funny a lot. He walked her to her door. He didn't try to bum rush her into going to bed with him, even though he was horny. Should be worth extra points, he thought. He politely kissed her, no tongue, said he had a great time and he'd like to do it again. To her credit, and showing infinite wisdom, she said she would like to do it again also.

He whistled that old Spinners song, 'Could it be I'm Falling In Love' on the way home. He felt good, real good.

***

After the second date, he asked her up for a nightcap while they were standing in front of her building. "You want to walk back to your apartment?" She laughed, as did he, when he realized his gaffe.

"Oops. Not very well planned for a guy with ulterior motives, huh?"

Terri agreed. "Poor at best. Want to come up?"

"You must have ESPN."

Terri asked, "Huh?"

"You read my mind."

Her floor was the fortieth and she had a great view of the park. Her apartment was beautifully decorated and he received the full tour. At her bedroom, he put his best move on her. That started a long conversation about one-night stands.

"Nathan, I like you but I'm not looking to get hustled. I don't want to be a conquest."

"Me either," he said, thinking he just wanted to get laid. "I'm always hesitant to go to bed with a woman. If they think you're too easy they won't ever call you. If we go to bed together, you promise you'll call?"

"Yeah, maybe." She laughed.

Nathan said, "Puts my mind at ease."

Terri asked, "Are we going to tell people we are romantically involved?"

Nathan laughed. "I'm plannin' to tell everybody in the bar I nailed you." He saw the strange look on her face. "Just kiddin'. Come on, this is supposed to be fun. Of course we tell people. You want to keep it a secret? You aren't proud of your conquest?"

"No, not that. Wanted to give you the free agent option. You know, you might meet somebody in the bar that you want to go out with. If people in the bar know, and one of us goes out with somebody else, makes the other look bad."

"So if we tell does it mean we have to go to different bars if we are lookin' around?"

She said, "Only if you're looking for someone else. At Jimmie's, we don't look."

He thought about mentioning blindfolds, but decided it wouldn't be in his best interest to be funny. "Deal. Now can I ravish you?" She kissed him and he took that for a yes.

Her body was even better than he thought. She was also considerably shorter with her heels off. He undressed her and moved her to the bed, gently pushing her back on to it. Nathan moved between her thighs and tasted her while gently caressing her breasts. She had huge, dark nipples that he rubbed between his thumb and index finger, feeling them harden with his touch. As his tongue moved in her, the nipples grew even larger.

Nathan loved short women. At six-four he felt like a beast when he was making love to a five-footer. He felt powerful. Kongish!

He was really into it until Terri, wanting to stay even on the oral sex, said, "Nathan, you're not Jewish."

He started laughing so hard he had to catch his breath before he could say, "I know. What made you think I was?"

"Your name. Nathan Melton. Isn't that Jewish?"

Nathan said, "No, not to my knowledge. Never researched it." He gently tried to remind her about what she was going to do before he started laughing. No go. The mood was blown and that was all that was blown, so to speak. To get even he almost mentioned that she wasn't a true blonde, but was glad he didn't.

Later, after a couple of drinks, they continued kissing on her bed. Afraid of what might happen if he moved between her thighs again, he rolled on top of her. He entered her slowly, not breaking the kiss. He continued his movement, slowly in as deep as he could, then slowly back out until she started bucking, moving her hips wildly.

She moaned that she wanted him in deeper and he leaned back, lifting her legs on his shoulders, then drove himself in as deeply as he could. Neither lasted long, Terri convulsing as Nathan came deep inside of her.

***

The next day, Petey was at the bar and asked "Jimmie, how'd our boy do with Terri? They finally went out, right?"

"Yeah, they went out last night. Haven't talked to him."

Petey said, "Can't figure Nathan. Big guy like that. He acted afraid of her."

"He's full of shit like everybody else. Nice guy, though!"

Petey asked, "How's Betty and Dotty doin' in Florida?"

Jimmie said, "Great place. All kind a' stuff for the residents to do. Keep 'em active." He cleared his throat and said, "Toughest fuckin' thing I ever had to do, Petey." Jimmie scratched his head and went back to stacking glasses.

***

The next night at Nathan's apartment, Terri met Chucky. Little bastard didn't even try to bite her. Instead, he crawled up in her lap and growled at Nathan every time he got close to her. They developed a rapport. Knowing Chucky, it made her a little suspect, he thought.

CHAPTER EIGHT

Terri lived on West 57th also, but on the other side of Sixth. Since they both went in early and worked late, they started walking together to work and back home. Nathan felt like her protector on their walks. Or she was his. Either way, they were never mugged.

One night walking home from the bar, Terri said, "You know there's much more to New York than 53rd and Madison, the bar, Chucky, your apartment and mine. And Barry White."

Nathan asked, "Barry White! You sure?"

"I'm talking New York, Nathan."

"I sort of know New York. I know about the airport, both of 'em. I know about Yankee Stadium, Shea, Jimmie's, the Garden, the New Jersey airport, Hooters and the Meadowlands. And I know Barry White. That's not enough?"

She looked at him like his second grade teacher used to look. It was something approaching a mixture of scorn and pity. "Sundays will be tour days. We'll hit all the big tourist spots and broaden your horizons."

Nathan grinned, "I love it when you talk sexy.

I'm happy with the broad I'm with. But if you want to introduce me to more broads, okay by me."

The comment earned him a shot in the ribs.

In a ten-block radius, he had everything he wanted. Who's to say? The world may be flat and you could fall off, he thought. The gym was on 51st, so he'd been well past Park. He hit the Financial District regularly in dealing with the Street. Fuck it. He'd actually walked down to the big famous store on 34th once for the hell of it. He'd go to these places once with her. Couldn't hurt. He was getting laid regularly. He knew she was lying about Barry White, but why push it.

They began his education on Sunday. A three-hour wait to catch the boat for Ellis Island and see the Statue of Liberty. He kept reminding himself about the 'getting laid regularly' part.

To his surprise, he had fun. A lot of fun! And when he got home, there was Barry White. 'Can't Get Enough of Your Love Babe'!

***

Terri introduced Nathan to the other members of her little clan in dribbles. He discovered what Jimmie meant when he told him Terri was a collector of people.

Ray Lucci was the first person Nathan was introduced to in Terri's group. Ray was your basic, average, everyday asshole, he thought at first. Ray's saving grace was he had Giants and Jets season tickets. If not for that, Nathan didn't think he'd have a friend in the world. Get in close and Nathan figured he could broaden his horizons to include the Meadowlands regularly.

At well under six-feet tall and well over three hundred pounds, Ray was built like an Italian fire hydrant. He was in his mid-forties with long, dark hair worn slicked back like Pat Riley, the basketball coach. He had a really long nose and ear hair and thick eyebrows. Unfortunately, his eyebrows met in the middle of his forehead and made him look like a caveman. Or the guy that editorialized on Sixty Minutes.

Ray was vaguely associated with car sales and bragged about his murky, undefined Mafia connections. Petey had never heard of him, but the Mafia wasn't such a small world.

Ray bragged about his female conquests and anything else he could think of. He was a walking advertisement for Italian clothiers. Everything, his shoes, hats, slacks, belt, shirt and probably underwear, was Italian made. None of it looked good on him.

Nathan loved Italian clothing, but Ray somehow found the gaudiest colors imaginable, none of which matched. Petey told Nathan that he had no idea where Ray shopped. He'd never seen anything like it or heard of the labels. They determined that Ray had a little Italian Gypsy in him. Or that his clothes came from the bottom of the barrel in closeouts.

Ray also loved jewelry and never appeared without at least five rings. Of course, both pinkies were ringed, but they were so covered with hair, you had to look close.

"So you're the guy Terri was tellin' us about,"

Ray said, in his first conversation with Nathan. "Guy with the three-legged dog." He had a very gravelly voice, sounding like he had to spit and was saving it, or learning French. "Why don't you put that fucker in the circus?" Nathan ignored the question, thinking he'd like to see Ray put Chucky in the circus. Italian fucking sausage is what Ray would be. "Played ball for the Skinnies. I looked you up. You were a sub." He yelled to get everyone's attention. "He played on the kickoff and punt team. No big deal, I tell ya'. Guy was a sub." He had a deep, goofy laugh.

"That's exactly what he told me he was, a substitute, not a star. For thirteen years he played in the NFL. Still, pretty damn good," said Terri, taking up for Nathan. "What did you ever play, Ray?"

"Skin flute," said Jimmie, passing to wait on another customer.

"Is that offense or defense?" Terri leaned over and whispered to Nathan, not wanting to appear sports-challenged.

Nathan said, "Tell ya' later."

"Never mind. It's a guy thing, right?"

"Yeah. More of a guy and guy thing." Nathan laughed at his wit.

She started laughing. "I get it." Terri was like that. She was smart, but sometimes it took her a while. As Jimmie passed, she yelled, "Skin flute. Pretty good, Jimmie." He waved, but was too busy to stop.

Like most bullies, when he found out the crowd wasn't on his side, Ray became friendly. "Must've been something. All that pussy you guys got. Interviews and shit."

"Yeah, Ray. It was glorious." Nathan thought about his old football days. Waking up around noon on Mondays. Coming out of bed on his knees after waiting as long as he could, finally crawling to the bathroom. Peeing bright red blood for fifteen minutes. Facing the rest of life at thirty as a cripple. Yep, it was glorious.

"Listen, you need a car let old Ray know, huh?

Heavily discounted, titled, any state." He hit Nathan in the ribs and winked. "Really hot deals if you know what I mean?"

"Thanks, Ray." Nathan moved away muttering, "He hits me in the ribs again I'm splitting his nose. Right down the middle. Show him some glamour."

Ray was okay once you got past his bluster. And the fact that he belched, constantly lied and never bought a round of drinks. You stood up to him and he backed down quick. He was harmless.

Nathan introduced his new NYPD buddies to Ray and Terri. Love at first sight it wasn't. Ray, with his shady past, made himself scarce. Terri did too, although for reasons Nathan found out later. Apparently, Ken tried to pick her up before Nathan came into the picture. Terri knew Ken was married but he wouldn't take no for an answer and she dumped a drink on him one night.

Nathan sat on the other side of the horseshoe bar to get away from his new friend Ray. Stuart and Jimmie followed him over.

Stuart said, "I didn't know you played ball."

"Some detective," said Jimmie.

Stuart said, "Should've figured it, I guess. You're big enough. How come you never told me?"

Nathan shrugged, "It's no big deal."

"The hell you say," said Jimmie. "It's a damn big deal. What did you play?"

"Linebacker and I didn't play much. I spent most of my time on the taxi squad. That's what they had back then. It was kind of like the developmental guys now. When I played, it was mostly kickoff and return teams."

Stuart said, "Thirteen years, you had to have Somethin'." Nathan let it drop there. He didn't know why he was always embarrassed about semi-celebrity status, but he was.

**

The next person he met in the group was Gail Morales. Gail had the body of a model, which she was. Tall and thin, a six-footer, she was a combination of German and Puerto Rican descent and was in her mid-thirties. She had long dark hair that hung down to her waist and large breasts, which Nathan thought were illegal for a model to have. She also had one of those pouty looks, a real turn-on. Truly beautiful, rumor was she was kept by a big wheel in the garment industry. Being a model, she dressed either down or up, never in between. She could be in jeans and a ratty sweatshirt or in a designer dress with jewelry dripping off her.

"Got to be a fascinating business," Nathan said to her after being introduced. He could fake interest with the best of them.

"No, not fascinating. Actually sucks, but who's gonna' turn down the money idiots want to give you for looking a certain way?" His opinion of her went way up. "It's an ugly business. Kind of like sports, except I guess you guys don't have to fuck for your jobs."

He started to tell her to go ask Ray, but didn't.

"Tough to constantly stay in shape."

"Yeah. That and you're old quick. Money dries up as fast as it comes to you. You're young and you don't realize it right away, so very few are prepared financially when it happens. Hence, my current living arrangement," she said mysteriously.

He let that pass over his head, but told himself to ask Terri about it later. The word hence always intimidated him. Kind of like "genre." "Hell maintaining a certain weight. I wrestled and it was rough."

Gail said, "It was miserable, but I was lucky.

Great metabolism. Had to watch it, but I splurged on occasion." He was checking out the split in her skirt. Trying to figure out whether she was wearing panties or not. She spoke for another five minutes, but he couldn't remember what she said. He did determine that she wasn't wearing panties. Definitely no bra! Perky nipples you just wanted to hug. Much, much later he found out how intelligent she really was. And how tough!

He came out of his coma as she said, "Probably don't remember, but I saw you first. I was in Julian's with Terri. I was a blonde then." She shook her head so her hair splayed around her head.

"You mean the Halloween place? Everybody wearing black?" He decided to flatter her. "You look too cool for those kinds of places."

"Thanks," she smiled. "Used to go there a lot when I was a model."

Nathan said, "You don't still model?"

She said, "Not the runway stuff anymore. I do mostly catalogues and magazines now, a lot of legs and hands. Not meaning to change the subject, but your background is interesting. Terri told me all about you."

"She did?"

Gail said, "Yes. The Internet must be fascinating. New frontier. Do you think it'll really replace stores and shopping malls?"

Nathan said, "Not really. I think it affects the catalogue industry more. There's a segment that hates malls or doesn't have time and will shop us for some things. Most people would still rather fight the crowds. Got to have the experience of touching things before they buy." He was experiencing that same feeling just then. He wanted to touch things.

"Got to be a trip, though," she said. "New world to conquer and all."

He laughed, "IPOs aren't bad either with the right multiple."

She laughed. She had a great, deep, throaty laugh. "Your priorities are straight. When is the big day?"

"Too early to call. I'm looking at two years."

***

Later, on the way home, Nathan asked Terri about Gail.

"One of the things I like about Gail is her brutal honesty," said Terri. "She's the girlfriend of some guy in her industry. Married guy. Being an independent woman, I thought it was bad at first. Until I got to know her and found out how brutal the modeling industry is. Anyway, he set her up with an apartment. Lives a block over from us on the Park, next to Mickey Mantle's. It's in her name. She actually went out looking for the arrangement."

He said, "Kind of like a prostitute?"

"More like a past employee with a grudge. I think it's pretty cool. Milks this asshole for everything she can. Invests it well. Her nest egg for when he boots her for somebody younger. When I say milks, I mean it. I do her taxes," she said. "And besides, don't judge people unless you've walked in their shoes. Or however that saying goes."

"I could probably wear her shoes. She has some big feet." He thought she was playing, or at least she said she was, but she hit him right in the mouth.

She kissed him to make up and he said, "Did I tell you how good you look in that coat tonight?"

She twirled her new fur, modeling for him. "You like it?"

He asked, "Looks great on you. Is it like the first day for furs in New York?"

"Not that I know of, why?"

"Every woman in the bar had one on tonight. Just thought maybe it was like a Labor Day thing where you can't wear white anymore." She started laughing and he said, "What?"

Terri laughed, "Remind me to tell you someday. It's like a bar thing."

CHAPTER NINE

The next day, Nathan exited the building to meet Terri for the walk to work. She was early today, waiting on the corner for him. He leaned down toward her and kissed her hungrily. "Morning, baby," Nathan said. "Sleep well?"

"Wow. This is better than my normal peck on the cheek." She reached to wipe lipstick off Nathan's face and said, "You must've had a nice dream. Better have been about me."

He laughed, "Of course it was, Sugar Britches. You and me and the lady from 'Fox and Friends.' Little threesome action." His reply earned him a rib shot.

"E. D. is too tall for you, Nathan. You know you absolutely love petite women. Remember how you like to play Kong?"

Nathan smiled as they began their walk. "You're right. I was thinkin' one or the other of us spends the night on the weekend. It sure would be good to wake up next to you every morning. Do some major league snuggling. Snuggling is very important, fabric of our society." She had a contented look on her face and he continued. "I was, in fact, dreamin' about you. Jus' you. In my dream we were lying next each other, on our sides, spoon fashion. My penis was amazingly centrally located between your legs and vagina, arm around you, cupping a breast."

She stopped him on Fifth Avenue, tugged his arm and asked, "Which breast?"

"Huh? Oh, the one I can reach."

Terri laughed and said, "Nathan, you have long arms. I know it's your dream, but I'm in it. I want to visualize. Which breast?" She could see him trying to work it out in his head and tried to help. "Upper or lower? We're on our sides, remember?"

He grasped her meaning and smiled. "Oh yeah! Lower. I'm on my right side. Close to you. Slightest movement from you causes my penis to harden. That's it for sleeping and it's time to play. I lean back, upper torso away from you to attain the proper leverage for insertion. You place my penis inside you and I begin a slow, lazy rhythm."

She asked, "I'm just lying there, saying nothing?"

"You do have a smile on your face." Before she could ask another visualization question, he added, "I could see it in the mirror. In the dream the bedroom is mirrored." She laughed, hugging him as they walked and he continued. "At a particular point, you roll over on your stomach, pillow underneath you. I float above you, my penis in your vagina."

"Nathan, at your size you don't float."

Nathan said, "All right, hover. I try to find the L spot while massaging both breasts."

She asked, "L spot?"

"Yeah. One of those letters, L, J, you know, the somethin' spot."

Terri laughed, "It's 'G,' Nathan. It's the G spot."

They entered the building and were lucky this morning. The lobby was already crowded, but as they walked up to it, the elevator opened, and they were able to squeeze in. On the way up to the office, he held her hand. At her floor she squeezed his hand. Neither being at the "I love you" stage of the relationship, they just wished each other a good day.

On the three-floor ride to his office, Nathan thought about telling Terri he loved her. He wondered what her reaction would be. Would she respond with an "I love you" too? Or leave him flopping on the dock, completely embarrassed? He grinned, thinking he'd let her say it first.

***

His company had the whole floor and the elevator opened in the reception area. Stepping off, he shouted, "Love Mondays."

"Good morning, Mr. Melton," said the receptionist, Ruth Smalley.

He said, "Morning, Ruth," over his shoulder. He continued down the hall and into his office, greeting his long time secretary. "Yo Judy!"

She said, "Morning. How was your weekend? Do anything neat?"

"It was good, just restful, nothin' spectacular.

Hear from Ralph?" Judy was dating a broker who Nathan thought was married. He had strange hours and he never could spend the weekends. Nathan thought it was funny with the markets closed on the weekends, but he kept his own counsel.

"He worked all weekend. Seeing him tonight. I did your piles for you."

"I'll dance at your next wedding," he said. The piles were prioritized stacks. She loved to yell about his piles down the hallways, like it was a medical condition.

She said, "You look relaxed. Must've scored this weekend."

"Judy." Staring at her, he asked, "Did you do something? You look different."

"You mean other than lose eight pounds, color my hair and change the style? No, nothing different."

"Oh! Okay. You just look different. Smart ass!" Five minutes later, Harvey Walker, V.P. of Human Resources, stuck his head in. Harvey and Nathan had worked together for a long time. He, like Judy, had followed Nathan from Atlanta.

"What?" he screamed at Harvey, a standing joke. "Did you make a big deal about her hair?" Nathan gave him a vague look and Harvey said, "Judy!"

Nathan said, "I told her she looked different."

Harvey laughed. "Different? It's, like, blonde.

Major blonde. Hair used to be black." He paused and said, "Did you hear about the blonde who noticed the sign in front of the YMCA and said, 'They spelled Macy's wrong'?"

Nathan laughed, then asked, "You losin' weight?"

Harvey beamed. He said, "I joined your health club. Slim and trim for me. I'm gettin' a divorce." Harvey said, "Goin' to get a hot girl."

Nathan, amazed, said "You're shittin' me, right?"

"Nope. Definitely goin' younger."

Nathan said, "No. About the divorce."

"Nancy won't move from Atlanta. Now she's met a pilot, somebody from Delta. She told me we were never really happy anyway." Harvey scratched his head.

"I always thought we were. 'Just goes to show,' she said." Harvey shrugged.

Nathan started laughing. "She told you that you weren't happy? Actually told you that?"

"Yeah. Says we never were. Weird." Harvey was a year younger, an inch taller and about the same weight as Nathan. He wore his blond hair short, had blue eyes and a great sense of humor. He'd recently gone to a more casual look and quit wearing dark suits. Now Nathan knew why.

Nathan asked, "Have you found your 'hot girl'?"

Harvey said, "What I wanted to ask you about.

Where do you find one?"

Nathan smiled, "Don't ask me. Didn't like the places they hung out."

Harvey said. "I thought you met somebody?"

Nathan laughed, "Met Terri. She's my age."

"See if she's got some friends," said Harvey.

"I'll do it, Harv. If she does, probably gonna' be somebody our age."

"Never mind. Read an article says you shouldn't settle. Nancy said that's what she did with me." He scratched his head and said, "How's that fuckin' Chucky doing?" Harvey and Chucky had issues. Chucky had bitten Harvey on half a dozen occasions.

Nathan waved, "Chucky is Chucky. You want him?"

"Fuck no," he grimaced. "All I need is a 'Hitler Youth' dog." Harvey laughed, "Got a joke for you," he said. "It's a great New York joke. Lady goes into a bank and says she needs to borrow $5,000 for a week because she's going on a trip. Loan officer tells her they'll need collateral. She stands and says, 'Follow me.' She leads him to the bank window and says, 'See that Rolls parked in front? Will that do?' He says, 'Sure.' The bank does the paperwork, she gets the loan and he drives her Rolls to the basement and parks it. She returns the following week, pays off the loan and pays the $19.41 interest. The manager asks her, 'Why did you need the loan? We did further checking after you left and discovered you're a millionaire.' She says, 'Where can you park in New York for a week under $20?"

*****

Four blocks from Nathan's office, down Sixth Avenue at the bar, Jimmie hung up the phone. He'd had a disturbing call from his Parish Priest.

Petey and Sal Russo were sitting in what would've been Jimmie's spacious office. Instead, his office was cluttered with racks of suits and dresses, stacked TVs, microwaves and VCRs. Petey and Sal were having Italian coffees. Both were intently watching Sportscenter on ESPN to catch up on the scores from last night.

Sal, noticing the concerned look on Jimmie's face, asked, "What's wrong, Jimmie?"

"Father Donavan on the phone. Says a gang up 181st is givin' some a' the parishioners a hard time. They're robbin''em and stuff on the way to church."

Petey said, "The Heights. Sick fucks. Somebody ought a' do somethin'."

"You're tight with the cops, Jimmie. Make a call," suggested Sal.

Jimmie shrugged, "Father Donavan's tighter than I am. There's a Captain Rasmussen up there in that precinct. Won't do shit. Cops downtown tell him to, but he just gives it a lick and a promise. Sends out a couple of squads, does a couple of reports and that's as far as it goes. The Father says he just came from the church. Gang's on the corners now, shuckin' and jivin'. You guys want to take a ride up there, see what's up?"

They nodded and he stuck his head out the door and yelled, "Lou, watch it for a while. Be gone a bit."

Lou said, "Sure thing, Jimmie."

They took Petey's new Cadillac. In Petey's line of work, his car was equipped for what they needed to do. Arriving, they spotted gang members messing with people along the sidewalks close to the church. They rode around the block, scoping out any possible signs of trouble.

Petey pulled over at a curb a couple of blocks down from the church and said, "Looks like kids just having fun."

"Father Donavan don't get upset at the sight of kids having fun. You guys recognize the markings? Don't look like any gang I've ever seen," said Sal.

"I don't," said Jimmie. "What do you think, Sal?"

"Let me make a call. See if I can find out somethin'." Sal dialed a couple of numbers on his cell and had a couple of short conversations. Hanging up, he said, "Bimbo Washington with the Harlem Knights says he don't know shit about a gang in this area. Hector Ramirez says the Columbian Angels don't either. Says his people will take care of it from now on. I think it's most likely some jive-asses just making trouble."

"I counted fifteen when we rode by," said Petey. "If they ain't strapped, we can handle it right now." The other two men in the car nodded. Petey got out of his car, went to the trunk, came back and handed them baseball bats. Petey kept a bat for himself and got back in the car.

As he did a U-turn in the street, heading back for the gang, he said, "I'll take the left, you guys get the right."

Petey slammed on brakes in the middle of the street, blocking traffic. The doors opened and they jumped out. They charged at the gang members, swinging the bats. In less than a minute, six members were sprawled on the sidewalk or out in the street, dazed and scared. The rest were in full flight.

Jimmie yelled at their backs, "Show up again you'll get worse."

The ride back was eerily quiet. Going into the back door after arriving at the bar, Jimmie noticed a message lying on his desk. He picked it up, read it, and, smiling, said, "The good Father says thanks to each and every one of us."

Sal, leaning against the wall, asked, "If we'd have been caught doing the good Father's work, would he have put in a good word for us at our trial?"

Jimmie answered, "Well, no. Father Donavan couldn't very well do that, Sal. Use your head, man, it'd look bad for the church."

"What I thought," said Sal, pushing away from the wall. "Jimmie, you do too much for too many people. It could land you in trouble."

Jimmie tried to reason with Sal. "C'mon Sal, what did it hurt? Other than bruises on a couple of hard heads. We did the church's work. The Father thanked us, didn't he?"

"I need no thanks from the good Father Donavan, Jimmie," said Sal. "I did it to help out my friend Jimmie Collins."

Sal went out the door and Petey said, "He doesn't mean it, Jimmie. You know Sal, hardheaded sometimes."

But Jimmie stared at the door as Sal left.

Petey said, "He's worried about Cockeyed Phil, Jimmie."

"Phil Carmelotta? What's the problem, Petey?"

"You didn't hear? Cockeyed Phil is droppin' a dime. He got nailed with a key a' china white. Tryin' to buy some time back from the forty he's lookin' at."

"Piece a' filth," said Jimmie. "He's tyin' Sal in?"

"Got us all, Jimmie."

"Why in fuck's sake are you guys messin' with drugs, Petey?"

Petey shook his head and said, "At thirty a key, you can cut it five times and wholesale it. Jus' too much to be made, Jimmie."

Shaking his head, Jimmie said, "It's a health issue, Petey."

Petey shrugged. "Speakin' of health, you're startin' to look too skinny. How much more weight are you gonna' lose?"

"Been off the diet for a couple of months. Still losin'. Must be the change in my metabolism."

"Change it back, Jimmie. You ain't lookin' normal. Face all skin and bones."

"Petey, from anybody else I wouldn't of been surprised. Comin' from you, I'm amazed. Ya' fat fuck ya', you're jealous." Jimmie laughed, but Petey just shrugged.

CHAPTER TEN

Marie Kennedy and Dave Schultz were next to be introduced to Nathan by Jimmie. Jimmie threw them together after hearing of Terri's tour plans for Nathan. He called it marketing, a gimmick for creating customer loyalty for those living in the area. Others called it meddling.

Marie and Dave had been patrons for years. Nathan thought it odd that they both threw in the fact that they were Methodist when first introduced. Neither asked what religion he was.

Marie was fifty, not beautiful, but attractive. She was medium height and build and had dark hair flecked with gray streaks that she wore shoulder length. She reminded Nathan of Rizzo, the head of the girl gang in *Grease*. Not great looking, but guys still wanted to see her naked.

Marie was a great dresser, preferring suits to casual wear. She was meticulous in her surroundings and drove people crazy at parties with coasters.

She was also a jogger, but didn't have that jogger's attitude. Nathan knew the attitude. 'I'm superior in every way. How can you eat that? I'm telling the manager you're smoking. You threw trash out the window and I got your license number.' They made Nathan want to choke them. She wasn't like that at all.

Unbelievably, this kind, caring person owned a large collection agency. There were almost as many collection agency jokes as there were about lawyers and politicians. Most found that fact fascinating. Marie didn't.

Dave was fifty also, six-foot tall and in good shape. He had the body of a swimmer, slim with a well-developed back and great abs. He and Nathan discovered they both went to the same gym, he at night and Nathan in the early morning. When asked about the body differences, Nathan's excuse was that, as a strength guy, he used different machines.

Dave wore his blond hair short in a conservative cut. With his piercing blue eyes, he was the All-American guy, like somebody you'd see from the mid-West, solid. Born in Brooklyn, Dave was a successful divorce attorney and a sports fanatic. He jogged with Marie and played organized softball and basketball, with tennis and handball on the side. Unfortunately, he was just an okay athlete, average at everything. He was the type that was constantly looking to be accepted. Dave wanted to be a leader, but wasn't an inspiring, take-charge kind of guy.

Dave dressed well, although not as fashion conscious as Marie. If he saw it in a supposedly 'in' magazine, he wore it.

Nathan asked, "So you guys haven't done the tourist thing either?"

Dave said, "Nope. You can't do that stuff by yourself. Have to go in a group."

Nathan asked, "So you've just been waiting for the right group?"

"Yeah, that's it. The right group," said Marie.

Terri said, bragging, "Nathan's doing really well. Learning all about New York. He just loves it." She had a grip on his arm, daring him to say anything negative.

"Yep," said Nathan, showing off. "Did you know there's a TGI Friday's at the bottom of the Empire State Building that has really cold beer?"

"Shit, he is learning," said Dave. They 'high-fived', Dave missing in typical white guy fashion.

"Can I get in on this?" asked Gail, who'd just come in. "Can't leave me out."

"If you can't leave her out, you can't leave me out," said Ray.

"Me either," yelled Stuart, eyeing Gail's rear.

All of a sudden, this wasn't sounding like such a great idea to Nathan.

Jimmie stopped by delivering nachos and said, "Leave who out of what?" Nathan explained to him about Dave and Marie joining Terri's quest to educate him on New York. "I'm not doing anything Sunday," said Jimmie. "Okay if I come with you?" Nathan beamed. With Jimmie along he'd have a male to bond with. He'd already pegged Dave for a 'dweeb' and Ray was still iffy.

Gail said, "Only if you open early so we can get a buzz before we go? Can't do tours without a buzz."

"You got it, doll." Jimmie loved to do the Mickey Spillane deal. "How about I open early and the bar's a help yourself?"

"Good idea, Gail. With a buzz will be better,"
Nathan said. "Much better." He was wondering about her
undergarments.

Ken, checking out the rears of Gail, Marie and Terri, said, "Count
me in too. And my wife."

Terri snorted when Ken mentioned his wife. She said to Nathan,
"Not like the buzz we got at the first bar in Little Italy. Never made it
any further. I thought the bartender was gonna' kill you, Nathan." To
the crowd she said, "He kept yelling for a Don."

"A Don?" Jimmie asked, "You don't mean like the Godfather?"

"No," said Terri. "You know the beer? What was it called, Nathan?"

"Moretti," he said. "Italian beer. Got this old guy on the label
that looks like the Godfather, or actually Marlon Brando playing the
Godfather. Really good beer."

"Those people are serious about that shit," said Jimmie.

Petey said, "Believe me, Nathan. They don't play. Mafia is alive and
well in New York, especially Little Italy. Ask Ken and Stuart." They both
nodded.

Dave said, "I thought the only Italian beer was Peroni? That's what
it says in Playboy."

"That's an ad, honey," said Marie. Ray snorted.

Nathan said, "Au contraire, Dave. Moretti is the best. Ray can settle
it. Which is best, Ray?"

"Moretti. No doubt. It's like the Bud of Italy."

Ray scratched his head, "Guy does look like the Godfather. I mean
Brando. I never thought of that. But don't be yelling about the Don in
Little Italy."

Nathan asked, "Petey, you comin' along?"

"Yeah. Might be fun to see some of those places legit."

Dave asked, "Legit?"

"Yeah, ya' know, not workin' or nothin'." Dave still had a vacant look
and Petey added, "When I ain't collectin'. Ya' know," he made a motion
like swinging a bat, "collectin'."

***

On the way home, Nathan said to Terri, "I'm glad Jimmie's coming
with us. He works so hard. Needs to get away for a while."

"Yeah. Gives him an opportunity to forget his problems, at least
temporarily. Let's get Chucky and walk a bit."

They went upstairs to his apartment to get the little beggar. When
Nathan opened the door, the dog ran to Terri and growled at Nathan.

They got him outside quickly after he almost attacked an old lady in the elevator.

Terri picked up where she left off. "Jimmie really has major problems. You don't know about his family, do you?"

"Know he has a wife and kid. Never seen 'em."

Terri said, "His wife has MS and his daughter is seriously retarded. She's like in her thirties with the mind of a kid. Really sad. They live in an assisted living facility somewhere in Florida. Jimmie wanted them to be where it's warm. His wife hates the cold and they always planned on retiring to Florida anyway."

Nathan stopped and faced her, Chucky peeing on a bag on the sidewalk. "Never heard him complain."

"And never will. He believes you play the cards life deals you. That's why he works so hard, to make sure they have everything they want. Believe me, Jimmie makes plenty with the bar and investments. I do his taxes. But he has a lot of medical expenses not covered by insurance."

Nathan said, "Remind me to never ask you to do my taxes."

"Why?"

"If you're ever captured behind enemy lines you'll…." Terri tried to shut him up with a hand across his mouth, but smacked him instead, splitting his lip. Chucky growled at Nathan and bit his shoe.

"I'm sorry. My God, you're bleeding." She started wiping at his lip with a hanky.

"As long as you kiss it. Make it better." Hard to talk with his mouth full of hanky, but he was working on a sympathy thing here.

"Where does it hurt, honey?" He grabbed his crotch and got hit again. Her sense of humor was limited. Her punching power wasn't.

***

The Sunday tours soon became weekly occurrences. Jimmie was a regular on these trips and finally confided his home situation to Nathan, who acted surprised. After telling him about his wife and daughter, he said, "These little side trips help me keep what sanity I have. And that's not a hell of a lot. You don't mind me running my yap, do you?" he asked.

It was the first time Nathan had ever heard Jimmie complain about anything. "Hell no. What are friends for? Do I still have to pay my bar tab?"

He gave Nathan a look that would freeze water.

"Tell you what, I got a load of watches and jewelry the other day. Give you what you want at cost."

"Jimmie, I run a retail site. We deal in all that crap. I buy at real cost."

"Not this low," he said. Nathan humored him, agreeing to look at his stuff the next day.

***

The following day, Nathan had his merchandising people hook up with Jimmie. They loved his prices and they began selling most of the stuff he came across on the site. Jimmie's quantities increased dramatically. Nathan wondered about these great deals he was always coming across. One week TVs, the next cameras, carpets or furniture. Every once in a while he'd have art from some of the lesser-known name guys. Not his business where it came from, so Nathan didn't ask.

The staff from his office assumed he had some kind of deal on closeouts. They couldn't touch his prices dealing with manufacturers. Jimmie made a huge impact on the bottom line.

From then on, Nathan became Jimmie's bartender, listening to Jimmie's problems. Not that it was a burden or anything. He was glad to do it. With everything Jimmie had on his plate, he was flattered to be chosen as his confidant. Nathan wanted to do a "na na na na" to Terri. God knew she needed it. Now he had the inside scoop on Jimmie.

CHAPTER ELEVEN

Jimmie always woke up fast. This morning was no exception, especially when the sixth sense kicked in and he felt Betty looking at him.

His eyes opened, he turned toward her and she smiled. "Good morning, Jimmie."

He grinned at her, "How long have you been up?"

"A while, maybe thirty minutes or so."

"Couldn't sleep? Too quiet in Florida, ain't it?" He looked at the clock on the bedside table. "It's a little after five. Birds ain't even up."

"I'm okay, just thinking. You go back to sleep, you work hard, you need it. Got a long flight back to New York later." She reached over and touched his cheek, her other hand pulling the comforter up over his chest.

He smiled, saying, "I'm awake, Betty. What are you thinking about?"

"Just you. How you're getting cheated." He tried to speak and she shushed him. "Out of what could be a great time in your life."

"How am I cheated? I have everything I want in you and Dotty."

"Nonsense, a fine-looking man in the prime of his life. Your friends at the bar." Again, she shushed him. "Read in the financial papers about your friend Nathan becoming a genius with that Internet site. Think it was the Wall Street Journal or Business Week maybe."

He laughed, "You'd have to know Nathan, Betty. He's a funny man. He said it's easy to be a genius when everybody else is an idiot. He's like that. Very smart, but downplays it. Says the reason they killed the competition was they warehouse and ship direct. Didn't know, but most of the Internet sites drop ship; you know, direct from the manufacturer. Maybe he'll come down with me and you can meet him. You'd like him."

Betty said, "We've had this discussion before, honey. I don't want anyone to see me like this. Not now."

Jimmie said, "Like what, Betty? Just cause you need a little help getting here and there? Wasn't for that, nobody would know you were sick. Still my beautiful wife."

She smiled. "That's another thing, Jimmie. I know you have sexual urges, all men do. With my condition, I know I'm not very appealing. I don't want you deprived. If you have to take care of those urges outside our marriage, please do. Just don't tell me about it, okay?"

He stared at her. "Betty, you're more appealing than ever. Just didn't think you'd be interested with the sickness and all." He leaned over and kissed her tenderly. "How about now?" She giggled and he stopped her by kissing her again, this time with more purpose.

***

In mid-afternoon, Terri called Nathan. "So, 'Mr. Big Shot.' You couldn't go to lunch with me cause you were in a big audit meeting. How are ya' doin' now?"

"Miserable," said Nathan. "Lost every argument I tried with the friggin' auditors. Why do they call it an 'exit interview'? Their minds are already made up."

Terri laughed, "Sounds like you could use a drink?"

Nathan laughed, "Thinkin' the same thing. I'm headin' to the bar now. When are you getting off?"

Terri laughed, "It's only three, you just working half-days now?"

"Yeah. Half days for me. Don't want to appear as a working stiff. Me bein' a Big Shot and all."

"See you there. Don't get wiped. I have plans for you later. You going to walk Chucky first or you want me to go by when I get off?"

Nathan lied. "I'll catch the little beggar." He had no intention of going to the apartment first. Chucky could handle it. He had a little doggie door that he'd go through to the patio. Nathan had a six-foot by three-foot section of Astro-Turf on his balcony specifically for Chucky's use. Clean-up was no problem at all. Nathan would just rinse it off with the hose to get rid of the pissy smell. He was more creative with the other. After making sure no one was looking, he'd hit the turds over the balcony with a nine iron. He aimed for the covered skylight over the pool at the Plaza across the street. When the testosterone was flowing, or maybe it was the beer, he'd use a five iron. He'd try to hit the lines of people going in the foreign film theater down the block. Much tougher shot. You had to allow for wind, and get the right consistency from Chucky. Nathan was getting pretty good.

It was pretty quiet in the bar. Nathan hit the 'do nothing' time period between lunch and happy hour. The few people in the bar were nursing beers and staring at the TV screen. A couple of them were writers from the neighborhood battling writer's block. With the close proximity of the major networks, most were people from the technical side of TV: cameramen, directors and audio guys. They sat, hunched in a group, bitching about what assholes the "talent" they worked with were. One of the top literary agents in the city was sitting in a corner. He stared, glassy-eyed, until recognizing Nathan and waving.

Nathan sat at the bar and said hi to Lou, the regular daytime bartender. Lou was busily eating a bowl of soup while it was quiet.

Nathan ordered a Mick lite and then said, "Fuck it, Lou, I got it. Go ahead and eat." He got up and walked behind the bar to get his beer. A patron walked by the bar and threw a ten down on his way out. Nathan pocketed the ten and said, "Come back again."

"Saw that," yelled Lou.

Nathan took a one out of his pocket and threw it back on the bar. "Jimmie back from Florida?"

"He's back. He was around a minute ago. He and Petey were working on horses. Probably went to place their bets at OTB." Lou noticed the newspaper missing and added, "Or Jimmie might be in the shitter."

"Hope he washes his hands," said Nathan. He walked back to his stool with a cold beer.

Lou laughed, "You kiddin'? This is the service industry. Part of the allure of the job is making the customers sick."

"Always wondered," said Nathan.

"Good day or bad, Nathan?" Lou was Nathan's age and left the bar with more women than anyone Nathan had ever seen.

"I'm alive, must be good."

Lou O'Shea was a six-footer, medium build with a nicely-trimmed beard, and spoke with a strong, thick Irish accent. Women loved him not only for his looks, but for his bad boy image. Nathan never could figure out why women liked the bad boy image.

Lou was first generation Irish and rumored to be hiding out because of his IRA involvement. He did nothing to dispel the rumors and started most of them himself. Supposedly, he'd been involved in some gun deal. But Nathan knew the real reason he was hiding out. Lou ducked bail on a smuggling charge. He was bringing Cuban Cigars across the Canadian border illegally. The story changed as Lou's mood changed.

Lou was in the U.S. illegally, but so were most people in New York in the service industry. With his Irish background, Immigration and

Naturalization Service would never hassle him. Not in New York. It was much simpler for INS to run after the illegal Latinos.

"How's the love life, Lou?"

"I just broke up with my girl and the last thing she said to me was you'll never find another like me. I'm thinking, I hope not."

"What kind of soup is that?" Nathan asked as Lou slurped. "Sounds good."

After another loud slurp, he looked up at Nathan and grinned. "Alphabet soup. Right out of the can."

Nathan said, "Ever wonder if illiterates get the full effect of alphabet soup?" Lou ignored Nathan's question.

Looking around, then leaning closer to Nathan, Lou said, "Something I always wanted to ask you, Nate my boy. You know this is an Irish bar? Definitely Catholic in its leaning. Why would you, of English ancestry, hang out here? Don't take it wrong. I like you like a brother. But in the old Sod, we couldn't have a drink together." He looked up and said, "I hope I haven't offended you?"

"Not a problem. I come in here because I like the people. Never really thought about it," Nathan said. "Prejudices are weird. My only prejudice is those Baba Rum Raisins in the airports. Ones that replaced the Moonies. Besides, I'm Irish/German."

Lou looked at him. "You are?"

"Yeah."

Lou asked, "What religion are you then?"

"A mix. My old man made us go to church when I was a kid. Any of 'em. Whatever was close. Didn't matter. Baptist, Methodist, Episcopalian, Catholic. I've been in all of 'em except for a mosque or synagogue."

Lou laughed. "I thought you were Jewish," he said. "That's the good of America. It's a shame the rest of the world isn't like this. Coming here has really opened my eyes. Of course, when I go back it'll be the same."

"Did you tend bar in Ireland, Lou?"

"Fuck no. Too dangerous. Breaking up fights all day long between the fuckin' dart players, TV watchers, mad husbands and the like. Fucking Catholics arguing that Jameson's best, Protestants always yelling for Bushmill. No Nathan, I was a banker."

Nathan was stunned. He never thought of Lou as something like a staid banker. He started to ask him about being a banker when Jimmie yelled at him, coming around the corner of the bar. "Nathan, what are you doin'? Fuckin' with a workin' man. Want everybody to get the same reputation as you?"

"And what reputation would that be, James? Smart, energetic, great in bed. Has Terri been bragging again?"

"Talk about full of the blarney," said Lou.

"Sit down, young James, and I'll buy you a drink," said Nathan.

"You're buyin'? I'll have Jameson, Lou. The whole bottle," he said, as Nathan choked on his beer.

Nathan yelled, "He's cut off, Lou."

"Right 'o," said Lou, ignoring Nathan and getting Jimmie his drink.

"How was the trip to Florida?"

"Great. Betty and Dotty are doing well. They really like the place." Jimmie asked, "Where's Terri?"

Nathan said, "I tried to talk her into playin' hooky with me, but she's too diligent."

Jimmie nodded, "That she is. Fine girl. Any plans for the future?"

"Yeah. Plenty. I've given up on the presidency. Thinkin' about Pope. May become a fireman if you don't have to climb ropes. Wonderin' if ownin' a horse is a good investment?" Nathan stopped after seeing the sour expression on Jimmie's face. "Oh, you mean Terri and me?" Jimmie glared. "Nothin' immediate. So Dottie and Betty really like it down there?"

"Betty and I made love for the first time in months this morning. That's all you need Nathan, a good woman."

Nathan asked, "What's Betty doin' later on tonight?"

Jimmie snorted, "Don't know why I bother tryin' to talk sense to you. Now as far as Terri is concerned, you'll never find a finer woman. Don't know what she sees in the likes of you. Should light a candle every night is what you should do. Oh, got a good one for ya. Two ninety-year-olds had been dating for a while, when the man told the woman, 'Well, tonight's the night we have sex.' And so they did. As they are lying in bed afterward, the man thinks to himself, 'My God, if I'd known she was a virgin, I would have been much more gentle with her.'

Next to him she's thinking, 'If I'd known the old bastard could get it up, I'd have taken off my panty hose.' Pretty good, huh? There's nothin' like the Irish and our talents for tellin' jokes."

"I'll give you that. Not to change the subject, but something I always wondered, are you related to the Irish hero, Jimmie Collins? You know, the guy Liam what's his name played in the movie?" Lou, back from waiting on customers, and Jimmie both laughed.

Jimmie said, "No. I think there's a Jimmie Collins in every Irish family somewhere. At least, all the ones with the last name of Collins. He was a great man. I'd be proud to be related."

"He was a tough guy. At least he was in the movie. I loved the way they painted their faces before they went into battle. In all honesty, and don't take this wrong, I thought Robert the Bruce should've had his ass kicked. He should have stood up to his old scabby-assed father."

"Wrong movie, Nathan. That was Scotland. Big difference. Those boys were tough, though. Of course, the Irish were much tougher than the Scottish with their silly painted faces and fuckin' kilts. Sissy things to wear, they are. Always blowin' up and showin' their bumpy arses. The Irish are tougher than ten-day-old dog shit," said Lou, leaving to wait on a customer.

Jimmie said, "Tougher than that. The movie didn't do him justice. Those were some bad boys! Believe me! Back in a second."

Nathan scanned the TV while Jimmie walked away. Red Sox were losing, Orioles losing, Braves losing,

Marlins losing. Damn! Figure with liking four teams, one of them would be winning.

Jimmie returned with a large bag of quarters. "Miss me?" Since it was so slow he'd decided to count the take on the video poker machines. The employees would be happy. They all got a cut off the illegal machines.

Jimmie said, "Did I tell you Ray wants me to set him up with someone now? Says I did so well for you he wants in on the action."

Nathan said, "Is there anybody you hate enough to set up with Ray?"

"Not off the top of my head," he said, continuing to count quarters.

Nathan laughed. "Little money makers, huh?" Nathan was watching him do his count. "You have to split with the guy puts in the machine?"

"Naw! Own 'em. Twenty-five hundred a piece those little babies cost. You can pay maintenance. I don't. Got a guy fixes 'em for me. They never tear up anyway. If one a' mine does, Sal switches it out for me."

"Expensive little bastards."

Jimmie said, "Not really. Pay for themselves in two weeks."

"You get bad weeks and good weeks?"

He looked at Nathan and said, "You kiddin'? Things are set at seventy percent. That's what they payout, rain or shine. My end's always gonna' be thirty."

"You can set 'em at different levels? What about a shutout every other week?"

"You're greedy, Nathan. Comes with your race, I suppose. Nobody plays the fuckin' things, what do you have? Fuck all is what you have. Some people set 'em lower. I set mine at max. No point in being greedy. I need to check out your website. Fuck, you must set everything at three hundred percent markup." Lou was starting to get behind with the customers so Jimmie got up to help him. As he was leaving, he said, "I need to talk to you about something serious so don't get pie-eyed on me."

Nathan said, "Wait a second." Jimmie turned back to Nathan, who said, "Are you saying you'd like me to be at one hundred percent?"

"Actually, over a hundred percent, Nathan."

"Well, in all honesty I've had difficulty with that expression. Countless coaches have often used it, but it's remained a mystery to me."

Jimmie stared at him and asked, "Why would that be, Nathan? It is a common expression."

"True, but let's think about it for a second. What exactly constitutes a hundred percent?" Nathan now had an audience of several listening to their conversation. He pulled a pen out of Jimmie's shirt pocket and wrote the alphabet on a napkin. He then wrote the numbers one through twenty-six under the letters and said, "Say we take the word H-A-R-D-W-O-R-K and add the numbers to the letters from the napkin. You know, like A is one and B is two." He pulled a small calculator from Jimmie's shirt pocket and added the numbers. "The total for hard work is ninety-eight. Close but no cigar." He looked up at Jimmie. "Let's use the word K-N-O-W-L-E-D-G-E." He again added the numbers. "Ninety-six."

Jimmie said, "Wait." He picked up the napkin and took his calculator from Nathan. He punched in some numbers and grinned. "How about the word A-T-T-I-T-U-D-E." He added, "Dead on a hundred. Mystery solved, genius," he said, handing the napkin to Nathan and pocketing his calculator.

Not giving up, Nathan grabbed the calculator and said, "Let's try B-U-L-L-S-H-I-T." He added the numbers and said, "Wow, look at this, a hundred three. Let's see how far A-S-S-K-I-S-S-I-N-G will take us." He now had everyone's attention as he added the numbers. "Damn, one eighteen." He looked up at Jimmie. "So James, one can conclude with mathematical certainty that hard work and knowledge will get you close. And attitude will get you there. But bullshit and ass kissing will put you over the top."

Everyone started laughing, except Jimmie who said sternly, "Watch that for me," pointing toward the stacks of coins on the bar in front of Nathan.

Nathan thought the downfall of America was the service industry. Whatever happened to the customer is always right and don't piss him off? Or make fun of him or tell him to not get pie-eyed? Hell in a hand basket is where this country was headed.

Second person today with "plans for him later." Why should another person's plans for you stop you from having fun? The nerve, he thought, getting up and heading for the bathroom.

Already a bit tipsy, he had trouble walking, but it was his business and nobody else's. He stood in front of the mirror. Looking closely, he studied his image. All these people thinking he's Jewish lately.

He muttered at the mirror, "What's up with that?" He didn't see any Jewish features. "Maybe my nose is big. Hell, a big nose could mean you're Arab. Or Roman. Or that you just had a big nose."

Laughing, he said, "Fuck 'em," as he stumbled out of the bathroom.

CHAPTER TWELVE

Nathan was stewing over what Jimmie said and decided to get pie-eyed to show him. The couple next to him moved over a stool closer and the guy said, "He's right, you know."

"About what?" If it was another pie-eyed comment, this guy had just purchased a super-sized ass whipping.

"About the machines. My father has a store and he's got a couple in his back room."

"Couple a what?" He was sure now the guy was heading for the ass whipping and Nathan was sizing him up. No way could some curly-haired, hat-wearing goober stand his onslaught, the beer said to him.

The guy said, "Video poker machines. I don't mean to get involved in your conversation. I overheard."

"You are entirely too nosy. And I don't mean that literally," said the lady sitting next to him. "Mind your own business."

Nathan thought it was a great reference. The guy did have one big schnooze on him. Hate to do coke lines with this guy and him go first. He started laughing at his wit. "Not a problem. Please let me get you a drink." He was glad he didn't have to fight. When drinking, unlike more than half the population, he was in a mellow mood. Everybody was a friend. Well, almost everybody. He reached over and messed Jimmie's coin piles up. Recounting would teach him humility. "Lou, my good man, some service down here would be sorely appreciated," he yelled. "A shame we don't have a professional bartender back there," he added and laughed again at his wit.

The couple introduced themselves and they talked about what a nice bar Jimmie had. His name was Avi, hers was Julie.

Avi was late twenties, orthodox right down to the ringlets, six feet tall and thin. His long dark beard made him appear thinner than he really was.

He was a real estate broker with his own business. He also did a lot of volunteer work for the Jewish Defense League. He'd spent time in Israel living on a kibbutz and served in the military there. Some kind of intelligence role he was vague about. His father fought in the Israeli war of independence in 1948.

Avi's voice was surprisingly deep for such a slight man. Nathan, judging all Orthodox Jews by his board chairman, found him surprisingly laid back.

Julie was a fox. Mid-twenties, above medium height, she was slim with long, dark, flowing hair. She looked like a taller Elaine on Seinfeld, but without the goofy eyes. Hers were very sexy, dark, but not huge.

Julie was an attorney and practiced property law with her father in the family firm. Two brothers and a sister were also in the firm. All had come to the U.S. within the last ten years.

Julie and her siblings were born in Israel. She still had a little bit of an accent, kind of a French sound to it, which made her even sexier, Nathan thought. Her parents also had fought in the war of independence. Her mother was killed in a terrorist move against the kibbutz where they lived, and the family came to the U.S. shortly thereafter.

There was bad blood between their families. It was apparently a Jewish Hatfield/McCoy thing that started so long ago no one could remember what it was about. They were forbidden to see each other, and obviously were paying no heed. They liked Jimmie's because it was far enough away from their families that they didn't worry about being seen.

Avi's parents lived in the Bronx and Julie's lived on Long Island, or 'Lon-guy-lan' as they said in New York. Both worked down Sixth Avenue. Out for the evening, they had time to kill before their movie started and popped into Jimmie's. Of course they were going to the French theater where Nathan sometimes aimed his five-iron.

After they left, Jimmie came back over. "Sounded like you were drumming up business?" He sat down and pushed a plate of super cheesy chili nachos toward Nathan.

Nathan was still mad at Jimmie, but decided not to turn the nachos down. "Better talk quick. I'm three sheets to the wind."

Jimmie said, "It can wait. I need you sober."

"Just kidding. If you don't tell me now, it'll kill the rest of the night."

Jimmie said, "I'm thinking about selling the bar. Moving in with my family in Florida."

Nathan said, "I thought they lived in a hospital."

"It's kind of an adult community. I'll like it there. All kinds of things to do. Shuffle board, tennis, like that. Place is outside of Miami, close to Shula's restaurant."

"That's good. I'm sure you'll enjoy it. Golf and stuff. What made you decide?"

Jimmie looked at him and said, "My wife will get much worse. Now she has trouble doing things she's done all her life. Can't remember, things like that. Towards the end she'll be incontinent. Know what that means?"

"Yeah, but I wouldn't call Florida incontinent. Still in the states. Be like Europe or something, if you're incontinent."

"Dumb ass. Incontinent means you can't control your body functions."

"I know what it is. Just screwing with you.

Lighten the moment, you know." Nathan paused and said,

"It's got to be hell. Them down there, you here."

"Nathan, at least I'll be able to do somethin' for them. Feel helpless here."

"You did your part, Jimmie. Fought the battle for a long time. Done everything you can do. No need to feel guilty." But Nathan knew that's what he was feeling. "Least you'll spend some quality time with her."

"Well it won't be soon. I'll get everything in order here, sell the bar. Keep it to yourself for now okay?"

Ken and Stuart walked over and Nathan asked, "What are you two up to this fine night?"

"On a friggin' stakeout," said Stuart. "Came in to get a quick bite."

Ken said, "Got a joke for you, Nathan. A young ventriloquist is touring the clubs and one night he's doing a show in Arkansas. With his dummy on his knee, he's going through his usual routine when this blonde in the fourth row stands on her chair and starts screaming. 'I've had enough of your stupid blonde jokes. What makes you think you can stereotype women that way. Asshole. What does the color of a person's hair have to do with her worth as a human being? It's guys like you who keep women like me from being respected at work and in the community. Your perpetual discrimination affects not only blondes, but women in general, and keeps us from reaching our full potential as human beings. All in the name of humor. You should be ashamed.' The ventriloquist is embarrassed and begins to apologize when the blonde yells, 'You stay out of this, mister. I'm talking to that little short bastard on your knee.'"

"Ken, I got to admit, that's good," said Terri, coming up unnoticed from behind. "Ken, why do men masturbate?" She paused, waiting for his guess, which didn't come. "It's sex with someone they love."

***

After they left, Terri said, "I was talking to Stuart on the way in. He's so cute. Wants me to set him up with Gail."

"Stuart?" laughed Jimmie. "Exact opposites. No way will she go out with him."

"You might be surprised," said Terri. "She says she's always looking for a regular guy and Stuart is as regular as they come."

"I think they'd be a perfect couple," said Jimmie. Slapping his head, he said, "Damn! Madeline was in earlier looking for Ken. Forgot to tell him."

Nathan asked, "Madeline?"

"Nathan, you don't remember Ken's wife? Nice looking," said Jimmie. "Went with us to the Statue of Liberty."

Terri said, "Nathan, I know you don't remember her. You, Ray and Dave were ripped. She was a bitch."

"She's all right," said Jimmie. "A little full of herself maybe. Probably trying to impress us."

Terri said, "She didn't impress me."

Nathan said, "Damned if I know who we're talkin' about. I remember going to the Statue of Liberty."

Terri said, "You were arguing with Ray and Dave about people lining up."

"I remember that. New Yorkers don't line up worth a shit," he said. "Line up good down south."

"You want to line up, Nathan, go south," said Jimmie.

"Speaking of south, how's Betty doing, Jimmie?" asked Terri?

"Doin' great. Getting harder for her to get around."

Terri said, "Between this place, traveling to Florida every couple of weeks and worrying, you're running down. You're almost gaunt. What do you weigh now?"

"Enough. Terri, I'm okay."

"When's the last time you saw a doctor?"

Jimmie said, "Been awhile."

"Make an appointment, Jimmie. You don't, I will," said Terri.

CHAPTER THIRTEEN

The next morning, Jimmie, Sal and Petey sat around the bar before opening time. They were all staring into their Italian coffees.

Jimmie asked, "Bad, Sal?"

Sal shrugged. "Cost of doing business. Could be worse." Sal, Petey and three men from Sal's crew were notified six months earlier of an indictment. It was the IRS, tax evasion, and Sal knew they were goners.

For the past few months, they'd had their attorneys trying to cut a deal in a plea bargain. "Cut it to twenty. Good time, I'm out in eighteen and a half. Petey," he gestured toward him, "is getting five."

"Do that standing on my head," said Petey. "That is, if the fuckin' judge accepts the plea."

Sal said, "Got that right. Friggin' fed judges are a law unto themselves."

Jimmie said, "Never could figure that out. Work a deal with the prosecutor and the judge don't have to take it. Turn around and throw the book at ya' anyway." Shaking his head, he said, "And the shit of it is, you're on record as cuttin' a deal based on your guilt."

"At's why they call 'em feds, Jimmie" said Petey. "Ain't s'posed ta' make sense." Grinning, he added, "if their lips are movin', they're lyin'."

"What about Cockeyed Phil?" Jimmie asked, "How bad is he gonna' hurt ya'?"

"Who the fuck knows?" said Sal. "My attorney is feelin' the prosecutor out. Maybe I'll plea out ta' somethin'. Save Petey and the boys some time."

Jimmie asked, "Ain't that gonna' really bury you, Sal?"

"Not if I can do it concurrent." He shrugged, "Fuckin' Carmelotta don't deserve a nickname no more. Bastard should get cancer."

Jimmie said, "I can talk to him. We used to be close."

Sal said, "Jimmie, stay away from that prick. He remembers your name, he'll deal. Give 'em some shit happened twenty years ago. He's liable to try and walk on your back."

Jimmie said, "I can maybe get somethin' goin'. Maybe give 'em a permanent headache."

Sal yelled, "Do not do any shit like that. You gotta' take care a' Betty. Stay the fuck outta' this. Capice?"

Jimmie asked, "If they accept the plea, when's sentencing?"

"Probably hold it off for a while. Maybe a couple of months," said Petey.

Jimmie shrugged, "I'm gonna' be there." Sal started to speak and Jimmie cut him off, "Don't give a shit what you say, Sal. Been friends too damn long to expect me not to come. I'd be pissed you didn't come if I was being sentenced."

Sal smiled and held his hands up in a helpless gesture. "Ya fuckin' Irish Goombah, give me a hug."

After the mutual hug, Jimmie asked, "Anything you guys need?" Both shook their heads no. "Sure? How bout I send you commissary money, somethin'?" They both shook their heads no. "That way your wives won't have to screw with it. Let me do it, a couple hundred apiece a month ain't gonna' hurt me a bit."

Sal said, "Do me one favor. All I ask, Jimmie, is one favor."

"Anything, Sal."

"Get your ass to Florida and quit fuckin' tryin' to solve all the world's problems. Biggest damn social worker I ever seen in my life. Will ya' do that for me?"

"Sure, Sal," Jimmie said. All three broke up laughing, seeing Jimmie's lie for what it was.

"Ya' couldn't quit," said Sal, laughing, "if your life depended on it."

"What we gonna' do with him, Sal?" asked Petey.

"He's fuckin' terminal," said Sal.

***

That night Nathan and Terri went to the bar early and ran into Ray. He waved them over and they sat on stools along the bar with him. "Did I tell you guys Jimmie is lining me up with Agnes?"

"That's great, Ray," said Terri. "She's nice."

Nathan asked, "Who's Agnes?"

"She's a librarian," said Terri. "Tall, slim."

Nathan almost said 'you mean Olive Oyle', but didn't. "Yeah, Ray. That's great." Agnes was a good foot taller than Ray. Over six feet tall, she weighed a little over a hundred pounds and wore her hair in an old fashion bun style.

"Thanks," said Ray. "When are these people comin' in? Your buddies, Nathan?"

"Soon. Didn't give me a time."

Old buddy Ray was always the same. "So you say this Jew girl is fuckable, huh?"

"No Ray, I said she's beautiful. She's also engaged to Avi."

"Beautiful, fuckable, same thing, ain't it? Think she's easy?"

"Yeah. Waiting for you to swoop in and knock her off her feet, you silver-tongued devil." Fuck him. Let him make an ass of himself. Julie could handle him and his big, three hundred pound double-wide ass. Suave bola.

Ray said, "Is she better looking than Gail?" Gail had just arrived and turned to hear Nathan's answer.

"Nobody's better looking than Gail, Ray. I meant she's beautiful for a normal person." Politician is what I am, he thought. If Nathan had said yes, Gail would've gone after Julie with a meat cleaver.

As it was, she was smiling and gave him a big hug. No underwear, she was rubbing her hard nipples against his chest. "Thanks, big fella'," she said. "Always nice to hear. Most men are like place mats. They only show up when there's food on the table, but not you, Nathan."

Returning later from the bathroom, Nathan sat beside Terri and said, "Big crowd tonight. Third time I've gotten up and somebody took my seat."

"Cause you get up too much. Stay seated."

Nathan nodded, "That would be one answer."

She gave Nathan her 'the only answer' look. She leaned against him. "Hey, I'm horny. What do you think my chances of scoring tonight are?"

"Got to be good with this big a crowd. Just jokin'," he said, before she could hit him. "Want to play some games tonight?"

"Yeah. What do you want to play?" She had a glazed look in her eyes. He loved that look. Made her look very sexy.

"How about Daddy's little girl?"

She giggled, "I like that one. The plaid jumper's back from the cleaners. Patent leathers are in the closet."

"Giddy-up."

She said, "Are those your friends?" He swiveled to look at the front door. "No, coming in the side." He rose to greet Avi and Julie. Before he walked across to them, Nathan leaned close to Terri and said, "I noticed that 'your friends.' You're jealous because I met them first. Now you aren't goin' to be friendly? Might have to spank my little girl."

"Oh, Daddy." She rose, taking his arm to walk across the bar to meet them. "Promises, promises. Of course I'll be friendly. If you promise to spank me."

Nathan introduced everyone and let them wander around, getting to know each other.

"What do you guys do for the JDL?" asked Ray. "Any kind of top secret shit? Is Israel going to end up with a large oil field soon?"

"Maybe. If the friggin' Arabs don't wise up that they don't have their Russian protectors anymore. Of course, we would hear about it the same time you did on FOX or CNN," said Julie. "No, we don't do anything really neat. Just smile and dial. We're fundraisers."

"I like Israel," Nathan said. "Was in Tel Aviv on business and extended it into a vacation. Visited Jerusalem. Great. Could feel the history running through you. Finished up at the LaRomme Hotel on the sea with a bunch of naked Scandinavians."

Avi said, "Must've been Eilat. Really great for naked Scandinavians. How'd you like Tel Aviv?"

"Really enjoyed it. Terrific restaurants except they name them funny. Great steak place called the Pharmacy on Wisenheimer Street, or something like that." Avi and Julie winced at his pronunciation. "Went in for Tylenol and had a terrific meal."

"Except for the women have hair under the arms," said Ray. "And they don't shave until the beginning of the knee."

"Oh yeah?" Julie raised her skirt up to show Ray all Jews didn't practice that policy. He giggled.

Jimmie said, "You know, I always wanted to go to Israel. People got to be somethin'. Must be fun."

"Not sure about fun. Not fun like you guys have," said Julie. "America is so refreshing. Jews have a tough time just letting go. Always worrying about somebody taking your country. Annihilating your race. It's a bitch."

Gail said, "You guys do need to chill. Enjoy life. It's so short."

Score one for Ray, who said, "Especially with your race being annihilated."

"It's not all serious," said Julie. "Something happened in the synagogue Saturday that was funny. The Rabbi announced he wasn't renewing his contract at the end of the year. Said he was going to a much more prosperous synagogue. Mr. Edestein, who owns several auto dealerships, said if the Rabbi stayed, he'd throw in a new car every year. And a mini-van for his wife.

Mr. Golden, an investment banker, stood and said he'd personally double the Rabbi's salary.

Mrs. Goldfarb, who is ninety-six years old, stood and said, 'I'll give the Rabbi sex.'

I was sitting next to her and couldn't help laughing. I asked her what that was all about, giving the rabbi sex.

She said she asked her husband what should be done about the Rabbi and he said, 'Fuck the Rabbi.'"

They all were pretty ripped at that point, but nobody was making a move to leave. Nathan leaned over and said to Terri, "You about ready?"

"Oh, honey. You remembered I'm horny. I love you. Ready for some monkey sex?"

He was kind of taken aback. That was the first 'I love you' between them.

***

As soon as they arrived at her apartment, Terri ran to put on her costume.

Nathan was looking through her CDs when Terri came back out. She wore a plaid jumper over a white blouse. Patent leather shoes and bobby socks completed her ensemble. She marched over and sat in his lap.

One of the things he loved about Terri, and hated about his ex-wife, was Terri was quick to orgasm. His ex, on the other hand, took three or four hours and that wasn't a given. She was just as liable to orgasm as to ask, 'You want to go for ice cream'?

"Has Daddy's girl been good?"

"No, Daddy, I've been real bad."

Nathan asked, "What has Daddy's little girl done that's so bad?"

Terri, in a soft little girl voice, said, "I let a boy look up my dress at recess."

Nathan asked, in a mad voice, "Did he touch you?"

Terri, with pouty lips, said, "Yes. He put his finger inside me."

"Inside you where? Show Daddy."

Terri lifted her dress and Nathan noticed something new had been added. Terri was shaved. He rubbed along her outer lips and said, "Is this where?" He gently probed her opening. She was already wet.

He moved his moistened finger up to her clit and asked a breathless Terri, "Did that mean old boy touch you here?" Terri quivered in excitement.

He laid her on the floor gently and parted her legs. He moved his mouth to her and began a gentle licking. Just under her clitoris, back up and around, gently sucking and flicking her with his tongue.

"Damn it, Nathan, in me, now!" Terri screamed.

He put her ankles, shoes and socks still on, over his shoulders. "Bam" as the guy with the cooking show says. All over except the shouting.

CHAPTER FOURTEEN

A few weeks later, Jimmie saw Terri coming into the bar and said, "Where's Nathan?"

"He was tied up so I came without him." She sat and said, "Is that okay?"

"Sure. Jus' normally see you two together. You can come in by yourself anytime." He placed a drink in front of her. Sensing something, he said, "I've never seen you so happy. Betty gave me hell about it, but my matchmakin' worked, huh?"

"Yeah, I guess so."

Jimmie asked, "Uh oh! Something wrong? The big Dufus hasn't picked his nose around the punch bowl has he?"

She laughed. "No. Just sometimes he's a bit much."

"Lots'a worse things. I remember some of the other guys you dated." She winced. "Want me to talk to him?"

"You're priceless, you know it?" She laughed and said, "No, I don't want you to talk to him. Did you know men are like government bonds, Jimmie?" He shook his head and she said, "Because they take so long to mature." They both laughed. "He's just overwhelming at times. Doesn't make him a bad person."

"Just overwhelming," said Jimmie.

"Yeah. Jimmie, are Great White Sharks found in the Atlantic Ocean around New York?"

"Why?"

"To hide the body," she said. "Honeymoon is definitely over. Don't get me wrong, I love Nathan. But he can't ever be serious, always jokin'. Just sometimes he's just, well, just…"

Jimmie smiled, "Overwhelming."

Terri asked, "Did you ever go to the doctor?"

"Yeah. Saw Schwartz two days ago."

"Jimmie, Schwartz is older than dirt. I'll make you an appointment with my guy."

***

Later that evening the usual group was sitting around the bar. Nathan said, "Damn Jimmie, a mentoring program for kids? Should've said something. I'll help."

"You have on many occasions, Nathan. I've been over charging you ever since you started coming to the bar."

"Seriously, I wouldn't mind mentoring a kid, putting them through college. If you can do three, I can at least do one."

"I'm not doing three by myself. I have help. Some prefer to stay in the background."

"Mafia guys, Jimmie?" asked Terri.

"Just because their names end in vowels doesn't mean there's anything wrong with them," he admonished Terri. "Shame on you." He turned to Nathan and said, "I'll get you started when I come back from Florida. Any of your people want to help, let me know."

"I just want you to know I think it's wonderful what you're doin'," said Nathan.

"Don't make me out a saint, Nathan. Maybe, all the wrong I've done, I'm trying to buy my way into heaven. Wouldn't be the first time someone tried it."

"Bullshit, Jimmie," said Gail. "Wrong? Stood by a family situation few would. You are a saint."

"Not you, Gail! Would've believed it out of one of these other sob sisters." He looked at them and saw they didn't understand. "I just believe when you're here, you should try to make a difference, that's all. Bad luck to you if you don't try. You guys feel that way, how about some of you helping me with the Christmas toys thing? Some of my other helpers are going to prison."

Terri asked, "Names ending in vowels doesn't mean there's anything wrong with them, but not Mafia guys, Jimmie?" He ignored her.

Nathan said, "Ray told me you set him up."

"Yeah. So?"

"What did Agnes do wrong?"

"You mean other than never payin' her bar tab on time and being surly to my help?" Nathan laughed.

***

A couple of weeks later, Jimmie was in the kitchen cooking some prime rib for sandwiches when Petey stuck his head in the door.

"What's up, Irish?"

Jimmie said, "Nothin' Petey. You still workin'?"

"Naw. Finito for me, bro'. Fuckin' tired a' chasin' stiffs."

Jimmie said, "Gettin' bad? Words out that Sal's goin' down."

Petey shrugged, "Nature of the beast. Sal's goin' in the joint and every 'mamaluke' in town figures he ain't gotta' pay." Petey leaned over Jimmie and pulled a hot piece of prime rib from the pan. "Cookin' dinner, Jimmie?"

"Makin' some stuff for Stuart and Ken. Pulled another stakeout, poor bastards. Wanna' come with me?"

"What else I got to do?"

Jimmie left Lou with the chore of closing the bar. After loading a thermos with coffee, he and Petey headed down to the stakeout site. With Dotty and Betty gone, he seldom went home anymore, preferring to sleep on a cot at the bar. Usually too keyed up after closing the bar, he'd watch cable for several hours.

Petey, a night person also, usually didn't go to bed until mid-morning. His nefarious duties for Sal left him with a schedule that would make a telemarketer cringe. He would often watch TV with Jimmie at the bar or go with him to the stakeouts.

***

Stuart and Ken were on a stakeout at East 53rd Street. The police had tried unsuccessfully to serve a warrant early the previous morning. Chances were, the suspect wouldn't return to his apartment. But, still in the doghouse with their lieutenant, they'd drawn the assignment.

"Fuck, I'm tired a' this shit," said Ken. "Every bullshit assignment comes along we catch."

"Could be worse. Could be in that friggin' diner."

"Damn, hated that place. I'm not sure sittin' in an unmarked Plymouth is any better. See the looks we're getting from the people live around here?"

"We're takin' up a prime parking spot," said Stuart. "Jimmie say he's coming by?" With his family in Florida, Jimmie often came over to their stakeout. He normally brought them food.

"Said he was. Want to go out and hit some in the morning?"

Stuart said, "Fuck no, ask Jimmie. I hate the fuckin' game. So do you. Speaking of, how're things goin' with Madeline?"

"Couldn't be better. Why?"

Stuart said, "Just curious. Was wonderin' how much longer you're goin' to play golf?"

Ken looked at him. "I'm not getting a divorce if that's what you're askin', Mr. Smart Guy." Stuart laughed. "Rough patch is all. It'll work out." Stuart smirked. "Don't see you exactly settin' the place on fire with Gail. Doesn't it bother you she's a kept woman?" He saw the look on Stuart's face and felt bad he'd purposely hurt his partner. "Didn't mean it like that, Stu." Someone knocked on the passenger window, scaring Ken. He rolled the window down and looked crossly at the person standing on the curb.

"Excuse me, Officer. I'm trying to get to Times Square. Family and I are in from Des Moines," the man motioned to his family standing on the sidewalk. "Can you tell us the quickest way to get there?"

"Cab! That'd be the quickest," said Ken as he rolled his window back up. Turning to his partner, he said, "Jesus Christ! Even a fuckin' hayseed made us for cops. So much for the undercover police cruiser "

"Too much TV," said Stuart.

The guy walked around the car and tapped on Stuart's window. He rolled it down and the guy said, "Your companion was very rude. My question is, would it be close enough to walk?"

"Buddy, we're in the middle of breaking up, so I apologize for my lover. Now what was your question?"

The guy says, "Are we close enough to walk to Times Square?"

"If I say yes, you're going to ask me how to get there, right?" The guy nodded and Stuart said, "I just don't feel like a long discussion, know what I mean? Ask somebody else so we can get on with our lover's spat." As he rolled up his window, he said to Ken, "I don't think this guy can just walk away. Five dollars says he asks another question."

"No bet." They both watched the guy standing on the sidewalk talking to his family and pointing at them.

Stuart said, "Hold the fort, partner. Gotta' run to the store on the corner and pick up some stuff for home. Right back." He got out of the cruiser and ran across the street to a Korean grocer who was open late. Entering, he nodded to the clerk, a young Korean girl, and walked the aisles gathering supplies in a shopping cart.

Finished, he carried them to the counter and laid them out for the girl to scan. He grinned as she scanned his purchases, a small tube of toothpaste, one roll of toilet paper, one frozen dinner, one can of coke and one box of cereal.

He said to the clerk, "Guess you can tell I'm single?"

The clerk said, "Why would I guess that?"

Smiling, Stuart said, "Because I'm buyin' one of everything."

The clerk looked up at him and said, "No, I figured it's because you're ugly."

He walked back to the cruiser shaking his head. He muttered, "What happened to foreigners jus' bein' glad to be here? Assholes are here a day and they get a mouth on 'em."

Once back in the car, Stuart said, "Now, to your earlier question about Gail being kept by another guy. Yes, it bothers me, but what can I do? It was goin' on before I got in the picture. Not like I didn't know about it. Can't say shit."

Ken said, "Look who's coming down the street."

"Jimmie!" Grinning, Stuart said, "Hope he brought food."

***

"Look at these poor mokes, Petey. You couldn't make 'em for cops, you got a room temperature IQ. City ought to do somethin' better'n this."

"Looks good to me, Jimmie," said Petey. "Remember, I'm on the other side. Why make it harder for the poor workin' stiff?"

"Good point," Jimmie said. They walked up to the car and got into the back seat from opposite doors.

"What's up, guys?" asked Ken. "Did you bring food?"

"No, Ken. Just walk around with a fuckin' grocery bag for the hell of it," said Jimmie, handing the bag across the seat.

Ken and Stuart dug in as Petey asked, "Who we watchin'?"

Ken pointed toward a brownstone up the street. Mouth full, he said, "White guy about six feet tall, slim, sometimes drives a Mustang."

"Real desperado?" asked Petey.

"Just serving a warrant. Guy's some kind of white collar criminal."

"Fuck," said Petey. "Thought we might get some excitement."

Stuart turned around to face Petey. "Fuckin' sorry we can't make it more excitin', Petey."

"Never know," said Petey, hoping for blood. "Still could be a shootout."

Stuart, losing it, said, "Jesus, Petey. Do I come on your job and root for the other guy? When you're bustin' some poor moke's balls can't pay the vig, do I cheer for him if he fights back?"

"Jeez, Stuart," said Ken. "Guy's jus' bored. Don't get so hostile."

Petey said, "He's right, Ken." Turning to Stuart, he said, "See what you're sayin', Stuart. No offense."

"Jimmie," said Stuart. "Been thinking about something. Ken brought it up earlier. My relationship with Gail is goin' pretty good. Wondering whether I should say somethin' to her?"

"Mean like askin' her to marry you?" asked Jimmie.

"Well, not quite yet. She's still hangin' with that dude. Bothers me."

Petey said from the back, "Would bother me too. No offense, Stuart."

"None taken, Petey. Thinkin', if I say somethin', is it gonna' blow the whole thing? I mean, I really care for her."

Jimmie thought for a second. "Seems to me you have to have an alternative. Far as the other guy, I wouldn't worry about that too much, I was you."

"How? No offense, but if it was your Betty, you sure wouldn't want her fuckin' nobody else," said Ken.

"Why I married her. Gave her an alternative. You're not ready to marry her, can't say nothin'." He tapped Stuart on the shoulder. "I was you, Stuart, I wouldn't worry about it."

"Jimmie," said Stuart, "you know somethin', tell me."

"Take me for a snitch, Stuart? If you tell me somethin' and ask me not to say anything, you think I'd tell somebody? Hell no I wouldn't and you know it," said Jimmie, answering for him. "Why you told me in the first place." Jimmie thought back to the confidence placed in him by Gail. Stuart had nothing to worry about, but Jimmie had gone as far as he could go.

Changing the subject, Jimmie said, "Ken, you got lucky with Madeline."

"Fuck, Jimmie! Me, lucky? In my first marriage, I bought a used car and my wife's clothes were already in the backseat." They laughed. "And that was the good one. I don't know, Jimmie. Things ain't going good. Jus' don't fit in her world."

"That's a problem." He thought for a second and said, "You both knew what each other did before you married. This ain't comin' as a surprise, is it?"

"Not for me," said Ken. "Seems like it is for her."

"Have you tried to include her in your world?"

Ken said, "A couple a times. Ball games and stuff. She hated it."

Jimmie sad, "She seemed to enjoy spending time with us."

Ken said, "Like when we were goin' on the tours? Said you guys were lame."

Jimmie snorted, "She said we were lame? Ain't like she's the life of no party or nothin'. No offense, Ken, but fuck her."

"None taken, Jimmie. I say anything about her friends, I'm an asshole."

"Can't imagine her havin' any friends. No personality," said Jimmie. Stuart started laughing and Jimmie asked, "What's so funny, Stuart?"

"Nothin', Jimmie," said Stuart, still giggling.

Jimmie said, "Nothin' hell. You're squealin' like a girl up there."

"Jus' somethin' funny."

Jimmie said, "Either let us in on it, or quit cacklin'."

Start tried to quit laughing and wiped his eyes, "A minute ago you were tryin' to talk my partner into savin' his marriage. Find out she thinks you're lame, now she should get fucked."

"She should," said Jimmie. "Wasn't jus' me she thought was lame. Would imagine her knowing you played a big part in the lame classification."

"Uh oh," said Petey. "Guy pulled up. Ain't a Mustang. See him, guy with a hat?"

Ken studied the man. "Don't think it's him." He paused a second, then said, "Nah! Walkin' right past the address."

They were in the middle of Ken's problem and didn't notice the man approach the car. He tapped on the passenger window, startling Ken, who turned and said, "Fuck. Captain Jensen." Ken and Stuart got out of the car and faced Jensen.

Jimmie and Petey got out the other side and started heading back down the sidewalk.

Jensen, a short, blond-haired man, said, "What the fuck's goin' on? You guys on stakeout and havin' a party?" Stuart tried to speak, but was cut off. Jensen yelled at Jimmie and Petey, "Don't wander off." They stopped, but came no closer. Jensen said, "I don't know who this gentleman is," pointing at Jimmie, "but I know this asshole," pointing at Petey. "Consortin' with known Mafia members. The fuck's wrong with you guys?" He motioned to Jimmie and Petey and said, "Get the fuck outta' here. Party's over." As soon as they turned and started off, he really chewed Ken and Stuart out. "You fuckin' guys like this shit? Bullshit stakeouts. Maybe ya' should think about another line of work. Fuckin' Fire Department or Port Authority. I ought a' suspend the both a' ya's."

CHAPTER FIFTEEN

In the bar the next night, Terri and Nathan saw Ray come in and waved him over. Nathan asked, "How's it goin' with Agnes?"

"Goin' great. Went out on our first date. Did the movie and dinner thing. Went well. Didn't push it. Goin' out again this weekend."

"You the man, Ray," said Nathan.

Terri asked, as Ray wondered off, "What did Agnes do to Jimmie?"

"Somethin' about bein' slow payin' her bar tab."

Terri yelled, "Lou. Over her when you get a chance."

Nathan looked at her. "You got a full drink in front of ya'."

Terri, digging in her purse said, "Not that. My tab's gettin' high. Pay that sucker off."

Nathan started laughing, then stopped. "Wait a minute, was your tab high when Jimmie introduced us?"

***

Later in the week, Gail came into the bar, spotted Jimmie, Julie and Terri and rushed over, saying, "Did you hear about Stuart? He and Ken were both suspended for havin' crooks in their squad car while on a stakeout."

Terri said, "Crooks? It was Jimmie and Petey."

"Oh! Dumb-ass Madeline! Ran into her at lunch and she told me crooks. Jimmie and Petey? They must have started blonde jokes because of her."

"Crooks? Well, I guess we are," said Jimmie.

"Nonsense, Jimmie. You're the best person I know. As to Ken and Stuart, no reason to suspend them," said Terri.

Julie said, "Well, technically I guess it was. Not sure, but I doubt it's okay to have other people in a squad car."

Jimmie asked, "Unless they're under arrest. Terri, you seen Nathan?"

"Yeah, Jimmie. Almost every night. Busy as hell with the investment bankers. They're about to do the IPO."

"When you see him, tell him I need to talk to him about somethin'."

"Sure, Jimmie. Reminds me, I'm supposed to meet him for dinner," she said, checking her watch.

Terri and Julie left for a restroom call and Jimmie said, "Gail, when are you going to come clean with Stuart? He thinks you're still being kept by some guy."

"Yeah! Guess I need to straighten that up."

"When, Gail?"

"Soon, Jimmie, real soon."

Julie and Terri returned and Jimmie left to help with the bar rush. Terri asked, "What's Jimmie on you about?"

"Fucking men," said Gail. "They should be like Kleenex. Soft, strong and disposable." She thrust her hands toward the sky in prayer and said, "Lord give me chastity." She thought a moment and said, "Just not yet."

Julie laughed and said, "Thought you and Stuart were doing well."

Gail said, "We are, that's the problem."

Julie said, "I know what you mean. Avi and I were happy then he hits me with marriage. The fun balloon went right out of it."

Gail said, "Thought Stuart was just looking to have fun too. Jus' spend a little time together. Now he's asking Jimmie questions, getting emotional or something. Guys I've known have always been like mascara. They run at the first sign of emotion."

Julie said, "Think you know somebody and they change." She slugged her drink down.

Gail said, "I agree. Fuck it!" She downed her drink and signaled Lou for another. "How are you and Nathan doing?"

Terri smiled, "Doing great. The strangest guy I ever met, but I'm having fun."

Julie said, "Strange? Nathan is hilarious." Frowning, she added, "Maybe a bit strange."

Gail said, "More than a bit strange, Julie. No offense, Terri. Nice looking, but he acts really goofy sometimes."

Julie said, "Must be nice having all that bulk against you in bed. Nice secure feeling? All I've ever dated are regular size or little guys."

Gail said, "Me too. Guess it comes with being tall."

Julie asked, "Why is it that short guys like tall women? It's embarrassing sometimes."

Gail said, "I know what you mean. When you're slow dancing, their noses are always between your boobs. Why are men like parking spots?" Terri and Julie shook their heads. "Good ones are taken and the rest are too small."

Terri said, "Nathan is different, but different is good. You know what I mean?"

Gail said, "Not really. He is different, though."

"Think about it, Gail. Most guys you meet, it's kind of a hustle. Maybe it's New York, but it's like everybody's keeping score."

Julie said, "Yeah. Like dating. You don't fully commit because if you break up, you can say you didn't really care about him. You aren't holding the bag."

Terri said, "Right. If you see it coming, you break up first so you can save face. Always better to be the "dumper" than the "dumpee.""

Julie said, "That's right. He's the loser, not you." She looked at Gail to see if she was following.

Gail nodded and Terri said, "Nathan's not like that. He's fun, no hustle, he's always up front. Tells you he's going to the ball game, he goes to the ball game."

Julie said, "That's nice. With Avi it's like 'I Spy.'"

Gail said, "Maybe Nathan's just not cool. Probably an 'out of town' thing. Maybe he doesn't care. Think about it."

Terri said, "No, that's not it. He's pretty secure in his masculinity. He doesn't care if he looks bad. It may be the fact that he's a big man, played violent sports. Just not afraid to look bad. He can laugh at himself."

Julie said, "He is funny. Cracks me up."

Gail said, "Well, I got to admit he is funny. Fuck, I don't know Terri, maybe I'm jaded."

"You aren't jaded," said Terri. "It's just this town." Gail nodded, and Terri said, "While we're on the subject of men..." She smiled. "When are you going to tell Stuart?"

Julie asked, "Tell him what? Did I miss something?"

Terri said, "It's a long story, but the short version is that Gail lets men think she's being kept by some guy."

Julie asked, "Like a sugar daddy or something?"

Gail said, "It's easier than if they think you have money. I've been hustled by some of the best." She laughed. "Writers, painters, even plumbers. All gainfully employed till they find out you have money. The next thing you know, they're parked in front of the TV all day, gettin' fat, don't shave and wearing sweat clothes."

Julie laughed, "And who started that 'three-day beard growth is cool' stuff? Nothing like a rug burn between your legs to turn you off men."

Gail said, "Oh God, I know. I absolutely require a freshly shaved face before I'll allow it."

"Seriously, you've got to tell him," Terri said. "When, Gail?"

"Why so serious, Terri? It's not like you at all."

"Stuart's a nice guy. You recall he came to me to set you guys up. I'm obligated as the 'set upper' to look out for both parties."

"Okay, okay. Soon." Seeing Terri's skeptical look, she added, "I promise, soon."

Terri looked at Julie and said, "While I'm at it, what are you goin' to tell Avi?"

Julie said, "Not a clue."

Terri said, grinning, "Love between two people is a beautiful thing."

In unison, Gail and Julie completed the old joke, "Between five is fantastic."

Jimmie returned from the bar rush and said, "You girls are having fun. Did I miss a joke?"

Gail said, "Terri was solving problems."

Jimmie snorted, "Terri?"

Terri said, "Don't start on me, Jimmie. I'll start smothering and ask you how you're feeling."

CHAPTER SIXTEEN

The IPO was completed. It was a tortuous four months and Nathan was rich. At least on paper.

That's when he discovered what a "lock-out" period was. A lock-out period was basically a way to screw the new company and its management. They couldn't sell their stock for a year after going public. It supposedly was a safe guard to keep management from dumping all their stock and leaving an unsuspecting public holding the bag.

In actuality, to Nathan, it was so the big venture capital and institutional investors could unload their stock, making a huge profit for their fund investors. Of course, this drove the price down for the public, as well as management, since the venture capitalists held the most stock.

You can't forget the investment bankers, thought Nathan. They got a block of free stock for taking the company public. As well as a huge fee. They also dumped their stock, driving the price down even further so Nathan and his management group were left with a huge, short-lived paper profit.

And the unsuspecting public was literally and figuratively fucked. They bought into an IPO and held their stock. Prices went down and they'd lost money.

Nathan took heart in the fact that his friends at the bar, and his brother, had done exceptionally well. They got in at the opening minutes of the IPO and cashed out at the same time the big boys did. Most, after prices had fallen, bought the stock again at a much-reduced price.

Nathan and the management group saw the handwriting on the wall early and planned accordingly. They held out sales over the two quarters before going public. During the Internet boom, sites weren't expected to make a profit. Companies were suspect if they did and Nathan took advantage of it.

So Nathan's management group decided they'd screw the big guys. Let them cash out at $16 a share. At the end of the lock-out, Nathan's group planned to bring the held-back sales forward. They'd look good and stock price would skyrocket as a result. And the people who bought in initially and had to hold their stock when the price went down would make money.

***

A couple of weeks after the IPO, Nathan walked into the bar and was surprised to find Terri already there. After kissing him, Terri said, "Poor baby. I saw that Internet stocks are way down. Yours fell to nine bucks. You lost a lot of your paper profits."

"Maybe."

Terri asked, "What does that mean? Maybe?"

"It depends on what you call a lot of money."

Exasperated, she said, "I'd call fifty million a lot of money."

"So would I."

"Nathan, you want to tell me something, tell me. Quit beating around the bush."

"I bought a bunch with you guys under another name. Sold most of it."

Terri said, "Taking a chance, bucko. Bet it was your brother Lynn. You guys think you're slick. You know they check stuff like that."

"Wrong answer. Was under Sal's name. Think I'm stupid?"

"Which Sal?"

"Big Mafia Sal."

"Does he know it?"

"Said I could."

Terri said, "You trust Big Mafia Sal?"

Nathan said, "Jimmie's idea. Sal is goin' away for tax evasion. If they check, a little more tax evasion ain't gonna' hurt Sal. Case closed." Seeing she was troubled, he added, "Me and the team decided it wasn't fair. We all bought some. Different names. I don't know who they used. Nobody told. Safer that way."

"Jesus, a little crime wave." She took a deep breath to calm herself and said, "Nathan, you're a grown man so I won't say anything. You are playing with fire. I can kind of understand why you did it. I know it may not get back up to where it opened at, but rules are rules."

"We took care of that too," Nathan said smugly.

"Not sure I want to hear this, but tell me anyway."

And he did, explaining, "We held back sales."

"Nathan, that's crazy."

"No way," said Nathan. "We aren't stealing the money. Just showing revenue from the sales we didn't post as other income. After the lockout, we pull it back and show it as sales. Sales will be high and the stock price goes up again." She was looking at him dubiously and he added, "Checked it out with a lawyer. Perfectly legal."

"This was an SEC attorney?"

Nathan laughed, "Nope. Real estate. Of course it was an SEC attorney."

Shaking her head she asked, "What about the 10Q for this quarter and your year end, the 10K?" She referred to the quarterly and annual SEC filings where management had to show how much stock they owned and sold during the periods.

"Showed what I was supposed to have, grants and options and stuff. Hell, I hope it goes down some more. Before the lockout is over, we'll buy as much as we can get."

Terri almost shouted, "That's insider trading!" She tried to calm herself, "And the guy that gave your team this advice is an idiot. Can't be a real lawyer from a real school." Seeing she wasn't getting anywhere, she said, "Drop it. Don't want to know. Hope it is legal for your sake."

Ray came in as Terri was heading to the restroom. "What's up, buddy?" Nathan asked.

"I'm great, Nathan. Thanks for all the stock tips and stuff. Made a bundle."

"Glad to help. How are things with Agnes?"

"Couldn't be better. Not gonna' believe what happened last night. Did a threesome with her and her roommate."

Nathan said, "Damn, you're a mover, Ray. How did you approach the subject?"

Ray started to lie, but decided against it. "Jus' came outta' the blue. Went to pick her up to go out and both of 'em were in robes when I got there. They asked me."

Nathan said, "Get out a' here. They asked you?"

"Yeah. Hey, maybe you can help me out. Ever tried Viagra?"

Nathan said, "Nah. My doc won't give it to me. High blood pressure."

"Goin' to see my doc and get a prescription."

"Let me know how it works," Nathan said.

Terri returned as Ray was leaving and said, "Did ya' miss me?"

Nathan said, "I'm horny."

She said, "What's new? Your mind's always on sex."

"Been doing it for a while. Easy to remember."

Terri asked, "When was the first time you had it?"

"Fifth grade?"

Incredulously, she asked, "You were getting it in the fifth grade?"

"Not steady."

She laughed, "Liar!"

"Girl named Lorrina. In the bamboo behind my house."

"You lured some little neighborhood girl into the bamboo? What did you give her, a Snickers?"

"She was a seventh-grader," he snorted. "Gave her an Almond Joy and bubble gum."

CHAPTER SEVENTEEN

Having volunteered to help with the Christmas Drive, Nathan was touring the Canal Street warehouse. "Man, I can't believe all this stuff. You guys did a great job organizing it. Age groups, gender, this is good."

Sal grinned. "Told ya', Jimmie. And this guy knows what he's talkin' about. Let me show the rest of the operation, Nathan."

As he and Sal walked away from Petey and Jimmie, Sal said, "Good of ya' to help us out. You know me and Petey and some of the other fellas will be going away for a while. It'll be jus' you and Jimmie from now on."

"We'll jus' have to work harder." Nathan stopped and turned toward Sal. "I've been wantin' to get down here. Hell of a thing you guys are doin'."

Sal smiled. "Hey, you do what you can. Jimmie's idea. Sometimes he tries to do too much. Me and Petey end up helpin' out to keep him from workin' hisself to death." They walked down a long row of triple-racked wooden pallets loaded with toy trucks and tricycles. "Fuckin' Jimmie talks about ya' a lot. Why I wanted to ask ya' a favor. I want you to take care a' Jimmie."

Nathan said, "I will, Sal. Not sure how much help he needs though. Jimmie handles himself well."

Sal waved away his comment and said, "What I mean is keep him from takin' on too much. People take advantage of his good nature. The church, all kinds of people."

"Got ya', Sal. I'll watch over him like a brother."

Sal, relieved, said, "Says yer' from the burbs. Atlanta, no?"

"Yeah. Wouldn't really call Atlanta a burb."

"Hey it ain't da' city," said Sal, grinning.

"Nah, it ain't."

"Been there once. Fuckin' people talk funny."

"They talk funny, Sal?"

Sal said, "Yeah, you know, slow, fuckin' twangy. Can't understand a word they say. Like a foreign country or somethin'."

Nathan smiled. "At least they don't use descriptions, Sal." Nathan saw he didn't understand and explained, "Like you're Big Mafia Sal. Jimmie, at least to you guys, is Irish Jimmie. We got Fat Sal and Fat Jimmie at the bar and a bunch of Doms, like Skinny Dom, Cheese Dom, Joey the Jeweler, Dom the Jeweler, Berti the Plumber, like that. Hell, they even put a 'y' or 'ie' on the end of everybody's name."

"They don't do that in this Atlanta?"

"Naw, just call em' by name."

"The fuck do they know who you're talkin' about?"

Nathan said, "By name."

Sal grinned, understanding. "More people here."

"Yeah, guess so." He scratched his head and asked Sal, "Wonder why nobody gives me a name? You know, like 'Genius Nate' or somethin'. Nobody even puts anything on the end of my name."

"You got a fucked-up name. 'Natey'," said Sal.

***

Sentencing was held in the Federal Courthouse in Manhattan. Jimmy sat deep in thought, not really seeing his friends Sal and Petey. Already, at eleven in the morning, it had been an eventful day for him. Tears streamed down his face as he watched his two best friends have years of their lives taken away from them.

First Petey. The judge didn't go along with the plea agreement and sentenced him to seven years.

Then Sal, who at least got the twenty-year sentence he'd agreed to in his plea bargain.

Jimmie knew they did the crimes. But they were still good men. Both gave to the church freely, both helped with charity functions. Was New York that much safer with these men off the streets? They were his friends and he was going to miss them. Especially now!

After sentencing, both men nodded and smiled at him as they were led away. Jimmie fought back the tears and smiled back. Not quite sure whether the tears were for them or him, he broadened his smile out of guilt.

***

At the bar that evening, Ray came in and Nathan waved him over. Terri leaned over and said, "Goin' to the Ladies'. You boys can have your talk."

"So how did the blue diamond work?"

Ray said, all smiles, "Great. Banged 'em all night. Tough day at work today and s'posed to go over again tonight."

"Don't overdo it," advised Nathan.

"Tired, but I gotta' go. Nothin' like this has ever happened to me. Afraid I'll wake up and it'll be gone."

Jimmie came over and said, "Nathan, can I talk to ya' in private?"

"Sure, Jimmie."

Ray said, "You guys go ahead and talk. Gotta' run. Due to see Agnes in an hour." Ray made a big show of pulling two blue pills out of a container. He popped both pills in his mouth and washed them down with beer. "One for each girl. Takes an hour to work."

As he left, Jimmie said, "Nathan, I'm dying." Jimmie was stacking coins from the poker machines.

"We all are, Jimmie."

"I'm serious, Nathan. I got cancer."

Jimmie's comment was better than a cold shower for sobering him up. Nathan exclaimed, "What?"

"Keep you're voice down. Why I waited for Terri to go to the ladies' room. Don't want every friggin' person this side of Eighth Avenue to know I have cancer. Terminal. Esophagus. I've got about a year if the guys at Sloan are worth a shit at guessin' these things."

Nathan said, shocked, "Fuck! I am so sorry. How long you known?"

"Since this morning. Went to the doc before Sal and Petey were sentenced. They ran the tests a couple of weeks ago."

"Heard about the sentencing." Nathan scratched his head. It was early September. By September 2001 his friend might be dead. Nathan, a tear in his eye, said, "Can I hug you?"

"No! No offense. I'm not good at hugging and I don't think you are either."

"Why do men always have to be such hard-ons?"

Jimmie said, "I'm not sure. Don't wanna' hug, okay?"

Nathan gulped, "I don't know what to say."

"Don't want you to say anything. Need some advice. I don't know whether you know or not, but I haven't necessarily been a perfect citizen. I've always kind of been on the fringe of a lot of stuff." Jimmie smiled. "Kind of in the gray area, so to speak."

"Gray area?"

"Things fall off trucks, somebody finds some jewelry, stuff like that. Not a fence, but kind of like one."

"I see," said Nathan. "And this pays well?"

"Put together a fairly tidy sum to take care of my wife and kid. Comes to three million dollars, all of it hid overseas and all for them. That and whatever I get for selling the bar and my apartment. Might not be much now that I don't have the luxury of holding out for a good price."

"Jimmie, I'd call that tidy."

Jimmie nodded. "I want to make sure my wife and kid get it. Don't want them paying no taxes and shit on the overseas stuff. Nor do I want them being hassled in any way."

"Sounds like you got it taken care of, Jimmie."

"Not quite. Need somebody. Like an attorney, to pay bills, like that. Somebody I can trust, since I ain't gonna be here. Can you help me?" He began counting coins again, eying Nathan warily. He was trying to decide whether or not to recount them. Unfortunately, Nathan had a track record and couldn't be trusted to not mess up the piles.

"I can try. I'd have to ask around. Do it in a way that your name won't come up. So that I understand, the money is overseas and you want it administered as needed, correct?" Things falling off trucks? Three million dollars worth of things falling off trucks? His buddy Jimmie was a major crime wave.

"Yeah. I mean, would that keep you from helping me?"

"Hell no. Just wanted to make sure I understood. Fuck, Jimmie, friends take care of friends. The stuff we've been buyin' from you, that was part of the stuff fallin' off of trucks?" He nodded and Nathan gulped.

Jimmie said, "That's exactly why I asked you and nobody else. Friends help friends."

"Fucked-up break. Anybody but you."

"Knock it off, Nathan. I start thinkin' like that, I'll never make the fuckin' year."

Nathan said, "Do what I can. Offhand, I don't know a lawyer that I would trust to do it. I need to look around."

"I got a couple of other people lookin'. Nobody in the group, so don't mention it to them. Sal is lookin'. May be more up his alley. You know Sal, right?"

Assuming Jimmie forgot about Nathan helping with the Christmas Drive, he said. "Of course I know Sal. Big Mafia Sal."

Before Nathan could say anything about Sal and prison, Jimmie said, "No. Sal Russo would be worse than you, big blubberin' sissy. I'm talkin' about Sal the bookie. You know who I mean, right?" Sal took bets in the bar. Mafia through and through, Sal was with another part of the Gambrelli family.

"Fat Sal?"

Jimmie nodded. "That's him. Says he knows a guy who lives here and in Miami. He's settin' up a meetin' next time I go down to visit my family. Figured I'd ask you in case that don't work out or you got somebody you know better. Don't mention it to Sal. He's funny that way."

"Let me work on it." Nathan would rather find somebody than have Jimmie dealing with Fat Sal. Nathan didn't say anything, but he wouldn't trust twenty cents with Fat Sal. Much less the money Jimmie was talking about. "Who's your doctor?"

Jimmie asked, "Why?"

"I want to talk to him. Find out what you can and can't do," said Nathan.

"Bullshit. You aren't gonna' do the Jewish mother bit."

Nathan said, "Nope. You and I are gonna' have fun. Just want to find out how much fun you can have."

Jimmie smiled. "You're a good friend. Rudolph's his name. I'll call and tell him to talk to you. Dummy up, Terri's coming back and he's her doc too."

Not a problem, Nathan thought, speechless for once in his life.

***

The next morning, Nathan talked to his brother Lynn, who was almost an attorney. Lynn came to his senses before actually entering law school. He now owned a fairly successful software company in Florida.

"Not a clue, but I'll check. You aren't laundering money, are ya'?"

"Be kind a' stupid, wouldn't it? Launder money that's been taxed?"

Lynn said, "Stupid is as stupid does. Quick joke. A girl was visiting her blonde friend who had bought two new dogs. The girl asked her what their names were. The blonde responded by saying that one was named Rolex and the other was Timex.

"The friend said, 'Never heard of someone naming dogs like that'.

'Hellooooo', answered the blonde, 'they're watch dogs.'"

"Lynn, you know somebody? Kind of urgent. My buddy is dyin' soon."

Lynn asked, "Why does it have to be an attorney? All he needs is somebody he can trust."

"True. I didn't think of that. He doesn't need an attorney."

Lynn asked, "Anything else earth shattering you need?"

"Nope. Just checkin' to see if your thinkin' process was workin'. I had the answer of course." To change the subject quickly, he asked, "How's Philo doin' with the Pop Warner deal?"

"Doing good. Made him a lineman, but he doesn't care. He likes to hit people. Starting him on weights. Think ten is too early?"

Nathan said, "Never start too early. Especially for a lineman. It's for sure with his Melton slowness gene he's not going to be a speed burner."

Nathan then called the doctor, who graciously made time for him to visit. After small talk, the doctor cut to the chase. He told Nathan that Jimmie had a squamous carcinoma of the esophagus. The doctor explained that it affected a small percentage of the population, 3 out of 100,000 white males with the rates higher in blacks. He told him it was mostly attributed to environmental factors, smoking and alcohol.

The doctor told him it took a long time for any symptoms to develop, which usually included a problem with swallowing. By the time Jimmie came in the disease was already advanced. He told Nathan that Jimmie would have to change his eating habits, take in less solid food and more soft food. He could expect to lose significantly more weight. As the tumor got bigger, even liquids would be difficult and he'd cough up blood and his voice would get hoarse.

"So what can you do for him?" Nathan asked.

"We're going to give him chemotherapy, followed by radiation treatments," said Dr. Rudolph.

Nathan asked, "What about surgery?"

"The stage is too advanced."

Nathan said, "He told me he had a year."

"That's about right."

"If he's terminal, why the radiation and chemo treatments?"

The doctor said, "It may increase his time significantly. In this type of situation, you're playing for time. Things happen, who knows? I've seen patients live significantly longer after treatment. Time is hope, Mr. Melton."

"Doc, he has family in Florida he's been visiting every other week. Should he keep that up?"

"Simple answer is no. I'm aware of his family situation. In his place, I'd continue visiting. If I suggested he save as much strength as possible, he'd go anyway."

***

That night Nathan tried to talk to Terri about Jimmie. "Honey, I know this guy who hid money overseas and now needs it back in the states. He's dying and has to take care of his family, a little at a time. He wants a lawyer, but I'm not sure he needs one to administer like an endowment."

Terri said, "So Jimmie asked you too?"

"Son-of-a-bitch. Is there anybody that doesn't know about this?"

Terri said, "Don't get upset."

"I'm not," he said. "It's just he swears me to secrecy and every fucking body in the world knows."

Terri said, "Not true. Just you, me, Stuart, Ken, Julie, Gail and Dave and Marie."

"The bookie knows."

"Ralph knows?"

"Ralph? No, the bookie. Fat Sal. Who's Ralph?"

Terri said, "Ralph's a bookie too. Who is Sal?"

"Older Italian guy. Comes in about seven every night. Big fat guy. Wears those Italian silk shirts out of his pants. Wears bedroom slippers."

"Is he a bookie? I thought he was some kind of pervert. Only one I knew was a bookie is Ralph. Comes in later. Thin guy. Hair greased back. Big cigar. Dresses about the same. Got the tattoos."

"Is he a bookie?"

"Yeah," she said. "Maybe Jimmie needs a wider circle of friends. Ralph always comes in with Louie the Fence. Always has all that jewelry he's trying to sell."

"Shit. I thought Louie was a jeweler." Nathan laughed.

"Nope. Has a pawnshop over on Seventh. Great rings. I've bought some from him. Good quality."

Nathan said, "We're gettin' away from what I was talkin' about. Are you doin' anything to help Jimmie? If you are, I'll quit asking around."

"I found a guy, but Jimmie hasn't talked to him yet. I'll volunteer to do it before I let that greasy pervert Sal set it up. I could at least do the overseas part." Terri thought for a second. "He will need an attorney to set up the trust for what he has in the U.S."

"So he does need an attorney for the trust part. Is that a lot?"

"Not right now. Just the money he made with you. When he sells the bar it should be. And his apartment around Battery Park."

"Think he'll get much?" Nathan asked.

"Hope so. No telling how long it'll take." She noticed the pained expression on his face. "You look like your dog died. Don't worry!"

"Well, if you're settin' this lawyer thing up I'll quit screwing with it."

***

The next evening in the bar, Nathan couldn't help himself. He let Jimmie have it. "Man, I'm busting my ass asking everybody and their brother to try to get you help on this secret shit and find out you've told everybody. Every fucking body! Can't believe you, Jimmie. Why didn't you just take out an ad? Call Ken's wife. Maybe she can get you a billboard. Maybe one of those beams so you can light up the sky."

"I'm sorry, Nathan. This thing's got me so worried I don't know what to do. Or what I'm doing. I appreciate your help. Listen, don't worry about it, okay? I found a guy."

"That's great, Jimmie. This the guy that Terri was tryin' to hook you up with?"

He turned away from Nathan. "All taken care of. Met with him Sunday. Load off my mind. Setting up a trust and all. Don't mention it. Okay?" Jimmie turned to walk down the bar to help Lou during a rush period.

"Sure, Jimmie. How are you feelin'?"

Jimmie turned back. "Don't do this."

"What?"

"Start being smothering."

Nathan threw his hands up and said, "I've asked probably everybody I've seen today how they're doin'. Can't ask you anymore? What's up with that?"

"Sorry. I feel like shit."

Nathan said, "What about the bar? Anything happenin' there?"

"Got people looking. A couple coming tomorrow." "Shit. Sounds so sudden," said Nathan.

"No tellin' how long it'll take. You wanna' buy it?"

Nathan asked, "What the fuck do I know about the bar business?"

"You got this end covered pretty good." Jimmie laughed. "Here so much you're on the vacation schedule in the back room."

"You're a funny guy. Funny guy Jimmie Collins."

Jimmie said, serious, "I placed it with one of those business brokerages. They usually close pretty quick."

Nathan asked, "They gonna' bring people through all the time? Like a house? We can't fart and sit around in our underwear anymore?"

"No. It's more of a look at the books deal."

Nathan asked, "How do your books look?"

"As good as anybody runnin' a mostly cash business. Kind a' keep it quiet, all right? Don't want to lose any customers."

Nathan asked, incredulously, "You're askin' *me* to kind a' keep it quiet?" Jimmie laughed. Nathan said, "If you or Terri would've been captured before D Day, we'd have all been speakin' German."

Jimmie said, "Yeah. And drinkin' good beer, too." He walked away laughing.

CHAPTER EIGHTEEN

Jimmie's health was going downhill fast. He was losing a lot of weight and seemed to have no energy. He was still pissy about being asked how he felt. Jimmie planned to go to Florida again the next weekend and see his family for his daughter's birthday. Nathan volunteered to go with him, but was rejected.

To brighten his mood, Nathan took him to a ball game. "Nice huh? Nice quiet night in Yankee Stadium," Nathan said in jest. Some idiot behind them had a loud, battery operated horn.

"Beautiful," said Jimmie. "Be better when the battery runs out on this horn behind us. The bar is sold, by the way," he added. "Almost three mill on the books, a little more off. The new owner takes over in two weeks."

Nathan said, "Two weeks? Pretty quick."

Jimmie said, "Nice people. You guys'll like 'em. A husband and wife team. Good Irish couple."

"Is three mill a good price?"

"Good for them. Not like I got a lot of time to dicker," Jimmie said. "I'll stay awhile and help 'em. Show 'em the ropes."

"Then you're goin' to Florida?"

"I hate Florida," Jimmie laughed. "Be nice to spend time with Dottie and Betty, though."

"Shame you can't go as soon as you close on the bar."

"Nathan, you do what you gotta' do."

Nathan said, "No Jimmie, you do what you can do."

He dismissed Nathan. "You know I never really had time for sports. I'm sorry I missed it."

"You did as a kid, right?"

Jimmie shrugged. "No. Definitely not. Growin' up, all we had time for was the troubles. Survivin'. Stayin' alive. Hatin' a bunch of people who hated us."

"Must have been tough?"

Jimmie said, "It's what you get used to. It was easier and certainly more fun raisin' hell with the Prods' than gettin' whacked by a nun in school. Now I wish I would've had the education."

"You did all right. Did damn good as a matter of fact." Nathan laughed, "Even without the stuff fallin' off the trucks."

Smiling, Jimmie said, "Yeah, but my mother sure would've liked to see me and my brothers go further in school."

"First I've heard of brothers. How many do you have?"

"Had! Three. None made it out of their teens. I probably wouldn't of either. There was a bit of a price on my head and I had to leave fairly early on."

Nathan said, "That's tough. Leavin' home."

"Hell no," he said. "Ireland's a poor, hard, miserable country. Missed my family and friends, but miss that ball breaker? Never!"

***

Nathan and Jimmie returned to the bar from the game just as Ray was running out the door.

Jimmie said, "Ray's lookin' terrible."

"He's doin' both ends of a candle."

Jimmie asked, "Huh?"

"Agnes and her roomie."

Jimmie asked again, "Huh?"

"Threesomes. Hard to imagine."

"Don't want to," said Jimmie. "Would be somethin' to see though. Fat ass Ray and skinny Agnes." Deep in thought, he shook his head. "Ray?" Jimmie laughed, "Guess the old sayin' is true. There is somebody for everybody." He snorted, "But Ray?"

Nathan laughed and asked Jimmie, "When are ya' gonna' tell everybody about the bar?"

Dave, walking past them, asked, "Tell everybody about what?"

Jimmie, after calling Nathan a big mouth, said, "Now." Jimmie announced to the patrons that the bar had been sold.

Dave said, "That's great. You'll finally get to enjoy life."

"Who says I'm not enjoying life now? Just took in a ball game with this big lug," he said, pointing at Nathan. "I'm gonna' become a regular now that I'm a man of means. I'm going to make it my vocation. Baseball and travel. Basketball too if I don't have to sit close to friggin' Spike what's his name."

"Great, Jimmie," said Julie. "See the world."

Jimmie said, "Maybe not the world. There are some places I've always wanted to go. Maybe some of you can get away and go with me."

Gail asked, "Where do you want to go, Jimmie?"

"Costa Rica. Saw somethin' on the History Channel the other night. Like to go there first. Then I'd like to see Israel. Hearin' you guys talk about it makes me want to go."

Julie said, "You'll love Israel, Jimmie. I'll go with you on that one."

"Me too," said Ray.

"Costa Rica sounds great," said Terri.

"Costa Rica it is," said Gail. "Who's going?"

***

Later the same night, Jimmie, Stuart, Ken and Nathan were watching a baseball game on TV. Ken yelled to Lou, "Turn up the sound. It's Jimmie's vocation."

Jimmie turned to look at the game on TV and asked, "Who's playin'?"

Stuart said, "Giants and Astros. Enron Field."

Jimmie said, "They try to screw up baseball. But people still go."

Ken asked, "What do you mean, Jimmie? Big salaries and stuff?"

"Naw. Not so much the pay the guys get," he said. "Take Houston. Started out with those God awful uniforms reminded you of the flu or a damn Tide box or something. Put 'em in the fucked up Astro Dome. Place was like a morgue. They get a new stadium and name it after a friggin' business. What kind of shit is that?"

Nathan said, "It's the thing now. Like the Giants and 3-Com. College teams are doing it too. One of the Kentucky schools, not Kentucky, but Louisville or Memphis. Maybe it was Western Kentucky. Anyway, one of 'em named their stadium after Colonel Sanders. It's Chicken Field or something like that."

"That's what I'm talkin' about," said Jimmie. "S'pose one of those companies goes belly up. Or maybe the Colonel's chicken kills a bunch of people with that disease chickens catch sounds like an Italian singer. Team's sitting there with egg on their face. Now, they don't do that in hockey."

"Hell they don't," said Stuart. "One of those Canadian teams plays in Molson Arena."

"Fuck it, Jimmie," Nathan said. "You go for the sports. Not the stadium name. Look at the Meadowlands. Think there was a meadow there before they built the stadium?"

Ken said, "Fuck no. Just Hoffa and a bunch of that radon."

Stuart asked, "Radon?"

Ken said, "Yeah, you know, the nuclear shit." Stuart had a confused look on his face and Ken tried to explain, "It's nuclear waste, Stuart. Buried all over Jersey. Why they all got pimples and bad complexions." Stuart still didn't understand and Ken said, "Need to read somethin' other than comics, bro'."

Stuart shrugged and said, "You're right, Nathan. Just go for the sports, not the friggin' name of the stadium."

"Forget it," said Jimmie. "I ain't gonna' sit some place I'd be embarrassed for somebody to see me cause of some pansy-ass name." Changing the subject he asked, "You guys like that duck?"

Ken asked, "Duck? What duck, Jimmie?"

"Fuckin' insurance duck. Walks around talkin' to people." Jimmie has a sour look on his face. "Fucker don't talk to Orientals though. Notice that? Eat him for sure."

"You mean AFLAC?" Nathan said, "They do great commercials."

"Great?" Jimmie says, "I'd strangle that little cocksucker he comes in here."

Ken said, "How about the one where this guy's got a friggin' Volkswagen on his head? They say 'He's got something on his mind and can't figure out what.' Fucker better get to a dermatologist and get that shit cut out and hope it's not malignant."

Jimmie asked, "How's Chucky, Nathan?"

"Chucky is Chucky."

"Worthless piece of shit," said Lou as he passed by.

Nathan said, "Heard a good Mafia joke today. A Mafia Don's kid is sitting at his desk doin' a Christmas list. His Dad told him always go to the top so he decided to skip Santa Claus. God was a bit over his head so he wrote, 'Dear baby Jesus, I have been a good boy the whole year, so I want a new...' He looks at the letter, crumples it up into a ball and throws it away. He gets out a new piece of paper and writes, 'Dear baby Jesus, I have been a good boy for most of the year, so I want a new...' He thinks about it and throws it away too. He gets another idea. He goes into his mother's room and takes the statue of the Virgin Mary off her dresser. He goes back to his room and puts it in the closet. He locks the door and takes another piece of paper and writes, 'Dear baby Jesus, if you ever want to see your mother again...'"

Jimmie said, "Man, I miss Sal and Petey."

CHAPTER NINETEEN

Gail surprised everybody with tickets to Costa Rica a week later. Her treat. All were going excepting Avi and Julie, who were still mad with each other.

They left from La Guardia and quickly discovered that Costa Rica is not a country you can fly to directly. What began as a happy, talkative group full of energy, degenerated into a quiet, tired group after connections in Dallas and Mexico City. On the last leg, all were lost in individual thought.

Gail was in a quandary over when, what and how much to tell Stuart about her former life. Stuart, certain he loved Gail, was having a tough time dealing with what he thought was Gail's former life.

Jimmie was thinking about his pending death. He was putting on a brave front for everybody, but he was truly afraid. A God-fearing man, he was troubled about his past and how that would sit with God on his Judgment Day.

Nathan and Terri were both worrying about Jimmie and how he would hold up on the trip.

Ray was worried that the flight attendants would run out of peanuts during the flight. He was hungry.

They arrived at Juan Santa Maria Airport in the late afternoon. They were traveling fairly light so they cleared customs quickly.

Each had gone through separately. Jimmie caught up to Nathan and leaned over and said, "Fuck. Sweating bullets over the passport."

"Me too," he said. Nathan was actually thinking about work and hadn't thought about Jimmie's fake passport. Forgetting worked in his favor. Nathan was the worst at hiding his feelings. He would've given it away by acting nervous.

Jimmie said, "Guess Avi knows what he's doing." Avi had supplied Jimmie with the phony passport.

For reasons not known by them, and never explained, Jimmie had a social security card under one name. He also had a driver's license under another name and now a passport under a third. None were under the name of Collins.

Oh, what a tangled web we weave, thought Nathan. "You told me it's none of my business and I respect that, but how do you keep the names straight?" His credit cards were under his real name. If Collins was his real name.

Jimmie said, somewhat exasperated, "Be a real stoop if I couldn't keep a little thing like that straight now wouldn't I, boyo?"

"Right, Jimmie. He never thought of that, Ed. How stupid of me, Bill. I can be a real dunce sometimes, Henry," said Ray, coming to Nathan's defense and both of them chuckled.

Jimmie gave them a dirty look, the finger, then a final, "Fuck the both of ya's," as he walked away, which made them giggle harder.

Ray asked, "What good are friends if you can't screw with them?"

They gathered the luggage and Gail suggested they all ride together.

Ray said, "You kiddin'? Anytime this many New Yorkers get into a cab together without arguing, a bank robbery has just taken place."

They caught a couple taxis. Nathan rode with Ray and Terri and left Jimmie to Gail and Stuart.

Coming out of the dirty airport, things improved dramatically. The countryside was beautiful and the roads excellent. This lasted until the outskirts of San Jose. The scenery became ugly and mean looking and got continuously worse as they entered San Jose. The city smelled like a nursing home. Old people shit!

After a short ten-dollar taxi ride to the hotel, and the promise of any type of drugs, woman, girl or boy they wanted, they arrived. At least the hotel was nice. Maybe not a five-star, but it was clean and the front desk people appeared adequate.

They had to wait while the rooms were readied. Ray joked that "readied" meant they were getting snakes and birds out of the rooms. Terri used the time wisely and rushed to the bathroom. The rest filed into a small bar off of the main entrance to wash the road dust off.

They'd just gotten beer when a staff member brought keys. Nathan said, "Before we split up, do we want to do something tonight?"

Stuart asked, "What do you have in mind, Nathan?"

Nathan said, "Schedule some kind of tour?"

"Let's go to dinner tonight and discuss it," said Gail. She handed him the guidebook. "Pick a spot, Nathan. Make it something good. I need a shower bad. Hot, isn't it?"

"Not bad," said Stuart. "Enjoying being wet. It's like a wet T-shirt contest outside. A lot of contestants. You'd starve to death with a bra franchise in this country."

"Stuart," said Gail. "You acting up? Remember what I told you?"

"Yes, dear. I remember. No cheating. Want me to come up with you and wash your back?" They'd been a couple for a while now and had a couple's cutesy way of talking to each other.

"I think that would be great, honey," she said, patting him. She gave the rest of them the "Stuart's going to get laid" smile as they left the bar.

The men watched her leave, as she knew they would, and Ray said, "I'd look good on that."

Terri and Nathan were shown to their room and Nathan tipped well. He loved to be treated like a God. He gave the bellhop two bucks, ensuring his deity.

After the bellhop left, Nathan said, "The guy was so happy I think he may have blown me."

"Hell, give him three," said Terri. "Take away the doubt. That way I can get some rest." She noticed the look on his face, and didn't help by saying, "Go on, go play." That was as far as she could take it and started laughing.

"Nah! Mustaches are a turn-off." The room was nicely furnished with all of the modern conveniences. Unfortunately, only half worked, but they were all new as the bellhop pointed out before he left. "Have I been wearin' you out?" He was grinning proudly.

"Can't wear out something self-lubricating," she giggled and kicked a shoe at him.

"Love it when you mix engineering and anatomy. Major turn-on! Want to fool around?" Nathan asked.

"Did you get horny on the trip? Or was it the bellhop?"

Nathan laughed, "You must be butter cause you're on a roll, huh?" He grabbed her and tickled her lower back. "Nothing else to do. Skeet shooting range isn't open yet."

"Well, I think you should wait for it to open Mr. -wise-ass-just-talked-yourself-out—of-some."

"I can forgo it. Shoot one, shot 'em all."

Terri said, "You sure? Don't want to see my sweetie deprived. Besides we don't have much time."

Nathan said, "I got absolutely nothing against quickies. Wanna' do it standin' up in the bathroom? You can use the mirror to do make up. Save some time!"

"Asshole," she said, heading for the bathroom.

"Good choice," he said, following her.

He was in her from behind. She was leaning over the sink. He was watching her breasts bounce in the mirror when he noticed her face.

"Terri, something I always wondered." Her eyes popped open. "Why do women close their eyes during sex?"

"Don't know about everybody." She pulled away and he slipped out. "I can't stand to see you having a good time." She was mad. "Nathan, I can't believe you. I was so close."

Nathan said, "Honey, I was serious."

"What you need to be serious about is your fucking performance. The hell is wrong with you," she said, pushing him out of the bathroom.

He volunteered to wait for Terri to dress, but she knew he was lying and told him to get the hell out. He called Ray and they decided to meet in the bar and decide what to do that night. Nathan was hopeless with the guidebook.

***

Down the hall, Stuart was climaxing after waiting for Gail to catch up. They were in the shower, Gail bent over at the waist and Stuart in her from behind. Tall women are great, he thought, squeezing the last drops of semen from his penis inside her.

As he pulled out, Gail sat in the shower and leaned back against his legs. "That was good, baby," she said.

"Always good!" He began playing with her hair. "Hand me the shampoo and I'll wash your hair."

"Not hotel crap, Stuart. Bag's on the toilet. Reach and get the blue bottle out." He did and began lathering her hair. "Honey, we need to talk."

"You have my undivided attention," he said, becoming aroused again as his penis brushed the back of her head.

"I want you to know that I'm not seeing anyone other than you."

"Do you have to move out of the apartment? You know you can move in with me, baby."

She smiled, "That's sweet of you. Stu, I own the apartment."

"Well yeah, but not technically. The guy's gonna' want it back. I mean, you aren't seeing him anymore."

For some reason this angered her. For him to think that she couldn't buy an apartment without some damn man's help. Fuck it! "You're right, Stu. Guess I need to move." Gail knew her temper and decided to drop it. She became violent when mad, very violent. "Stuart, let's talk about it when we get back? Just enjoy our time in Costa Rica?"

"Sure, baby," he said, lathering in conditioner. His smile would've lit up the room. He had his girl. As he was behind her, he didn't see the tear falling down Gail's cheek.

CHAPTER TWENTY

Ray was there when Nathan entered the bar and already one beer up on him. Gail and Stuart hadn't put in an appearance yet, Nathan noticed as he entered the bar.

As he walked over to the table Ray said, "Another American. Pull up a stool. Where you from, stranger? Wichita or somethin'?" Ray waved for two more beers.

Nathan said, "West Virginia. You?"

"I'm a big city boy. Know what the first words out of a West Virginia girl's mouth are just after sex for the first time?" He paused, "Daddy, get off me. You're crushing my cigarettes."

"Talkin' about my sister, asshole?" Nathan handed Ray the guidebook, sat and asked, "Where's your roomy?"

"Jimmie went to get some postcards."

Nathan said, "We'll be back before the postcards get to New York."

Ray said, "That's what I told him. Went anyway."

"Hey, how come you didn't bring Agnes with you on the trip?"

Ray's face darkened, "Fuck Agnes."

Nathan asked, "Things aren't goin' well?"

"Understatement. Went to see her just before we left. Her and her damn old roommate. Had it all set up. Took two blue pills before I went. Ready to nail 'em as I came through the door." He shook his head, "Bitches had dates. I went home. Had to go to the doctor the next day."

Nathan asked, as he was signing for the beers, "You hit one of the guys?"

"Nah. Damn Viagra. Bought a dirty movie on the way home. I was pissed, but my pecker wanted some action." Nathan laughed and Ray said, "Couldn't get it down. Whacked all night and now I got a scab. Don't tell nobody. Please?"

"Of course not. What do you take me for?" Looking at Ray holding his beer, Nathan added, "Might wanna' start puttin' lotion on those hands though."

Ray looked at his hands and said, "She wasn't for me anyway. Not my type."

Nathan asked, "Too tall?" It was a good guess. Ray was five-and-a-half-feet tall. Agnes was over six feet tall.

"Nah. She wasn't as hip as me."

Nathan spit beer all over the table. "Oh."

Stuart came in to a chorus of "another American, pull up a seat, stranger" and sat, smiling. "Gail's doing her makeup. Be awhile. Where's everybody else?"

Nathan said, "Terri's mad and Jimmie's buyin' postcards. Ray's buying beer."

Ray grimaced and told them Gail was starting to scare him. He'd sat across from her in an aisle seat on the plane. Jimmie and Stuart had the windows and were sleeping soundly. "All the way from Dallas she's playing with a fuckin' rope. Telling me how the knot has to be prepared correctly or it'll tear up the neck and face. Very scientific. Too much rope and too long a fall and the head could be torn off. She's got a fuckin' book on hangings. Supposed to tie it just right so the vertebrae cracks, making the death painless."

Nathan asked, "Thought it was s'posed to hurt. She don't want that?"

Ray said, "Yeah well, she's workin' with her knot so the bastard will suffer. Nathan, she's scary." He turned to Stuart, "If I was you, I'd sleep lightly. Forget the conjugal stuff, Stuart. Better not sleep at all, old buddy. Feel something easing itself around your throat, run like hell."

Stuart said, "Talking about my possible betrothed. Ain't funny, Ray. Nathan, want to trade?"

"Fuck no!"

"Want to trade what?" Gail had come up behind them, unnoticed. She put her arm around Stuart and sat down.

Quickly, Nathan said, "Seats. He wants to watch the senoritas pass." Thankfully Nathan's seat faced the outside window and he happened to be watching a senorita pass when she asked.

She grabbed Stuart's cheek between two fingers and said, "I don't put up with unfaithful men." They all laughed, but Stuart's sounded contrived. She looked at Nathan and asked, "Where are Terri and Jimmie?"

"Jimmie's mailin' post cards. Terri is waiting for the skeet shootin' range to open."

"The what?"

"Nothin'," he said. "She's putting on makeup. Older, so it takes her longer than you."

"Age has nothing to do with it," she said.

Ray asked, "Why wouldn't it? If you're older you'd have more to makeup, wouldn't you? Or how about if you're fat?"

She was saved an answer as Terri and Jimmie came into the bar. Terri said, "Let's go check out the town. We can go to the shopping district. I know where to go. They told me at the front desk."

Jimmie asked, "Sure, if you promise to help me pick out something for my wife and daughter. Then let's eat. I'm hungry. Ray stole my airplane peanuts while I was asleep." Jimmie's voice was very hoarse.

"Fuck, Ray," said Stuart, laughing. "Can't believe you."

"We'll be glad to help, Jimmie," Terri said, turning to look at Ray. "You got his medicine?" she mouthed so Jimmie couldn't hear her. "We'll go to the Mercado Central. Is that the way you pronounce it, Senor?" she asked the bartender who nodded in the affirmative. "I heard from the clerk there are good buys on leather goods. Maybe we'll get them a nice, handcrafted purse."

"That, and maybe Gail a whip?" Nathan suggested.

***

The Mercado Central sold virtually everything. It was a full city block square filled with small stalls. You had to dig through the wares until you came upon what you were looking for. The variety was terrific and the sanitation was poor. It was hot and very much overcrowded and unpaved. Dust from the dirt floors filled the shopping stalls.

The shopping spree was without incident although they saw several snatch and grabs. Jimmie was happy as Terri and Gail found him a leather purse and backpack for his wife and daughter. He bought a leather cowboy hat and bandoleer for himself. Stuart bought a bag full of wallets for the guys he worked with.

Nathan ran for the first beer stall he saw as they finished shopping. "Jimmie, I like your hat. The bandoleer might be a bit much," Nathan said as they caught up with him and joined him for a beer. "What did you get, Ray?"

"Crabs." Nathan left it alone.

While out, they decided to have dinner and caught a taxi to the Centro Colon back toward the hotel.

Terri said. "We want to try the fish at the Peruvian restaurant, Machu Picchu."

Ray asked, "How do we know they're fish? Could be cat."

Gail said, "So it'll be the first pussy you've eaten in a while."

They ordered and the waitress brought the food promptly. Nathan asked Ray, "How's your fish?"

"Alright. Nothing special," said Ray.

"Mine sucks," said Gail.

Ray said, "Wonder if we can go someplace and get a steak?"

"Works for me," said Terri as Gail began consulting the guidebook. "I've had about as much local culture as I need today."

"How about a hamburger?" Gail asked.

"Local?" asked Ray.

"Burger King," said Gail.

CHAPTER TWENTY-ONE

The next day they had an early tour planned. As Terri and Nathan were getting ready, there was a knock on the door. Nathan opened it and Gail rushed into the room.

Gail said, "I need to talk to Terri in private. Do you mind?"

"No problem. See you ladies in the bar."

As soon as he left, Terri said, "Gail, what's going on?"

"Just Stuart. Really pissing me off." She told Terri about the conversation on the plane. "This morning, he's, like, got me moved in with him. It's like I don't have any say in the matter."

Terri asked, "You talk to him yet?"

"Tried to. He's like every other man. Women are stupid, need a man to keep them straight."

"Stuart said that, Gail?"

Gail said, "Not in so many words, but that's what he meant."

You haven't told him yet?"

"I tried, Terri. He just jumps to conclusions."

Terri said, "If you like him, you are making it worse by not telling him."

Gail said, "Fucking men. You need 'em for reproduction and that's about it. Like fucking copiers."

***

They met the tour bus in front of the hotel. As they boarded the half-full bus, the guide picked up a microphone and asked the passengers what they were interested in seeing first. The group was mostly European, except for the six New Yorkers.

"Forts. You know, battles with guys killed. Interesting stuff like that," said Ray.

Most of the Europeans started grumbling about museums. But the tour guide aligned with Ray and said, "Perfect. There are a number of historical sites which should be of interest."

"Hold on," said Terri, "battles and forts are nice, but how about some cultural things?" That started an argument with Terri, Gail and the Europeans voting Ray down. Culture it would be.

The guide gave them a running commentary as they left the hotel. "The eastern part of San Jose has many fine old mansions. Most are now commercial buildings. This is also the area where the Children's Hospital and the Hospital San Juan de Dios are located. This part of town is pedestrian only. A couple of blocks away you'll find the inner city bus terminal. This is the red light district and is the roughest part of town. The Mercado Central is three blocks away. It is like the Souks in the Middle East." Terri commented that they'd briefly visited the Mercado Central and she and the guide compared shopping stories.

The tour guide continued. "Following independence from Spain in 1821, Cartago and San Jose fought a battle to be the capital. We'll visit that site this morning."

Terri looked over at Jimmie, who was sitting next to her in the van. He'd lost an amazing amount of weight. It seemed his voice was becoming more hoarse every day.

As if he could feel her looking at him, he turned toward her and said, "What?"

"How you feeling?"

"Terri, don't start this mothering bullshit. Listen to the lady. There'll be a quiz later."

Terri said, "When do you start the radiation treatments?"

"When we get back. Go to Florida and visit first, then start 'em. Now quit. Leave me alone. I want to hear the lady." A couple of minutes later she looked over and he was sound asleep.

Several hours into the tour, and after several museums, the guide asked if anyone had questions.

"Do a lot of foreigners live in Costa Rica?" asked Jimmie, now awake.

"It's very affordable," said Mimi, the tour guide. "A lot of Americans live here. Canadians too. Some Orientals, but mostly Americans."

"Are there any regular bars? Places where Americans hang out?" Ray asked from the back of the van.

"Certainly. One of the better ones is Stan's. We will pass it in a few minutes."

"You guys want to visit an American-type bar in Costa Rica?" asked Ray. Everyone nodded and Ray asked the guide to drop them off, much to the delight of the European tourists.

The guide said, "I'm afraid you'll find that most of the Americans don't come in until later. It's early afternoon, but you may catch a few."

Ray said, "We'll give it a shot."

The guide said, "We can wait for you."

"Not necessary." Ray produced a fifty-dollar tip that brought a big smile. Capitalist Dog.

***

They entered Stan's to discover country and western music blaring. Yep, an American bar all right. Stan seemed to think this was the way to go.

A very pretty waitress approached their table dressed like a sexy cowgirl. "Howdy, strangers. What's your poison?"

Nathan jumped in, not waiting for anyone else. "Beer. Michelob or Michelob Light." The look he received from the pretty waitress was one of amazement.

"Mick-a-what? If you want American beer we have Bud, Schlitz, Heineken, Old Milwaukee, Corona or Millers. Or we have good local beer. Or maybe some Jap beer? We have Chinese beer too. Taiwan Beer."

He didn't bother straightening her out on Heineken or Corona. With her looks, beer geography didn't have to be her strong point. "Bring me a Taiwan Beer." He'd spent three months in Taiwan on business. Almost became a vegetarian until he discovered they had a Dan Ryan Steak House. He did love their beer though. Taiwanese Beer regularly pissed the Germans off by winning the Munich Beer festival. She took their order, which was a challenge. Forget drinks. Order a bottle of something.

"Man, I am tired of looking at stuff," said Ray. "Rather sit around the pool."

"Well, it's a good thing this is Jimmie's trip. I'd be bored to death just sitting around the pool, you jackass," said Gail.

"Jeez Gail, lighten up," Jimmie said. "Ray was just thinkin' how good you'd look with a tan. Don't you think a tan would look great on her, Stuart?"

"You are so full of shit, Jimmie," said Terri. He was saved a further tongue lashing when the waitress finally brought the beers.

Nathan said, "Could we get different music on?"

"You don't like this song?" It was something about being left with six kids, a cum-stained pillow and a box of condoms and sung by some yoyo with a lisp.

"Don't like the music. Maybe put on some Earth, Wind and Fire or something? Maybe George Benson? Fuck, even the Beach Boys, I don't care. Anything but this twangy shit."

She laughed. "I'll ask my boss." She leaned down and whispered, "I don't like it either."

He sipped his beer and looked around. You had to pay attention with Taiwanese Beer. It came in two-liter bottles. A careless Taiwanese beer drinker had chipped many a tooth by hoisting the bottle too quickly. He toasted her from across the room as Billy Joel came on. Stan's was large, holding four or five hundred people easily. Half-bar, half-restaurant with a dance floor in the middle. Big sound system cranked up. Nice size outside dining area. Stan was doing well.

After two hours, and a return to country and western music, some Americans started floating in. There was a wide assortment of couples, old and young, and several single guys. One group, in particular, caught their attention as they sat next to them. Ray struck up a conversation.

"Hey, another gringo," said Ray, directed to their table.

"Yeah," Nathan said. "How you doin'?"

"Good, man," said the shorter of the foursome. "Live around here?"

"Naw, just a short vacation."

"You'll love it. David Brown," he introduced himself. "Carl Thornton, Stuart Vogel and Skip Weiss," he said, pointing at a short man, a balding man and a tall, well built man.

"Nathan Melton, from New York," he said, then he introduced everyone at his table. "Where are you guys from?"

"I'm originally from D.C.," said Stuart Vogel, the tallest of the four men. "Been living here three years since I retired. Talked Dave into coming." Stuart was balding and letting his hair grow long on the sides so he could comb it over. It didn't do much to cover his baldness on top. Could have done better with a magic marker.

Brown was a six-footer, maybe two hundred pounds, jet-black hair, mid to late forties. He wore those goofy glasses like John Lennon used to wear. Granny glasses, they were called. Looked like a hip used car salesman. Somebody you'd never trust.

Brown's buddies were carbon copies. All were retired CIA. They were all laughing loud and trying to be noticed by several women spaced around the bar.

Jimmie asked, "You guys come here often?"

"Here pretty much most of the time," said Thornton, the short guy. "Either here, playing golf at the club or chasing women."

"It's amazing, all you guys from the CIA. Thought you weren't supposed to tell people." Ray said.

"We're all retired," said Thornton. "Bunch of guys in Costa Rica from the CIA. Like a retirement spot."

Vogel said, "Not all were official. Some were contract and still do some things. Not us, though. Put in our time. We all mostly worked together."

Ray said, "Bet you guys got some stories."

"Those we can't tell," said Brown.

At the other end of the table, things weren't going so well. "Well, we're here. Stan's world famous, chicken shit bar. It's hot outside," said Gail. She and Stuart were pressed up against the wall. Gail had complained continuously all day about the lack of air conditioning in the bus. She'd been drinking since well before lunch and had a pretty good buzz on.

"You know your constant complaining about the heat hasn't cooled it down one degree," said Stuart.

"Want me to see if I can make it hotter, Gomer? I believe I can." Gail said loudly.

"That's okay. Just remember what we're here for, huh?" She ignored him. "C'mon, a little heat's not going to stop us from having fun. What's with this Gomer shit?"

She ignored the Gomer question and said, "You're right. I'm going to the bathroom. Order me a beer."

Stuart asked, "You sure? You might want to slow down a little."

"Just order me a beer, Gomer." She got to her feet shakily and went to the restroom.

While he was waiting for the waitress he thought about Gail. God, she could be a pain in the ass. A major pain in the ass! Always harping on someone. Not sure whether she was more trouble than she was worth.

The waitress showed up. "Howdy, Pardner. Ready for another?"

"Huh?"

The waitress asked, "Are you an American?"

Stuart said, "Yeah."

"That's not the way they speak, is it? 'Howdy pardner?'"

"No."

The waitress was pissed. "I told my asshole boss that, but he makes us talk like that. And wear these funky costumes." She had a short cowgirl skirt on, complete with toy guns and holster.

What is it with all these pissed-off women all of a sudden, thought Stuart. "It's cute. And so are you." This brightened her up considerably. "How about two more Millers?"

"Si."

"And hurry." Gail returned from the restroom.

Gail turned to Stuart just as he muttered, "Fuck it."

She put on her biggest, brightest smile and said, "What, dear?"

"I said fuck it. I'm tired of you being an asshole. Why don't you and I go back to the hotel? Let everybody else enjoy themselves."

"You go. I'm having fun." Stuart got up, stared for a moment and walked out. She started to follow, amazed that he'd left. She had the feeling she'd screwed up, but let him go anyway.

Nathan was coming back from the bathroom when Stuart brushed past him. Nathan grabbed his arm and said, "Hey, what's up?"

"Just Gail, Nate. I think I'll call it a night, catch a taxi back to the hotel."

"Man, don't do that. Don't end it like that. Gail loves you."

"Women, fuck it. No bigger fan of the opposite sex than me, Nathan. Got the alimony payments to prove it. Just choose bad, brother."

Nathan said, "I mean it. She loves you."

"Got a funny way of showing it." Stuart shrugged, "I'll just go back. Everything'll be cool in the morning. What's the name of the hotel?"

"Grano Oro. Something like that."

Nathan walked back into the bar as Stuart left, thinking out loud, "Women. Can't live with them. The neighbors see you if you bury them in the backyard."

Gail was looking at him as he approached the table. He gave her a "what's going on" sign, which she ignored. Half into his cups, he let it pass. He wasn't Dear Abby.

Ray wandered to the restroom and Nathan casually followed him. As Nathan entered, Ray was standing at the urinal. Nathan asked, "What's going on between Gail and Stuart?"

"Gail's being an asshole. She's drunk. And now she's making eyes at that guy Brown."

Nathan asked, "Fuck! You see a fight coming?"

"She's a big girl and can handle herself. That's what she wants, let her have it. I'd rather her stay with Stuart, but nobody asked me," said Ray.

Jimmie came into the restroom and caught them talking at the urinal. "Nate, I don't want to be the one to spread tales, but you're spending a lot of time in the restrooms lately. Some kind of problem?"

They drank for another thirty to forty-five minutes and got up to leave. Terri was worried about Gail, who was shooting pool with her newfound friends. She went over and told Gail that they were leaving.

Terri returned alone and Jimmie motioned toward Gail. "She says she wants to stay. Brown says he'll get her back to the hotel."

Jimmie said, "I don't like it."

"I'll get her," said Ray.

"Give her a couple more minutes," said Jimmie.

They had a couple more beers and Ray went over to Gail and said, "Let's go Gail."

Brown stepped in front of Ray and said, "Can't you take a hint?" He then pushed Ray to the floor.

Nathan got up and went across the room just as Stan was raising hell and telling them to leave.

Skip, the big one, got to his feet from a nearby table and got in front of him. "You looking for trouble, Dude?"

Nathan looked at Skip. "In a minute." He then turned to Brown and hit him with a short right-handed punch in the throat.

Skip caught Nathan with a long, looping right that grazed the side of his head. Skip was big, about Nathan's height, but Nathan had him by a good twenty pounds. Some fat, but a lot of muscle.

More reaction than anything else, Nathan nailed Skip with his own overhand right. He followed with a left hook to the mid-section and then really cleaned his clock with an uppercut, lifting him completely off the floor. It happened so fast, those who saw it didn't know what they saw.

He grabbed Ray and said to Thornton and Vogel, "I'm going to get him out of here. Unless anyone else wants to dance." He paused, looked around, but there were no takers. "Would you two gentlemen make sure Gail gets back to the hotel? Grano Oro." He looked at Gail, who turned away from him. "Take this anyway you want to, but if she doesn't make it back, or has a hard time, I'll come for ya'." He gave both men the old linebacker thousand-yard stare, freezing both. "Oh, and tell Skip and Brown I'm sorry. I'll buy them a beer tomorrow. You guys will be here?"

Thornton looked from Nathan to Skip and Brown and back. "Yes. Hey, sorry for the disturbance. We'll be here and I'll tell the guys. Don't worry about your friend. Kid gloves, okay? I'm sure the guys didn't mean anything. Just too much to drink."

"Like Gail. People who can't drink, shouldn't. She's a friend of mine and I really don't want anyone taking advantage of her. I'd really get upset. Know what I mean?" They nodded. "See you tomorrow."

"Yeah, see you tomorrow," they said in unison.

Now down to four, they left in one taxi, heading for the hotel. Nathan said, "Man, I hate leaving her alone with them." Ray didn't answer and Nathan looked over at him. He was staring. "Are you all right, Ray?"

Ray found his voice. "I'm fine. I've never seen anybody hit that fucking hard. You knocked both of their asses out." He kept it up all the way back to the hotel. "They had the first laugh, right? You know what they say, "He who laughs last has the best laugh."

Nathan said, "Always thought it was he who laughs last has not yet heard the bad news."

CHAPTER TWENTY-TWO

They arrived back at the hotel and were glad Stuart wasn't downstairs. They would have hated to tell him Gail didn't come back with them. It's always tough when one half of the couple feels more than the other. We've all been there before, thought Terri.

Ray said he'd wait in the bar for Gail to come back. Jimmie was beat, so he headed up for bed. Terri and Nathan had a beer with Ray and then, somewhat guiltily, went to the room. Their reason for leaving was a little different. Terri had bought a skimpy maid outfit at the plaza and wanted to try it on.

Walking out of the bathroom in her costume, Terri saw Nathan, who was lying on top of the covers naked. "Pardon me, Senor," she said, turning her head modestly away. "I'm sorry to disturb you." Head still turned away from Nathan, she said, "but I'm here to turn your covers. I'll come back later, si?"

"It's okay," said Nathan, stroking his penis slowly. "You may turn them now."

"Gracias, Senor. I do have many rooms and can't afford to lose my job." She did not look at Nathan as she walked to the side of the bed opposite him and turned the covers back.

Still stroking his penis, he asked, "Are all the maids at this hotel so beautiful?"

"Some, Senor," said Terri, smiling.

"Are all so young?"

Terri, still smiling said, "A few, Senor."

"You seem shy, are you a virgin?"

Coquettishly, Terri said, "Si."

"Lie beside me. Don't be shy," said Nathan. Terri moved beside him, Nathan still stroking his penis. "Have you ever seen a grown man naked?"

"Just my Papa. But his 'thing' wasn't so big. Are all Americans big, Senor?"

Nathan said, "You are a very curious girl. Would you like to touch it?" He reached down and lifted her hand, positioning it on his penis.

"It's very warm, Senor." Terri ran her tongue across her lips and said, "What shall I do now, Senor?"

"Squeeze gently and slowly move your hand up and down. Watch it grow bigger."

Terri asked, "Like this, Senor?"

"Yes," said Nathan, throatily, "Just like that." Moments later he said, "Would you like to kiss it?" He ran his hand up her fishnet stockings, past her garter belt and under her short skirt, fingers inside her panties. "Yes, kiss it. Now suck it."

***

The ringing phone woke both Nathan and Terri up. That's not exactly true. He awoke to noise and blindly felt for what he was sure was the alarm clock.

Terri got out of bed, walked to the phone on his side, picked it up and handed it to him wordlessly. She then did what any sensible person would do and got back into bed.

"Yeah," he answered.

"Nathan, are you awake?"

"Sort of. Who is this and what time is it?"

"If you have to ask, you aren't awake. Now wake up. I need you. There's a problem."

"Ray, that you? What time is it?"

"Better. I don't know what time it is. They took my watch."

Nathan asked, "Took your watch. Who?"

The mysteriousness of the conversation awakened Terri. She picked up the extension and said, "Ray, what's wrong?"

Ray, being polite asked, "Terri, how are you?"

"Ray, what the fuck's wrong? Now!" Terri screamed at poor Ray, who was trying his best to practice proper phone etiquette.

"I'm in jail and my phone time's up. Get me out. Huge roaches in here and I can't speak the lingo. Stuart is hurt. Get me out now." The phone clicked off with Terri in mid-sentence.

They dressed quickly, not saying a word, both lost in their own vivid imagination. Ray in jail? For what? Stuart hurt? Damn!

While waiting on the elevator, Nathan said, "Think we should check on Jimmie?"

Terri said, "I'll run by his room. You get a taxi. What time is it?"

"Four," he said to her back as she ran down the hall and the elevator opened.

She ran through the hotel lobby and out the door, finding Nathan with the taxi driver. The driver was trying to jack up the fare. He was talking about all the business he was losing. He and Nathan were arguing as she came up behind Nathan.

"Yo, Pancho," Terri said. "See these other ten taxis sitting here with the drivers asleep? You ain't losin' shit."

Then Nathan opened the door for her. "To the jail," he said.

The driver turned and said, "I was just kidding. We don't need the policio."

"Not about you, our friend's in jail. Help get him out and there's a hundred in it for you," Terri said.

"Jimmie okay?" Nathan asked.

"Yeah. Accidentally woke him. Told him I was just checking on him. Got yelled at," she said.

Nathan said, "The plight of woman," and regretted it instantly. She let it pass and he scolded himself, saving her the trouble, as they pulled up in front of the jail.

"Tell him what happened?"

Crossly, she said, "I'd have to know first, wouldn't I?"

"I can't fuckin' believe this," he grumbled.

***

Arriving at the police station, they went up to the front desk and the taxi driver explained to the cop that they were there to pick up Ray. The cop told him there was a fine they could pay, but Ray and the other gringo would have to appear in court for damages they'd done.

Terri told the driver, "Ask what he did."

The driver did, then translated. "He and the other man went to the home of an Americano and started a big fight."

"Ask if we can get a copy of the police report," she said.

They got it and the driver translated it for her while Nathan paid the fine for Ray. They discovered Stuart was in the Children's Hospital and Nathan paid his fine also.

The cop, after being paid, said they could forgo the court appearance tomorrow. He said for another tip they could pick up the other gringo from the hospital. They paid and he gave them a paper giving them authorization to get Stuart.

Poor Ray was led out with no shirt. His pants were torn and his shoes were missing. He was given his wallet, less the money he had in it when arrested, and they left.

Outside, Terri said, "What the fuck happened?"

"I was sitting in the bar. Been there for an hour after you guys left and Stuart came down. Got all pissed off about Gail and we took a taxi back to the bar. They weren't there, but the waitress, you remember our waitress, the cute girl in the outfit?"

Terri yelled, "Ray, what the hell happened?"

Ray said, "She told us where that guy Brown lived. Apparently all the girls have made the trip at one time or another."

"Ray, I don't give a shit about that. What happened?" Terri asked.

"We went and Brown tried to say Gail wasn't there. He and two of the other guys jumped us with bats. Think Stuart's arm got broke."

"How you can be so stupid I can't imagine," Terri yelled at the poor guy. "Fuck up a wet dream, Ray."

They were both glaring at each other when Nathan said, "Kids. You've got to play pretty or it'll be 'quiet time' for you both."

They got Stuart out of the hospital. He had a broken right arm and separated shoulder, and an eye swollen completely shut. They explained the situation to him.

"We gotta' get Gail," he said.

"How? If she don't want to come she doesn't have to," Nathan said.

Stuart said, "Maybe she's hurt?"

"Maybe she's not," said Terri. "Did you even see her when you and Bubba," she stared at Ray, "were there?"

"No, but she had to be there. Where else could she be?" Stuart was on the verge of losing it.

"Where to, Senor? Back to hotel?" asked the taxi driver.

"Hotel," Nathan said and looked at them. "All we can do is wait for her to come back. Probably waiting for the sunrise or something. Be back soon. Just watch and see." He didn't know if he had convinced them. It sure as hell didn't convince him.

Terri took Stuart up to his room to check his bandages and get him some Tylenol. Nathan told Terri that he and Ray would sit in the lobby and talk for a while. Adrenaline was running too fast to try sleeping again. She promised to call the front desk and put the tour off until the afternoon.

It was getting close to seven in the morning and the streets were filling with people going to work. A lot of those people were good-looking women.

They sat, not speaking, for a couple of minutes, two old men watching the girls walk by. Ray said, "Good-looking people. You know it?"

"They are. There's somethin' mysterious about brown-nippled native women. It's a turn-on."

"That it is, young Nate. Got damn healthy bodies too. I can see why Americans want to settle here. Not a bad place at all. Nice looking, friendly people. Loose morals. I could settle here."

Nathan agreed. "Me too. If it wasn't so hot. Think they have a winter?"

Ray said, "Too close to the equator. Always summer. They got good AC though."

"You haven't joined the Chamber of Commerce overnight have you, Ray?"

"Maybe." Looking at a particularly well-endowed woman on her way to work, Ray said, "Wish Julie had come. Think she wears a string bikini?"

"Don't know. Ask Avi."

Ray said, "So, what we going to do about Gail?"

"You mean Vlad the Impaler? Assholes deserve her. If she wasn't Terri's friend I'd say let 'em keep her. Serve 'em right."

Ray asked, "What about Terri? Is she still pissed at me?"

Nathan said, "Yeah. You'll probably be collectin' Social Security before she speaks to you again."

Ray said, "You never answered my question. What are we going to do about Gail?"

"Go to the front desk and get a rental car. I think I can find the bar. Let's go take a look at the house. Think you can get me there?"

"Not now. I need a drink before anything like that. Want to go to the bar and shoot the shit?"

"It's not open yet. Won't be for a while. What do you have in your mini bar?"

"Same as you. I also have Jimmie in my room."

"Let's go to mine. Get something before Terri gets back from Stuart's room."

They made it to the room. As soon as they entered, Ray said, "Get me a beer, too." Nathan went across the room and started digging in the fridge. "We need to get gloves," Ray said.

Nathan asked, "Why? Once we find out about Gail we don't give a shit."

"S'pose they aren't there?"

Nathan said, "We leave. Why do we need gloves?"

"Cops, Nathan," he said. "Can't jus' leave if they aren't there. We're going to have to break in. Don't want to worry about wiping down later. Easier to just wear them. I'll need some electrical wiring for the alarm.

Some tape, a couple of screwdrivers and penlight flashlights. It'll be day, but we might need them."

Nathan said, surprised, "Cool. You can do that?"

"I practice some in case the car business goes in the shitter."

The door opened and in walked Jimmie. "What are you two Mulligans up to?"

"Terri gave you her key?"

"Fuck no. Don't need one if you got the touch." He neglected to tell them that he'd discovered, by accident, that any room key opens all the hotel doors. "Now answer my question and don't lie. Terri told me the whole thing." He saw the looks on their faces and said, "Wasn't her fault. I had it pretty well figured out. People checking on my health in the middle of the night. I'm dying, but I ain't there yet. Now what are you two up to?" Ray started to bullshit him, but was cut off. "I heard you talking about gloves and cops, so don't even try, Ray. You're plannin' on breaking into somethin'. I better go with you or you'll screw it up."

"You can't go, Jimmie, you're sick," Nathan said.

"Have either one of you poofters broke in to anything before? Other than your old man's booze?"

"No way are you going," Nathan said.

"We'll let Terri decide then," he said, walking to the room phone.

Ray said, "Wait. Nathan, he's got a point. I never have broken into anything. Have you?"

"No. It's beside the point," Nathan said.

"Bullshit. It is the point. I can do the alarm because a guy showed me. Yeah, Jimmie's sick, but we won't be in a situation where we have to run or something. If they're home, we don't go in."

Nathan said, "When we get in, we just get Gail or look for signs she's been there and get out. No screwin' around. Understand, Ray?" He nodded. "Jimmie?"

Jimmie nodded and said, "What if they've hurt her?" He looked at them and neither said anything. "One thing, if they've hurt her, we're doin' them. Don't have to be careful putting things back. Destroy the fucking place for all I care."

Jimmie got a beer from the fridge and handed them both another. "Drink this, then we go. How about you and Terri?"

"How about us?"

Jimmie asked, "You goin' to get married?"

"Not again, Jimmie."

"Nathan, this is Jimmie!"

"Like her too much to marry her. I think I'll find a woman I don't like and give her a house instead. Easier and quicker. Same she'd get in the divorce."

"Nathan, this is me, Jimmie. Terri is a friend of mine."

Nathan answered, "Fuck, Jimmie, so am I."

"I've known Terri longer."

Nathan countered, "I spend more in the bar."

"True. Any plans on increasing your expenditures?" He noticed the odd look on Nathan's face and said, "You know, still trying to make up my mind."

"What are you fuckin' guys doin'?" Ray said, "Tell him, Nathan."

"Who knows?" Nathan asked. "Marriage is a big decision. What was she like before I came into the picture?"

Jimmie asked, "You mean guys?"

"Yes. None of my business, but yes," asked Nathan.

"Weren't very many. She'd date, but rarely would she date a guy more than a couple of times. I think back then her job was kind of it," answered Jimmie.

Nathan said, "That's good. I like her. Maybe even love her. She's got a temper."

"Fuck," said Ray. "They all do." They had depleted the mini fridge. Didn't take long. They were down to wine and nuts. "Guess we better be goin'. Before Terri gets back and we have to answer a bunch of questions."

Nathan said, "Could go hit your mini fridge, Ray."

"Fuck no," he said, heading for the door. "That stuff's expensive." Nathan hit him right between the eyes with a pillow.

**

Following Ray's directions, driving to the home was a breeze, sort of. Other than getting lost a couple of times and finally paying a taxi to let them follow, they found it. Nathan drew the short straw and had to watch the home for movement.

At the surveillance post...Nathan liked that, 'surveillance post'...he squinted at what he thought was movement. He wished he'd brought a pair of binoculars with him. Four men. With his bad eyesight he could just pick them out. They'd come out the front and then were hidden by a partial courtyard wall. They cleared the wall and he could make them out. It was Brown and his three friends from yesterday, Stuart, Carl and Skip. All of them were in golfing clothes, Skip with a bandaged nose, which made Nathan smile. They got in the last car in line, a large Mercedes Diesel, and backed out of the drive.

They were leaving the suburb. Nathan sat watching in the rental car parked three doors down from Brown's home. He turned to his companions. Jimmie was asleep beside him and Ray was stretched out in the backseat. Both were snoring.

Nathan said, through cupped hands, "Oh, yoo hoo!"

"What the fuck was that," yelled Jimmie, sitting straight up in the seat. Ray's reaction was the same, but more pronounced, as he bumped his head on the roof of the car.

"That was our signal, remember?"

"I remember telling you we don't need a signal. We're in the car with you," said Jimmie. "Damn!"

"At's what I remember too," said Ray, rubbing his head. "They left?"

Nathan said, "Yeah, just pulled away. Looks like they're leaving the neighborhood."

Jimmie said, "Give 'em a little time. Make sure they don't come back for something."

***

Twenty minutes later, on the greens at the San Jose Country Club, Brown's cell rang. "Hello," he answered.

"Dave, this is Sam. You on scrambler?"

Brown hit a button and said, "Am now."

"Got that info back you asked me for. Can't find anything on the names you gave me. Anything other than what they told you. All check out in New York. The one guy's traveling on a false passport, but that don't mean nothin'. Definitely not DEA."

Brown said, "I can just barely hear you on my cell. Can you hear me?"

"Yeah. Coming in five by five."

Brown said, "Me and the guys are on the first tee at the Club."

"Watch that fuckin' Vogel. He'll move his ball on ya'."

"Caught him three times already." They both laughed. "You know how it is, Sam. Can't trust anybody in this line of work. Keep on it. May be innocent. Could be just a coincidence. You know what they say about coincidence?"

"All right, Dave. I'll have 'em put a little screen up, see if anything comes up. How you going to handle it now?"

"Just chalk it off, most likely, unless you come up with something. You'll have the two hundred and ten keys in Yuma day after tomorrow if I don't hear from you."

Brown pushed end on his cell and turned to the rest of his foursome. "Sam says the dudes from last night are clean."

"Told ya," said Vogel. "Just a bunch of dumb-ass vacationers."

"I got a score to settle with one of those 'dumb-ass vacationers'," said Skip.

"Bullshit," said Brown. "Got your ass clocked once. Might want to leave the big guy alone. I know I do. The coke leaves on time for Yuma and you'll be shadowing."

"Maybe you can find yourself a nice small whore to beat up in the meantime," said Thornton. They laughed and Skip scowled.

CHAPTER TWENTY-THREE

Jimmie, Ray and Nathan decided it was time. They collected their tools and headed for the house. Thankfully, their movements were mostly concealed with lush gardens and a recessed courtyard around the front door.

Nathan asked them, "You want to explore the grounds a little?"

"No," Ray said. "I'm too nervous. Let's just get it over with."

Nathan asked, "You get a good look at the security system?"

Ray said, "Stinking home alarm. Piece a' cake."

"Both you guys shut up," said Jimmie.

Ray disconnected the alarm with no trouble, surprising Jimmie and Nathan. Jimmie, "Mr. Experienced Cat Burglar", used a thick screwdriver to pry open the door. It gave with a thwack that Nathan and Ray were sure could've been heard in Spain.

Nathan said, "Damn, Jimmie. We could of done that. Thought you were going to do somethin' really slick. What happened to all that experience?"

Jimmie said, "I was thirteen when I robbed my first and last house. Next-door neighbors. Got caught."

"No fucking wonder." Ray said. "What you use then, a cannon?"

He gave Ray his "you're an idiot" look. "Couldn't let Laurel and Hardy do it by yourselves. Knew you'd screw it up."

Nathan said, "Somebody could've heard."

Jimmie said, "Nobody heard. Nobody came to investigate. It don't really matter. We're in."

Nathan headed immediately to the left of the house while Jimmie went the opposite way and Ray went down the middle. A quick look around and they'd be out.

***

Ray and Nathan heard two screams, one behind the other. The first, a high-pitched scream, sounded like a woman. The second was Jimmie.

Ray and Nathan arrived in the kitchen area about the same time and saw Jimmie lying on an enormously fat woman.

Both laughing, Ray said, "Jeez Jimmie, join one of those Date Clubs or somethin'. You can do better than that." Nathan cracked up and fell on the floor.

Jimmie turned toward them and said, "You blithering idiots. The poor woman fainted." They were still laughing as he went back to trying to revive her.

It was just one of those situations. Like church giggles when you're a kid. They couldn't stop laughing. Jimmie rose off of the woman, felt for a pulse and stood. "She's dead."

The laughing stopped. "Holy shit," Nathan yelled.

Ray screamed, "Huh?"

"Dead, you sure?" Nathan rushed over, grabbed her leg and felt frantically for a pulse.

Jimmie looked at him. "May have better luck feeling in the neck. Very seldom do you get a pulse around the knee."

"Fuck it," Nathan said, dropping the woman's leg. "I'll take your word for it."

"How about you, Ray?" Jimmie asked, "You want to take a pulse on her foot? Feel her tits a little?"

Ray said, "Not me. Not touching a dead fat lady. We got to get out of here." Ray started to run.

Nathan grabbed his arm and said, "Let's do what we came here for. We didn't kill her. Probably died of a heart attack."

Ray said, "You're some kind of doctor now?"

"My doc told me I was too fat and going to have a heart attack. She's fatter than I am." Nathan was miffed at the questioning of his medical prowess. The knee thing was an accident, a blip on the radar.

Jimmie said, "I agree with Nathan. Let's take a look for Gail and then get the hell out of here."

"Fuck that," said Ray. "This is like all those TV shows. You know, innocent person hangs around and then gets blamed for a murder."

"Ain't no murder. She died of a heart attack." Jimmie thought a second and said, "Okay. Makes sense Gail would've heard the commotion. Let's look for signs she's been here."

Ray asked, "What kind of signs? Body depressions on the bed? Ass tracks on a chair?"

"Just look," said a pissed Jimmie and they scattered to look.

Nathan found the master bedroom. Next to the bed was a desk with a computer. Facing the bed was a dresser with unopened mail on it. He picked up the mail and looked at it. Two letters to a Donald Rosen, one from an Austrian bank and one from American Express. He opened the letter from the bank. "Thank you for choosing us," it said. "New account opened for $4,718,256.89." Had his account number, transaction confirmation number and everything. "I'll be dipped in shit," he said out loud. "Brown's using a fake name." He pocketed the letter.

He turned on the computer and wished he had one of those software programs that figured out the password. No telling what they'd find here. He turned off the computer. He didn't have a zip drive so he couldn't copy anything even if he had the magical software.

He went to check on the guys and show them what he'd found. Ray was still in the kitchen. He was on the floor eating a half-gallon of ice cream next to the dead lady.

"Jesus, Ray! Ice cream?"

"I get nervous, I eat. And I am damn sure nervous," said Ray.

"What kind is it?"

Ray said, "I don't know. The label's in Spanish."

Nathan said, "I meant what flavor is it? Not who makes it. Dick!"

"Butter Pecan. It's good. Want some?" He was holding the container and a spoon out to Nathan.

Nathan thought about it and said, "Save me some." He told him what he'd found. Ray told him he'd found nothing so far.

"Duh! Ain't gonna' find nothin' in that ice cream container."

Nathan went back to the bedroom and started rifling through drawers. He found a matching pair of Colt 45s, an Ingram MAC 10 and a leather attaché case with a ton of money in it. A quick count revealed in excess of a hundred thousand dollars. He stuffed the money in a pillowcase.

Jimmie yelled and Nathan ran toward his voice. He found him in the den. "Look at this shit," Jimmie said.

Nathan moved to the closet he was pointing at. He saw a mountain of brick-sized white stuff wrapped individually in thick cellophane. Ray bumped into Nathan and he jumped back, screaming.

"Shut up," said Jimmie. He shook his head and looked up towards the ceiling. "I'm puttin' my ass on the line with two pansies." Looking at Ray and Nathan, he said, "Probably just the neighborhood knows we're here. Don't want the next block to know, now do we?"

Ray said, "Was him screamed. Not me. I'm not a pansy."

Nathan said, "Me neither. Big ass Ray sneakin' up on people. Gonna' start a heart attack epidemic."

"Both of ya' shut up. Either of ya' found anything?"

Nathan told Jimmie what he'd found, including Ray eating ice cream and asked, "What do you want to do?"

"These guys are drug dealers," said Ray.

"Big time from the looks of it," said Jimmie. "We better get out of here. Gail's not here. We're in way over our heads."

Nathan said, "What about the dead lady?"

Jimmie said, "What about her?"

"They're gonna' know we were here. Or somebody," he said. "Won't they be able to get our prints?"

"Not if we wipe the place down," said Ray.

Nathan said, "Or if we'd of worn those fuckin' gloves you stole from the maid's cart at the hotel. They're stickin' out of your pocket."

Jimmie and Nathan stared at Ray as he reached in his back pocket and pulled out the gloves. He handed them a pair and started pulling his on. "Let's wipe it down," he said.

"Idiots!" Looking back up toward the ceiling, he said, "I'm surrounded by idiots. Ray, go to the garage. There's a gas can by a big riding lawn mower. Bring it here," said Jimmie.

Ray left mumbling about mowing the lawn and Nathan said, "Wouldn't a cleanser be better? Saw Lysol in the bathroom. Something scented with a nice smell?"

Jimmie looked at him and said, "Yeah, it would if we were goin' to clean the house. But we're not, are we, Nathan? We're goin' to burn it. Take care of the prints. No use wipin' it down. We'd miss somethin'." He laughed, "You tryin' to get the maid a raise with your fuckin' scented Lysol? You're late. Nathan, I never noticed how much you talk before."

Ray returned with the gas can and said, "Yeah Nate, you're a regular Chatty Cathy."

Jimmie said, "Knock it off. Let's get on with it."

And that's just what they did. Even made the dead maid look like a hero. Put the fire extinguisher next to her and placed her outside the back door. Poor thing had a heart attack trying to save her employer's home. Jimmie got her purse and took her identification so they could send something to her family.

They turned the gas burners on the stove. Then they poured gas all around the kitchen and down the hallway to the den with the dope in it. Jimmie lit the fire and they got the hell out of there, taking the money with them.

As they were driving away, they stopped at a roadside store with a public phone in front of it. Jimmie told Ray to call and report the fire.

Ray screeched, "Now?"

"Been five minutes," said Jimmie. "Time to get a good blaze going. Don't want it to burn down. We want them to find the dope. Give Brown and them somethin' to worry about other than the fire."

Ray got out, went to the booth and was back in minutes. "What do you think the emergency number is here?"

"Got to be 911," Nathan said.

"What I tried. It's a garage." Then they heard sirens coming from all directions. Two fire trucks and a police car passed them.

"Get in, Ray," Nathan said. "Neighbors must have called. Let's get the fuck out of here."

"What's the plan?" Ray asked, "What do we tell the others?"

Jimmie said, "Play it by ear. We don't know enough to plan."

***

They made it back to the hotel. Didn't get lost once. They ran through the entrance and hurried toward the elevator. As they passed the bar, Terri yelled, "In here. We're in here." They went into the bar and found Terri and Stuart. "Where have you guys been?"

The jig was up and Nathan decided to come clean. He turned toward Jimmie and Ray and they were no help. He looked at Terri and Stuart sitting, waiting for an explanation. "I don't know how to tell you this, so I'll jus' throw it out. Stuart, I know how you feel about Gail. She's been abducted by a bunch of drug guys." It was out and he felt better.

It took Nathan a second to see their reaction wasn't what he'd expected. They were laughing. He started to get pissed.

Stuart said, "She came back to the hotel last night. She checked into another room because we'd had a fight. Been here all night." He looked up and yelled, "Come here, honey, you got to hear this."

Jimmie, Ray and Nathan turned to see Gail coming out of the restroom. She said, "What's up, guys? Where have you been? Nathan, I'm surprised at you. Poor Terri was so worried."

"Comin' back with some half-cocked story really makes me mad," said Terri, throwing a roundhouse right and connecting with Nathan's forehead. She stormed out of the bar as the bartender turned the TV sound up.

There was big fire on the screen and several homes burnt to the ground. Unfortunately, it was in Spanish, but the neighborhood looked familiar.

Ray said, "What's goin' on, Julio?"

Julio, the bartender said, "Some rich gringo's house burned. Five more with it. A brave house keeper died trying to put out the blaze. Almost burned the whole neighborhood. Policio made a big drug raid."

***

Not wanting to hang around Costa Rica anymore, they mailed the drug money to the maid's family. Then they caught the first flight out.

On the plane, Gail finally came clean with Stuart. "I'm not a kept woman."

"Not anymore, you mean," he hugged her. "I'm proud of you, baby."

"Stuart, just listen okay? Don't be a man for a second?" He nodded. "While modeling, I kept my ears open. Lot of rich ladies go to the shows. Wives of CEOs, heiresses, stuff like that. So I listened. Picked up a lot of stock tips. Invested my money. Stuart, I own the building where I live."

He sat up. Still holding her hand, he said, "Why didn't you tell me to begin with?"

"I don't know. I thought maybe you were like all the other men. Try to play me for my money."

Stuart said, beaming, "I love you and I'm very proud of you."

"I love you too, honey. See, all blondes aren't stupid."

From behind them, Nathan said, "All blondes aren't blondes either."

CHAPTER TWENTY-FOUR

A week later, Nathan was in bed with Terri when she said, "I love your hairy chest. Promise to be careful always? I don't want anything to happen to it."

Nathan was going through that uncomfortable, for men, after-sex cuddling period. "Of course I'll be careful. When have you ever known me not to be careful? I'll wear a condom the whole time I'm not with you."

"You are so funny. Such a funny fucking guy." She got out of bed and stormed to the bathroom, slamming doors.

He yelled to her back, "You're right, honey, not always safe. Good friend got hit by a bus wearing a condom." He knew it was stupid when he said it but couldn't snatch it back. She was mad.

"Honey, what's wrong?" He got up and went after her, catching her in the bathroom. She was just getting in the shower.

"Not with your fucking friends in the bar now, Mr. Funny Man. Leave me alone. I'm going to shower and go home."

"What's wrong?" No answer. Shit. He climbed into the shower. She turned away from him. "Playing hard to get, huh? Well, I'm just going to wash your back until you speak to me." She laughed lightly and he knew he had her. "I'm sorry. I do joke too much. It's primarily because I'm scared. Defense mechanism." He continued washing her back, then stopped, reached around her and started washing her front. One thing led to another and he decided they fit well together.

Later, lying in bed, he started laughing and Terri asked, "What's so funny?"

"Sorry. I was thinking about how women take showers. You're so thorough, everything exactly right."

She asked, "Well, how do women take showers, Mr. Smarty Pants?"

He said, "It's just so planned. You take off your clothes and place them in a sectioned laundry hamper dividing the light and dark clothes. Then you walk to the bathroom wearing a long dressing gown. If you see me, you cover up any exposed areas. You always look at your body in the mirror, critique it and say you're goin' to do more sit-ups at the gym.

"Finally you get in the shower. You use all assortments of washcloths; a face cloth, arm cloth, leg cloth and pumice stone. You wash your hair once with cucumber and sage shampoo 'cause it has forty-three added vitamins. Then you wash your hair again to make sure it's clean. You condition your hair with grapefruit mint conditioner cause it's enhanced with natural avocado oil. You leave it on your hair for the prescribed five minutes exactly."

Terri asked, "Got it down, huh?"

"Oh yeah. You wash your face with crushed apricot facial scrub for exactly ten minutes until it's red, like it says on the box. You wash the rest of your body with ginger nut and the body wash stuff." He laughed and continued, "Then you rinse the conditioner off. You shave your armpits and legs with proper up-strokes, never sideways. You turn off the shower and squeegee off all the wet surfaces. Then ya' spray the shower walls with Tilex. Can't have any mold, right?

"Then you get out of the shower and dry with a towel the size of a small country. Afterwards, you wrap your hair in another towel cause the first one has dead skin on it or somethin'.

"You carefully check your entire body for zits and tweeze all unwanted hairs. Then it's back to the bedroom wearing a robe with the towel still on your head. If you see me along the way, you cover up any exposed areas." He laughed. "It's a riot!"

"Well, Mr. Know-it-all, men are no walks in the park."

Nathan said, "You're jokin'."

Terri laughed. "Nope. My turn. You take off your clothes while sitting on the edge of the bed and leave them in a pile. You walk naked to the bathroom. If you see me along the way, you shake your dick at me and make that stupid 'woo-woo' sound. Then you look in the mirror and flex your arms. You pull on your dick and scratch your ass. You get in the shower and wash your face, maybe your armpits. You always blow your nose in your hands and let the water rinse it off. The worst part, the part I absolutely hate, is you make fart noises. I guess you're makin' them. Could be the real thing.

"Then, Nathan, you spend the majority of time washing your privates and surrounding area, maybe including your butt. Not sure about that one sometimes.

"You leave your pubic hairs stuck on the soap. Then you shampoo your hair, play with it and make a shampoo mohawk. You pee, rinse off and get out of shower. Most of the time your back is still dry. You always fail to notice the water on the floor. It's there because the curtain was hangin' out of tub the whole time. You leave the wet bath mat on the floor. Of course, the light and fan are still on.

"On you way out of the bathroom, you can't pass the mirror without flexing somethin' and admiring your dick.

"When you come back to the bedroom, you always shake your dick at me and make that damned 'woo-woo' sound again. The topper is, you always throw the wet towel on the bed or at me."

He said, "Well, I didn't make it as personal as you did."

She laughed and said, "You know what our friends will say when we get married?" He looked up at her expectantly and she said, "Thank God they married each other and not one of us." Nathan rented a limo and picked Jimmie up after seeing Terri off Sunday morning. Jimmie had spent the weekend in Florida with Betty and Dotty. He was due to start chemo treatments on Monday.

***

Flying into LaGuardia, Jimmie stared out the window of the plane, lost in thought. Returning from Florida, it seemed he had the weight of the world on his shoulders. He had no idea how much longer he had with the cancer. Wasn't much, that was for sure. And Dotty. What would become of Dotty? he wondered, as the tears slowly ran down his cheek. At least he'd finalized things for their long-term care a while back.

A flight attendant noticed his tears and asked if she could help. Wiping his face, he tried a smile and told her he could handle it. As he watched her walk up the aisle, he mumbled to himself, "Don't I always handle it."

Jimmie was tired, tired of being the strong one, putting up the front. He wished he could just let it go, but he'd been taught men, real men, didn't do that.

As the plane taxied to the gate, Jimmie mentally strained to pull himself together. Nathan would be meeting him.

***

The change in Jimmie was unbelievable. He looked as if he'd aged ten years in the two days he was in Florida.

Nathan asked, "Good trip?" trying to make small talk. Jimmie grunted and Nathan let it go. When they got to Jimmie's apartment, Nathan told the driver to wait.

"I'm going to carry your stuff up and you can come home with me for dinner."

"I don't really feel like it, Nathan. I'm really tired."

"That's cool. You can spend the night." Nathan didn't give him a chance to say anything. He got out of the limo and went to the trunk to get the bag. He went up to Jimmie's apartment and put the dirty clothes in a hamper. He then grabbed some clean stuff out of the dresser and went back down.

In thirty minutes they were at Nathan's apartment. Nathan got him in and settled Jimmie in a recliner in front of the big screen TV, handing Jimmie the controls.

"Want a beer?" Jimmie nodded and Nathan got them both one. "How about some chicken soup for dinner?" Nathan asked as he sat down to watch TV with Jimmie.

"Sounds great. What is it with Jews and chicken soup?"

Nathan said, "I don't know. They love it, though."

Jimmie asked, "Didn't your mother make it for you when you were sick?"

Nathan said, "Sometimes."

"Did she show you how to make it?"

Nathan said, "Yeah. She just opened a can. Put it in a pot on a burner and waited for it to bubble. My mother was a terrible cook."

"A can? What kind of Jewish mother is that?"

"Jewish?" Nathan said, "My mother is a Baptist. So was I at one time."

"Always thought you were Jewish. Name and all. Way you took to Avi and Julie."

"Nope. I'm a mixture."

"You sure?" he asked, looking at Nathan.

"Positive. You want to see my pecker?"

Jimmie yelled, "Freeze on the Willie Johnson. Damn! Sure thought you were Jewish. You gonna' make the soup out of a can?"

"No. Terri's gonna' make it and bring it over. She's not Jewish either. Is that all right?"

He gave Nathan a sour look. "Of course it is, you idiot."

Terri came over later in the evening with the soup. They both teamed up on Jimmie, as planned, and talked him in to living with Nathan for a while.

"You'll love it," Terri said, after they wore Jimmie down. "Be like boys night out. You don't have to put up with the hassle of the realtors showing your apartment."

"Be helping me out too, Jimmie. You know how scared I get at night." Nathan gave him his "cute" smile. To their surprise, he agreed.

CHAPTER TWENTY-FIVE

The arrangement went well. Nathan's apartment was less than a block from the bar. Jimmie could go in anytime he wanted.

Worked out well for Nathan also. He enjoyed the company. He thought, you never really know somebody until you live with them. He'd found that out the hard way with assorted women. Jimmie never once hung wet panty hose in the bathroom. Jimmie even got along with Chucky. Or as well as could be expected.

The new owners took over the bar and nothing really changed. They knew a good thing when they saw it. They even kept the same name on the bar. Jimmie moved into the background after a week or so. A month later, they told him they'd release him in two more weeks. By then, he was having a tough time making it to the bar. His friends tried to get him to use a walker. He wouldn't hear of it. He was almost finished with his six weeks of radiation therapy and said he'd feel better then.

"Race you," Nathan said one day. He'd come up behind Jimmie on Sixth Avenue, moving slowly.

"Just like you to pick on cripples."

"That's a terrible thing to say to your best friend. I ought to kick your big crippled ass."

Jimmie said, "Just as I said. Probably rob me too."

Nathan looked at him. This man he'd known only a short while had gone from being big and well-muscled to just over one hundred sixty pounds in a matter of months. He was just making it down the sidewalk.

"Don't give me any ideas. Come on and I'll let you buy me a drink. Save you an ass-whipping."

"Sounds a winner. Better get all you can out of me. After that, you'll have to come to Florida to sponge off me soon. By the way, anyone ever mention how loud you snore?"

"I plan on coming to Florida to sponge and I don't snore. You grumpy old fuck."

"Can't come to Florida. You got to work, Junior."

"Lockout's over next week, baby boy. I'm free to do anything I want. Be a fireman, jockey, go to the North Pole, whatever."

Jimmie said, "You know what I'd like to do? Go to Israel while I still can. Want to go before I settle in Florida. Go with me?"

"Hell yes. You promise not to kill any old fat women?"

Jimmie smiled, "Sure you want to go with an old cripple?"

Nathan said, "Might sell your ass to white slavers."

Jimmie laughed, "They won't give much for me."

Nathan said, "Parts maybe. Penny saved is a penny earned."

The new owners were in, both sitting at the bar on a slow, early Friday afternoon. "How are you two today?" Sean O'Malley asked us as they walked in.

"Fine," Nathan answered. "You guys look like you're working hard." The truth was it was nice to see them resting. Running a bar is rough work. Makes for a close marriage because you are always together working. Close, but short.

"Feeling lazy today. Nathan, be my guest and get me one too," said Sean. "Jimmie, how you feeling?"

"Like a sissy on a battle ship, four months in on a six-month cruise."

Nathan went behind the bar and got them both a Mick Light, Jimmie a shot of Jameson. "Glass, Sean?"

"No, I'll rough it. More shit to wash."

Sean O'Malley was late thirties and pudgy. The bar business would take care of that. Red hair, blue eyes, just under six-foot with a great sense of humor. "Did ya' see the Knicks won? Jersey lost at Boston."

"Caught some of the game at lunch."

Helen O'Malley said, "Nathan, you're taking your business to another bar? Shame on you." Helen was also late thirties and had long, flowing red hair. Green-eyed, she was tall and thin.

The couple looked more like brother and sister than husband and wife. Sean, a former stockbroker and Helen, a nurse practitioner, invested their life savings and were heavily mortgaged to buy the bar. Childless, they'd both always wanted their own business. Now that they had one, it was more like a life sentence than a business.

"What's he forcing you to do today, Jimmie?" asked Helen.

"Cleaning his damn old stinky apartment all day." Helen shook her head and he continued, "Close as I could get him to help was to go across the street to the package store. Where he buys most of his groceries."

"Nathan's still a growing boy," said Helen.

"Grows anymore I'm gonna' have to get a wheelbarrow to haul his fat ass around in."

Nathan laughed, "Come on. I'm in good shape. Round's a shape, right? Besides, I just started a new workout routine. The Fonda workout. Peter Fonda. That's where I wake up, take a hit of acid, smoke a joint and go to my sister's house to beg for money."

They laughed and Sean said, "You know, Nathan, you're a regular guy. Important rich guy like you might be expected to act different. You're somebody, but you don't act snooty."

"Sean, I always wanted to be somebody."

Jimmie said, "You should a' been more specific. Maybe done better."

"You know, roomy, you're turning into a real cranky shit."

Jimmie said, "Nobody knows you better than me and don't you forget it. All those redneck yokels you used to pal around with in the South didn't have a clue. Married to their cousins and shit, no wonder. Nothing against them. Hell, they had stupid cousins."

***

Later, they headed home. During the short walk to Nathan's apartment, Nathan asked, "What would you like to do tonight, James?"

"How about I make my chili?"

"Perfect. Haven't had heartburn in a week," Nathan said.

"You love my chili."

"It's Irish chili, Jimmie. You aren't supposed to put potatoes and lamb in it. More like Brunswick Stew or somethin'."

"You want to cook?" Jimmie asked and Nathan said nothing. "All right, my chili then."

"Careful with the peppers is all I ask."

***

The next day, there was a bit of a cool snap and it was nice in New York. Everyone was dressed for success and there were some delightful creatures pounding the pavement. Nathan whistled "I'm a Girl Watcher" walking along the sidewalk with Jimmie.

"Feeling good today, Nathan?"

"That I am, James. I got a special consultant to do my work. It's a life of leisure for me."

Jimmie and Nathan met Terri at the corner. After greeting her, Jimmie moved ahead to give them some privacy. "I'll start the coffee, Nathan," he said, walking down the sidewalk.

Terri asked, "What's he in a hurry for?"

"He's my new special consultant. He's going to help me. Talked about it last night."

She smiled. "You're a good man, Nathan Melton. Most of the time you hide it well, but you're a good man. Nice giving him something to do."

"Don't sell our boy short. Said he was tired of sitting around the apartment. He's not spending that much time at the bar anymore. Said he needed something to do. Keep his mind off things the next two weeks before he heads to Florida for good. He's getting worse, Terri."

"How so?"

Nathan said, "Little things. Like forgetting to turn the stove off, leaving water running, things like that."

"Any time you need some help, give me a yell."

"I will," Nathan said. "Got a joke for you."

Before he could begin, Terri cut him off. "Aren't you ever serious, Nathan? Jeez, I get tired of all the damn jokes. Just too much." Nathan's expression changed from a smile to hurt. Terri said nothing and they continued to walk to work, both quiet.

***

Judy came in thirty minutes after Nathan and Jimmie arrived at the office. "Good morning," she said, carrying two cups of coffee. Nathan usually made the first pot, which was situated in her office. Jimmie would take over making coffee as special consultant now. She brought him his second cup of the day. "I have donuts, little boy. Those burnt coconut ones."

Nathan asked, "Marry me?"

"I like you too much. Besides, you're too damn old for me."

"I'm a couple a' years older. Bugger," said Nathan, sticking out his tongue.

"What did I tell you about name calling? It's a shame," she said, holding the bag in front of him. "Two of these donuts used to be yours."

"I'm sorry," he said, snatching the bag from her and greedily wolfing down one of the donuts. "Did you speak to our new special consultant?"

"I didn't see anybody but Jimmie in the foyer. He was reading the paper."

"That's him. New special consultant."

She smiled. "I'm going to go give the special consultant some donuts."

As he was eating the other donut, he asked her, "How come you and I never got to know each other in a biblical sense?"

"It would be unnatural. We're too much alike. We'd kill each other within weeks," she said, leaving his office and taking the donuts to Jimmie.

"What a way to go, baby."

She stopped, turned to him, gave a really sexy look, and said, "Don't talk with your mouth full," and left his office.

He yelled, "That's the best you got?" She may have heard him. He was glad she'd left. She couldn't see him wiping donut crumbs off of his shirt.

Harvey came into Nathan's office with a cup of coffee. Nathan yelled, "What!" then said, "Look like you lost some more weight."

"Naw. Just going to a good tailor. Your guy upstairs."

Nathan asked, "How's the hot girl search comin'?"

Harvey said, "I've settled for not-so-hot. My divorce is finalized."

"All right, Harvey."

"Nancy and the pilot broke up. Says she wants to come to New York now."

Nathan looked at him. "Is that what you want?"

Harvey gasped, "Hell, no. Told her tough titty. How are you and Terri doin'?"

"Fuck if I know. Told me this mornin' I joke too much."

Harvey shrugged, "So stop jokin'."

Nathan said, "Did you see the Braves lost again?"

"Four in a row, but Chipper's hitting again. Bobby Cox should be manager of the year again. He won't get it. Press and other managers hate him. Jealous bastards."

Nathan said, "That they are. All those division titles and people act like it's nothin'. He and Tony in St. Louis ought to tell 'em to kiss their ass.

Harvey said, "Gotta' blonde joke. Blonde's house catches on fire and she dials 911 and says, 'My house is on fire. Come quick.' The operator says, 'Calm down. Just tell us how to get there.' Blonde says, 'Duh! In the big red truck.'

***

At lunch, Nathan and Terri walked a couple of blocks to Harley Davidson on Sixth Avenue. Terri asked, "Where's Jimmie?"

"Getting a crash course in the Internet business. Been with Merchandising all morning. Said to bring him back tuna on rye."

Terri said, "Wow. He's really gettin' into it."

She was quiet so he asked. "We have a problem?"

"I'm sorry. I'm still kind of pissed about this morning. Sometime you are a little overbearing. You never act serious."

Nathan said, "Guess maybe I don't. Defense mechanism or somethin'. Because people are large, other people don't think they're sensitive. I am, just try to hide it with humor. Maybe a nervous reaction," he said.

She said, "Maybe I was wrong in getting mad at you."

He said, "You've been doing that a lot lately."

"What?"

He said, "Getting pissed. Are you looking for an excuse to dump me, Terri?"

Terri answered, "God, no."

He said, "Well, at least you aren't losing your mind."

She laughed. "No. Not that I know of. I've been on edge lately. I know you have too. Jimmie mostly. We don't have any problems."

"Good. I don't want there to be problems. I kind of, sorta like ya'."

Terri asked, "Want to go steady?"

"Thought you'd never ask," he said. "I get your school ring and a chain to wear it around my neck?"

"If I can have your letter sweater?"

Nathan laughed, "Fuck yes! I got a bunch of them."

"I got a bunch of rings too," she said.

"Works great," he said.

"Want to play hooky this afternoon?"

He said, "Can't. But I'm free after an audit meeting."

"It's a date. I think our problem is we aren't getting enough. We'll rectify that tonight," she said. "You ready to head back to the salt mine?"

"Get your purse and pay the bill. Time's a wasting."

She asked, "Why do I have to pay?"

"You wanted to go steady."

***

Harvey popped into Nathan's office later in the afternoon and asked, "Want to go to a ball game Saturday? I got great seats from a vendor. Yanks and Boston. Afternoon game."

"Yeah. Meet you at Jimmie's like noonish? Is it all right if Jimmie comes?"

"Certainly. See you there, old cheeko."

Shortly after Harvey left, Judy burst into Nathan's office and said, "Nathan, they've taken Jimmie to Columbia Hospital. Your doorman Whitey called."

He rushed out of the building and caught a taxi to Columbia where he was told Jimmie was in the Emergency Room.

He was allowed back and found him in a cube. He was sitting up in bed and Nathan said, "What happened? You okay?"

"Yeah. Feel fine. Just passed some blood and that fuckin' little Nancy doorman of yours freaked."

"Why didn't you tell me you were going home?"

Jimmie said, "Just had a friggin' headache. No biggie. I gotta' tell you everything?"

Nathan, excited, said, "Yeah, you do!" The doctor came in then and saved them both from saying things they didn't mean and would regret.

"I'm going to release the patient," he said to Nathan. "I talked to his doctor at Sloan. He wants him to make an appointment and come in and see him as soon as possible." He looked at Jimmie. "Mr. Collins, if you'll promise to do just that, we can have you out of here in a few minutes."

"Of course I will, Doc," said Jimmie.

Nathan asked, "Doc, I've been taking him to work with me. Is that okay or does he need to stay in bed?"

"I think, as long as he feels like it, going in with you would be the best thing for him. Keep him active."

Nathan took Jimmie home and made the appointment with his doctor for the next day. Then he told him, "You either have to use a daytime nurse or come to work with me and stay. I don't want you alone. If you come to work with me and want to leave, you have to tell me. I'm having a motorized scooter delivered. Your choice."

"Let's go back to work."

CHAPTER TWENTY-SIX

Nathan met Terri after work for the walk to the bar. It had been raining and the city had one of those rare, clean smells that wouldn't last long.

"Terri, time is right if you want to buy my stock. It's down. I'm buying like crazy."

"Thanks, Nathan. I started buying when you told me what you were doing, but I'll get some more. It's still dropping like a rock."

"That's good, but I feel bad. Kind of hurts my feelings," he said.

Terri asked, "Did Jimmie get off for Florida this morning?"

"He knocked on my door and told me he was off. My office set him up with a limo."

"Do we have plans this weekend? I'd like to screw our brains out," Terri asked.

Nathan winced. "I'm going to a ball game with Harvey tomorrow afternoon. Harvey's getting a divorce and I think he's kind of lonely. I'll be back early evening."

"That's cool. While you're gone, I'll go shopping and check in on Chucky. Need a new whip and some batteries."

"You're in a fabulous mood. Is it the going steady thing? You didn't think I could face a commitment?"

"That's exactly what it is." She stopped to look in the window of Ferragamos'. "I like commitments."

He said, "Shit! You like shoes more."

"Yep. Buy me something, Daddy." Hello, monkey sex.

Terri and Nathan walked in the bar and were greeted by Ken and Stuart. Lou had also seen them come in. He had Nathan's beer and

Terri's Tom Collins sitting there for them as they made their way to the bar.

"Welcome home, Nathan," Lou said.

Nathan took a long draw on his beer. "Dusty trail," Nathan said, motioning for another. Turning to Ken, he said, "What's New York's finest up to?"

Ken said, "Just killing eight on another shitty assignment."

"Shitty assignment? Been guarding the bar all day," Lou said.

***

The next morning it was raining like hell. Nathan looked out of his window and figured there'd be no ball game. He started to call Harvey, but decided to meet him at the bar anyway.

"So this is the famous Jimmie's? Pretty nice." Harvey was waiting on Nathan when he arrived. With the rain, Terri was watching Chucky. No whips and batteries for her.

"I don't know about famous. Just a place close to home."

"I'm going to buy a place in Manhattan. Tired of that commute from Lincoln Park everyday," Harvey said. Lincoln Park was in Northern Jersey and he caught the train, like millions, everyday.

"Can't blame you there. I hate commutes. Going to be giving up green in both senses." Nathan had been to his condo on a couple of occasions. Beautifully landscaped, on a lake, close to cross-country snow skiing. His development was kind of like Florida two months out of the year. "I can give you my realtor if you want. She did a great job for me."

"She fuckable? I'm becoming a dangerous man."

Nathan said, "Yes, as a matter of fact she is. If you like Hungarians,"

"Ugly Eskimos at the moment would look pretty good."

Nathan said, "She's not ugly. You ready to shell out some cash moving here?"

"Well, thanks to the IPO, that's not a problem." Harvey made ten million on paper with the IPO and stood to make considerably more when the stock price headed north.

Nathan asked, "Is the soon-to-be-ex going to share in your riches?"

"You'll get a kick out of this. Her father left her about $800,000 when he died and she made me sign a pre-nuptial agreement. She's trying to fight it now, but it's not a happening thing."

Nathan laughed, "That's beautiful. She smarted herself right out of big money."

"This was your buddy's bar." Harvey looked around. "Looks like a money maker. Guess he deserved it with the bad luck on the wife and daughter."

"Yeah! He's a great guy. Not everybody would've stayed given the cards he was dealt."

Harvey asked, "You want to go to Hooters? Grab a burger and look at some orange?"

"I just got here. You tell me it's a great place and want to leave? Besides, it's raining, Harvey."

"Kind of dead. No women here. We can take a taxi if you want. Just a block away."

"It's a long block." Nathan looked at the sad look on his face. "You buying Mr. Pre-Nupt?"

They walked and got drenched. It was a long block, but uphill. With an umbrella, they had a choice of getting the back of their heads or their knees wet.

They finally made it and got two seats at the bar. "Have you seen this yet?" Harvey asked, pointing at the TV. Nathan nodded no. "Great commercial. ESPN uses Jeff Kent. He's talking about how proud he is they would ask him to do the commercial. They're flying all kinds of banners and stuff across his face. Guys are funny. I don't know who does their commercials for them. Whoever does is great."

Nathan watched the commercial and laughed. "I got into trouble trying to explain ESPN commercials to Terri not long ago."

"You guys havin' problems?"

"Not anymore. We're goin' steady," said Nathan.

"Steady? Fuckin' women. It's the old bounty thing," Harvey said, eying a cute young waitress, clad in the obligatory orange, across the room.

"You know, Harv, the station is changing. ESPN. All the announcers try to be funny now. Trey and those guys. Kind a' name is Trey?" Nathan looked at Harvey, but he was staring at orange. "All copying Dan Patrick and old what's-his-name, Oberman or somethin'. Used to be you had Dan Patrick and the other guy. Remember the guy that got suspended and said he couldn't tell the difference between a paid suspension and vacation? Went to another network. Not a clue where he's at now. Was really funny."

"Yeah," said Harvey. "I know who you're talkin' about. Can't think of his name. Keith somethin'. Looked like Clark Kent." Harvey took a drink of beer and said, "Most of those guys aren't funny and should just do the sports. Stuart Scott is funny. Guy with him too. Straight-looking guy."

"Yeah. Rich something. He's funny. Dude Kenny is too. Kind a' out there, though."

Harvey said, "Guys I hate are the PTI guys. One dude is a black supremacist and the other's just stupid. Should have the guy Max that does the fights. Him and the guy from the Miami paper, Dan something. Or Stat Boy. Should fire the other guys."

"Ah, they're okay. Wilbon's good if he's not on the race thing. Tony is funny in a weird way. They jus' scream at each other too much." Nathan stood and said, "Gonna' make a restroom call, Harv." Harvey nodded.

When he came back from the restroom, a waitress was sitting with Harvey. "Nathan, this is Glenda. She just got off work."

"Harvey, game's a rainout. You and Glenda enjoy the afternoon."

"Sure thing, buddy." Harvey immediately turned his attention to Glenda.

Nathan couldn't remember anybody happier to see him leave. He walked back into the rain smiling.

CHAPTER TWENTY-SEVEN

A week later, Nathan was in Terri's apartment. "Are you gonna' spend the night, big boy?" Terri smiled coyly.

"Not the night, but I can stay a while. Dave and Marie are taking Jimmie to dinner and bringing him back later. Sunday, Avi and Julie are taking him to Bingo. He's spending the night with Julie Sunday."

Terri said, "Glad to hear they got back together."

"Yeah. Weird deal. Julie won't marry Avi, but said she'd do a trial thing with him. They won't see anybody else."

Terri laughed, "They weren't anyway. So what's Jimmie doing Monday? I miss him."

Nathan said, "Monday Julie's taking him to the doctor. Might be free Monday night."

Terri asked, "You got him all planned out."

"Everybody is pulling together. Really helps, but you know what? I get jealous sometimes."

***

"Sir James," Nathan asked. "What would you like to do tonight? Something nice and relaxing?" They were eating Saturday breakfast, his big treat. Weight-wise, Nathan splurged on Saturday morning breakfast. Sausage, eggs, grits. All heavily loaded with cheese. Once a week, then back to a sensible diet of steaks, ribs and chili cheese fries.

"I think if you're trying to relax, the best way would be with the opposite sex. Terri being a fine representative, spend the night with her. Don't worry about me, Nathan."

Nathan asked, "What are you doing?"

"Nathan, you're doing the smothering thing again. I'll let it pass because I love you like a brother, but for God's sake you don't have to baby-sit me. I'm going on stakeout with the lads." Ken and Stuart were helping out with Jimmie and on occasion were taking him on stakeouts. It was a way to give Nathan some space, but also spend some time with him.

Nathan said, "Got to be exciting. Think they'd mind if I tag along?"

"The more the merrier. I'll call Stuart just to make sure," said Jimmie. "As far as exciting, I don't know. Usually we just sit around, tell jokes and shoot the shit. Maybe laugh at each other's farts to break the monotony. Tonight might be different, though."

"Yeah. They on to something?"

Jimmie said, "Got a location staked out right around the neighborhood where the perp has been hitting. It's just down the block, other side of Fifth."

"Is the guy a robber or somethin'?"

Jimmie said, "He's a friggin' whacko. Breaks in and exposes himself to women. Makes them watch while he whips skippy. Sick fucker should be put out of his misery."

***

Stakeout. What a miserable way to earn a living. Especially if you had a nine-minute attention span like Nathan. They were in an apartment facing an alley and the back of another building on East 56th. The perp displayed a talent for getting into tough places by climbing. He had struck a couple of apartments in the area the week before. The cops were hoping he'd strike the same area on the same night of the week again.

Stuart and Ken were happy for the company. Stakeouts were the most boring and dreaded part of police work and they'd blown any semblance of conversation years ago.

"So this is a stakeout," Nathan said, bored to tears and struggling to make conversation. "Kind of slow." He'd previously thumbed through the dog-eared Penthouse, Playboy and NRA magazines they kept in the car for distraction.

"Ninety percent of our job is like that," said Ken. "Remember when we met you? We'd been in that friggin' diner for a week. Ugly, ugly, ugly! I was havin' nightmares about the waitress, who was a piece of work, by the way."

"I couldn't handle it," Nathan said. "You do nothing for most of the time and then you got to put it on the line. In football, you knew when it was going to happen and you could pump up for it."

"We appreciate the company, believe me. Helps to have some extra eyes," said Stuart. "New conversation ain't bad either."

Nathan volunteered for the first watch. He was so bored he actually volunteered. The apartment they were in was empty so the owner had allowed the city to use it for the stakeout. There was no furniture except for a blow-up mattress, a card table, three chairs and a telescope.

He asked, "What am I looking for?"

"See the third-floor window, directly across from us? One that's lit up?" Stuart said, "Just stay trained on that window. That's the one we hope the mope hits."

"Oh yeah. Good-looking blonde sitting in a bra on the couch," Nathan said, finding it with the glasses. "Window wide open like that. Got to be crazy."

"That's the one," laughed Ken. Jimmie and Stuart laughed too. Jimmie had been on this stakeout a couple of times. They were playing three-handed Tunk, a game Nathan couldn't figure out. Seemed you just yelled a lot and threw cards around the room.

"What's this guy look like?" Nathan asked, letting the laughter pass.

"That's a problem," Ken said. "Descriptions vary. So do times. Got him in two places at the same time. Fuckin' guy hits a couple places an hour some nights."

"Some stamina," said Jimmie.

"Think a guy like that does Viagra?" Nathan laughed.

"People are excited," said Stuart, laughing, "and fuck up the description and times. Guy is anywhere from five-and-a-half feet to six feet tall. Weighs one-fifty to two-thirty."

"Damn! That's a stretch," Nathan said.

"Like I said, people are nervous. You got a weenie whacker standing over you, you're naked, makes it difficult," said Jimmie.

"I can understand that," Nathan said. "You have a tough time deciding where to focus. You'd think at least you'd have a description of the guy's pecker."

Ken said, "We do. Described as big." He laughed and said, "You guys see Tyson yesterday? Guy's an animal! Went after Lewis."

Nathan said, "Wish he'd of got him. Smug ass Lennox Lewis with his accent."

"Shortest book in the world," said Stuart. "*Dating Etiquette,* by Mike Tyson."

"Naw," said Jimmie. "Janet Reno's *Beauty Secrets* would be shorter."

"No way," said Stuart. "*Things I Love About Bill,* by Hillary."

Ken said, "You want political. *My Life's Memories,* by Ronald Reagan."

"*Wild Years,* by Al Gore," said Stuart.

Ken said, "How about *My Plan to Find The Real Killer,* by O J?"

"*Spotted Owl Recipes,* by the EPA," Nathan said.

"*All The Men I've Loved Before,* by Ellen de Generes," Ken said.

Stuart asked, "Is she the one...?

Ken said, "Yeah, yeah. A carpet muncher."

Nathan almost shouted, falling out of his chair, "Guys, got some movement in the alley."

Ken and Stuart jumped up, pushing Nathan away from the telescope. "He's right," said Ken. "Could be our perp. Yeah, that's the guy," he shouted. "Climbing up the rain spout. Let's see, one, two, three windows down to the right. Going for it." Stuart was on the radio as they rushed for the door. "Nathan, you're a good luck charm. Two for two."

Nathan shouted after them, "Yeah, but I got hurt last time."

He turned and Jimmie had moved his scooter over in front of the window. "What's happening?"

"Guy's climbing. Man, he can move. Wait! Another guy," said Nathan. "Climbing, five windows down from the other one." He looked at Jimmie, "Shit. We got to tell Ken and Stuart," Nathan said, running for the door.

"Better stay here," said Jimmie, but Nathan ignored him.

Nathan made it to the alley in record time. For him anyway. It was pitch black and he couldn't see ten feet in front of him. He looked up to get his bearings and all he could make out was the lit up third-floor window. He didn't see anyone. Ken, Stuart, other cops, nobody. All he could think to do was try to protect the blonde on the third floor. He didn't yell because he didn't want to screw up Ken And Stuart. He looked around, picked up a rock and threw it toward the window. Missed by four feet. That's why he played linebacker. Couldn't throw for shit. He found another rock and threw it and busted the damn window.

The blonde came to the window, looked through the hole where he'd busted it with his trusty rock and said, "What the fuck you doin', Mack?"

Nathan looked up and shouted in warning, "The blonde's got a mustache. The blonde's got a mustache." He turned just in time to be hit in the head with a two-by-four and his world went black.

***

He regained consciousness several hours later. As his eyes opened and he tried to focus, he was aware of being in an inclined position in bed. The first face he recognized was Terri's. Then Ken came into focus, followed by Stuart. He heard Jimmie's voice. Then a stranger was over him and he thought, *is this the weenie whacker?* He tried to move and couldn't.

The stranger had a penlight flashing it across his eyes. "Follow the light, Mr. Melton." He followed it wondering how the weenie whacker knew his name.

"Concussion," the man said to the others around the bed.

"Good thing he's got a hard head," said Jimmie. Nathan reminded himself to be mad at him later.

"He's damn lucky." Turning toward Nathan, he said, "Mr. Melton, I'm Doctor Winthrop."

Nathan tried to rise, couldn't and said, "You're not the weenie whacker?"

There was laughter in the room and the doctor continued, "You're at Lennox Hill Hospital. Be still," he said as Nathan tried to move. "You are going to have one hell of a headache."

"It won't hurt half as much when he sees the side of his head where you guys shaved it," said Jimmie.

Doctor Winthrop frowned at Jimmie then turned back to Nathan and said, "Your friend is right, Mr. Melton. We had to shave the side of your head to stitch you up. Twenty-three stitches. Not a small area, but you'll be fine. We'll keep you here for observation and, barring anything traumatic, you'll be released tomorrow. You have friends here so I'll let you spend some time with them." He turned to Terri. "No more than twenty minutes. I've given him something for pain, so he'll be asleep shortly."

Terri asked, "You okay, honey?" He didn't answer her damn fool question.

Ken moved into his line of vision. "Officially two for two." It sank in to Nathan that he'd been involved in two stakeouts and hurt on both; the mugger at the ATM and this one. "Got our guy. Both of them. Two of them operating as a team. Jimmie told us you tried to warn us. What the hell were you yellin'?"

"Blonde had a mustache and was in on it."

"The 'she' was Officer Pete Donovan. The stakeout was a decoy," Ken said.

"Who hit me?" Nathan crooned.

"Patrolman Lon Malloy," said Ken. "He thought you were the perp and whacked you with a board. Lieutenant busted our ass when he found out you and Jimmie were helping us. Suspended again. This time for two weeks."

Nathan said, "Sorry to hear that."

Stu said, "Works out well. I'm doing some work for Gail in the building. Ken is gonna' help."

Nathan was released the next morning and Terri and Jimmie took care of him all weekend. He felt fine, but kept walking into walls.

CHAPTER TWENTY-EIGHT

It was Monday night and Nathan was in bed with Terri at her place. "You don't love me anymore," said Terri. "You're a million miles away." She leaned over and started rubbing his chest, then the fuzzy section on his recently shaved head.

"Naw," he replied. "Just thinking about a ton of stuff. Wondering how long Jimmie has. Why Jimmie and not somebody else? He does all this great stuff, stuff for the church, his employees, kids with the mentoring program, the Christmas Drive. The guy has had nothing but bad breaks, but keeps on doing good things. His daughter, his wife and now him. Why him?"

She said, "I'm no theologian, but it does seem unfair. If you asked him, he wouldn't change a thing."

"Probably not. I would, I'd be mad."

She rubbed his head again and asked, "When do you get the stitches out?"

"Friday. Itches like a bastard." He turned and looked at her. "Just not fair, is it? Jimmie's barely making it now. I don't know how he'll make it through this next round of chemo. He's planning to go to Florida for good after this session. Asked him if I could go with him for a while and help out. Know what he told me?"

"I can guess," Terri said.

"Told me to piss off. Get on with my life." He wiped at a tear running down his cheek and turned away from her.

She pretended not to notice. She thought, why are men like that? Afraid to show a human side. She put her arm around him and said, "Jimmie will be alright."

They lay for fifteen minutes in complete silence. Terri rolled over on her side and put an arm across Nathan. "You tired of being sad?" She reached down and started rubbing the head of his penis, feeling him stiffen. "It's a good look for you, but kind of leaves one horny." She moved beneath the covers and took him in her mouth. At first she teased and then got serious, taking him all the way in. After a bit, he tried to move her from underneath the covers so he could make love to her, but she wouldn't budge.

After his orgasm, and feeling the quid pro rule in effect, he moved under the covers. She was ready for him and already moist. She tensed as he slowly moved his tongue over her clitoris.

The great sex led to a nap and later they walked the neighborhood, making a very usual stop at the bar.

"Listen, I need to talk to you sometime tonight," said Lou, as Terri and Nathan entered the bar.

Nathan said, "Want to do it now?"

"No. I'm on break in about an hour. Maybe we can do it then?"

"Certainly. I'll be here a while," Nathan said.

Lou laughed, "What a surprise."

He and Terri kibitzed with Stuart, Avi and Dave until Ray came in an hour later. "Here's my buddy," Nathan said, seeing him coming up behind him. "What's up, Ray?" Nathan turned to shake hands with him, but was enveloped in a huge bear hug.

"Here's my buddy, Chatty Cathy," Ray said. "Did he tell you his new name?"

"Chatty Cathy?" Terri asked, "What's with that?"

"Sometimes he gets on a roll and just doesn't stop. On and on he goes. Ask Jimmie. But I love him." He raised one of his meaty paws and messed up Nathan's hair. Thankfully the side of Nathan's head that was not shaved. "Ain't that right, Nate me boy?"

"Yeah, little buddy. That's me. Chatty Cathy. Guess it's a nervous reaction." He thought about mentioning Ray's propensity for ice cream at odd times, but didn't.

"God knows we had stuff to be nervous about," Ray said. "Lotsa stuff." The Costa Rica story had grown since their return.

Lou came up to Nathan and said, "Got a second?"

"Yeah."

They walked out to the sidewalk in front of the bar and Lou said, "You still think it's a good idea to buy the stock?"

"I'm still buyin' if that answers your question," Nathan said.

"Other thing—Jimmie's telling everybody he's goin' to quit taking the chemo and go to Florida. Says maybe he'll finish this round of treatments down there. You think that's a good idea?"

Nathan answered, "We kind of half-assed talked about it. Thought he'd decided against it."

Lou looked at Nathan and said, "Question, Nathan. If he's terminal, why is he taking the damn treatments anyway?"

"Doc said it might increase his time. Maybe not." Nathan grimaced. "Thanks, Lou. I'll talk to him. He can't make that trip right now. If it wasn't for his scooter he couldn't make it the half-block to the bar."

A half-hour later Jimmie motored into the bar. Like a celebrity, he took a while to get to Terri and Nathan's position at the bar, meeting and greeting old friends.

When he finally made it, he beamed and told Nathan, "Closed on my apartment today. Put a nice fat check in the bank."

Nathan asked him, "Jimmie, what's this about you quittin' treatments?"

Jimmie said, "Treatments are a waste of time."

"Not what the doc said and you know it."

Jimmie said, "Don't know anything of the sort. Need to see my family, Nathan!"

Nathan looked at his friend and his wasted body. His body was emaciated, but he still had his hair, and was proud of it. That was all that remained of this once-powerful man he'd met not long ago.

"Tell you what," Nathan said. "I'll check with the doctor and we'll go as soon as he says you can."

"You know what he's going to say. I feel good."

"We got to go by what the doctor says."

"Not when you're dying." Jimmie looked at Nathan over the ridge of his glasses, another concession to the cancer that racked his body. "Nathan, this is something I want to do," he said pleadingly. "I don't know how long I have left."

Nathan looked at the group for help in arguing his case. Dave, Avi and Terri jumped in to help Nathan. They talked to Jimmie as parents to a child when the kid wants to do something and the parents know it's bad for them. They gave some strong arguments. Saving his strength so he'd last longer, feeling better when he did go to Florida after taking the treatments, quality of life and all that.

To his credit he listened to them. When they had finished, he looked at Nathan and in his severely hoarse voice, said, "Okay Nathan, you win. But promise me you won't try to stop me when the treatments are over?" Then he motored out of the bar, leaving Nathan feeling like the lowest form of life.

The rest of the crowd saw how Nathan felt and tried to cheer him up, but it wasn't going to happen. He felt he'd let his best friend down.

Terri said, "He'll finish his chemo session and we'll have a going away party for him. Big sendoff before he goes to live in Florida."

***

At work the next day, Nathan's company released the news about the huge increase in sales for the quarter preceding the lock-out period. The stock price started rising. Within a week, share price pushed past $20 a share. In two weeks, it was above $30 and the institutional funds jumped in. Nathan and Jimmie started cashing out at $30.

Jimmie was down to one-hundred-ten pounds and really looked like a cadaver. His eyes were sunken and he was passing blood daily. His doctors didn't hold out much hope and said he would probably be gone by the end of the year.

CHAPTER TWENTY-NINE

Jimmie didn't make it to the end of the week. He died in his sleep two days later with a week left on his treatments. Jimmie never saw his family again.

Nathan discovered him when he went to wake him up for breakfast. It was tough. Nathan had grown really close to him in the time they lived together. He cried when he first found Jimmie. Jimmie would've laughed himself silly. Probably would have told everyone. Nathan didn't care. He was more than a friend, he thought, cradling Jimmie's head in his arms.

He was trying to say goodbye to him in his own way and crying like a baby. "Damn, I'll miss him," he mumbled, tears flowing. Knowing him like he did, how proud Jimmie always was of his appearance, he carefully shaved and dressed him. He wanted his friend to look as good as possible before people saw him.

Finished, he dialed two digits of the number for the ambulance people and stopped. He just wasn't ready to say goodbye to Jimmie, to let him go. For a full thirty minutes he talked to his friend, saying all the things he wanted to, but couldn't say when Jimmie was alive. Why, he thought, sitting on the bed next to Jimmie, is it wrong to tell another man you love him? Why the stupid stigma? And he cried.

At some point he called Terri to tell her Jimmie was dead. He actually couldn't say the word "dead" and started crying again. Terri made the call to Jimmie's doctor and the police, who told her what to do and who to call.

Nathan wanted to make the funeral arrangements. He knew what Jimmie wanted. He waited until the body was taken away. He started to call the funeral home, but Terri told him not to. It was up to his family, she told him.

"We are his family," he protested. "I promised him I'd spread his ashes on the roof of the bar. He asked me to, Terri."

"Nathan, call the nursing home. No, I'll call the nursing home. I'll have them find out what Jimmie's wife and daughter want done," said Terri.

Nathan argued, "What if they don't want what Jimmie wanted? I promised him."

"They're his family. We're his friends. We have to do what they want."

The staff at the nursing home talked to Jimmie's wife and called Terri back. The family wanted his body cremated and returned to them in an urn. They asked her to send Jimmie's belongings to them at the home. Terri agreed to dispose of the other possessions that weren't of a personal nature.

Jimmie and Nathan had cleaned out the apartment when he moved in with Nathan. He'd given most of his possessions to Goodwill so there wasn't much left. Nathan took it hard, but Terri insisted that family wishes came first.

Nathan and Terri made the arrangements. After the ceremony, which was well attended by his many friends in the city, they brought the urn back to Nathan's place. They organized an around-the-clock wake for him. Jimmie would have really enjoyed it, Nathan thought.

***

At the wake, Nathan listened, and then joined in with his own Jimmie stories. Interesting what you can learn about a guy from his friends. A lot of these people Nathan didn't know. He'd seen some of them in the bar, but there were a lot that he'd never seen before. The many different perspectives were amazing.

"My favorite," Nathan told a small group "was when I met him. I walked into a stakeout, got hit in the mouth a couple of times. Stuart and Ken took me to his bar for a beer afterward. Jimmie gives me his big marketing spiel about not letting a customer buy his first drink in the bar. Says he's got them for life. I ask him what happens if they don't come back? He gets this weird look and says that would screw up his theory." He laughed and said, "Or the time he was acting like some kind of big time cat burglar. He told me and Ray he could pick any lock in this hotel we're at. Come to find out all the locks had the same key." He nodded at Ray and they both started laughing.

Ray said, "Nathan, remember when we thought Jimmie should join a dating club?"

They were both rolling and Marie said, "I don't get it."

Ray started to explain but, remembering the circumstances, said, "Had to be there," and he and Nathan started laughing harder. He looked at Nathan, tears in his eyes and asked, "What kind a' ice cream is it?"

Nathan yelled, "I don't know. It's in Spanish." Laughing, Nathan continued, "Or when I'd just started coming to the bar. One night I walk in and every woman in the place is wearing a fur."

Terri said, "Nathan asked me was this like a Labor Day thing where after a certain day everybody wore furs?"

Julie started laughing and said, "Everyone of 'em hot and Nathan thinks it's a New York tradition."

Nathan said, "Funny how you just got used to that at Jimmie's. Maybe thirty guys with the same suit on, all new."

Avi said, "Remember his coin piles?" He turned to the crowd and said, "Jimmie would be countin' the coins from the video poker machines and when he'd turn around Nathan would mess 'em up." Looking at Nathan, he said, "You never knew, but he knew you were doin' it."

Nathan said, "Why didn't he say somethin'?"

Avi said, "He knew you got a kick out of it. He laughed about it."

Nathan said, "Fucking Jimmie, I'll sure miss him." A chorus of "here, here" went up from the crowd as Nathan wiped a tear from his eye, everyone toasting Jimmie.

Another man said, "Great guy." Nathan didn't know him, but most of the room did. He was head of a New Jersey crime family. "He and I, Sal Russo and some of the other guys were about the same age and kind of started out doin' the same shit." He saw Nathan's expression and said, "Don't get me wrong. Jimmie wasn't into anything bad. He worked as a bartender at a club I used to make book at. Knew how to mind his own business. He saved his money and bought his place. Used to be real rundown, but he worked hard and built it up. Now I'm not saying Jimmie was an angel. Jimmie would fence some stuff, buy other stuff, but no drugs. He wouldn't fuck with drugs. Just the occasional clothes, funny money, jewelry, stuff like that. It'll kill Sal and Petey, not bein here."

Another big Mafia guy said, "Jimmie was honest. Wouldn't play games with the machines or put too many swag cigarettes in. Never more than two to one, even though we tried to tell him. Paid his taxes on a lot of the money he made. Even some of the cash. He was a regular John Q. Public, Jimmie was." He saluted Jimmie's urn, and took a long pull of whatever he was drinking. "Me and the boys stayed away from the bar, not wanting to embarrass our friend," he said as he wiped away a tear.

A leader of one of New York's main Mafia families said, "Remember when a bunch a' cowboys tried to horn in on Jimmie? Tried to pass themselves off as bein' with one a' the families. Fuckin' Jimmie didn't call nobody. He beat the shit out of 'em and threw 'em out in the street. Sal Russo found out and got mad at Jimmie for not tellin' him. Old Petey and some of the guys caught up with 'em and now they swim with the fishes." He turned, saw a police captain listening to him and said, "Jus' between us, Tim." The captain nodded. "He ran a straight business there at the bar. Didn't need somebody like me ruining his business with my reputation. Why me and a lot of the boys never came in durin' business hours. Jimmie was a brother to me." A tear rolled down his cheek. With his reddened eyes, it wasn't the first.

Later, Nathan ran into Jimmie's priest, Father Donovan, a real old-fashioned parish priest. "Jimmie talked about you often," the father said. "And why is it we don't see you around the parish?"

"Been meaning to get by there," Nathan said.

The priest said, "See that you do, young man."

"Certainly will, Father," said Nathan. "I was surprised that Jimmie was a big churchgoer."

"Morning mass, three, four times a week. Jimmie was devout. He also contributed heavily to our charities. None finer than Jimmie Collins, God rest his soul." He made the sign of the cross and said, "Jimmie told me a lot about you. Said you were one of his best friends. Is it true?"

"I was honored to be Jimmie's friend. I may have made him mad toward the end there, tryin' to take care of him."

Father Donovan said, "Nonsense. Jimmie used to brag about the way you and the rest of his friends took care of him."

"Small confession, father. I was jealous of his family. Made excuses to keep him here. I was the reason he didn't get to see his family again. Had him stayin' to take the useless treatments. I feel bad about it," admitted Nathan.

"Consider yourself absolved. You wanted what was best for Jimmie and it's over now."

Nathan spotted one of Jimmie's old employees across the room crying heavily. He walked over and put his arms around her and said, "Gloria, he's in a better place."

"I know, Nathan. He was such a good man." Gloria Ringwald was Jimmie's first employee and had stayed with him until he sold the bar. Early sixties and stout, she'd put four children through school while working for Jimmie. "Did I ever tell you all the good he did for his employees? The man was a saint. No way I could've put my children through school if it weren't for him." She sniffled and buried her face in his chest. "He was always helping us. Sick or behind on bills, you could always expect a little something extra in the pay envelope. Kids sick, the same. The man was a saint."

Ken, seeing Gloria crying, came to Nathan's aid. "Gloria, Jimmie Collins would've been sorely pissed at you. Crying at a wake."

"You're right, Ken," she blew her nose. "Wakes are supposed to be happy occasions."

Nathan snuck away while Ken was telling Gloria a joke and ran into Stuart. "Nathan, come over and meet the captain. Lot of brass here tonight, Deputy Commissioner, lieutenants up the ying-yang." He walked over and was introduced to Stuart's captain, a beefy, red-faced man. "Nathan, this is Captain Mahoney."

They shook hands and Mahoney said, "Nice send-off for poor Jimmie. You're a credit as a friend."

"Thank you," said Nathan. "Did you know him well?"

Mahoney snorted, "Yeah, I knew him well. Came over illegal-like… IRA and all…so me and the boys, mostly the Irish, turned our eyes a little. I started out as a beat cop, chasing him and his friends." He looked around. "A good many here tonight. They were always stealing off the back of trucks. Jimmie was a rogue of the first order, always in the middle of some caper. A rogue, but a likable rogue was our Jimmie."

Nathan said, "Funny, I always heard he was honest."

Mahoney said, "Don't get me wrong, he was honest. You catch him and he wouldn't lie about it. Wouldn't snitch any of his fellow rogues out either. He was a man of principle." He lifted his wrist, moved his cuff and showed Nathan a gold Rolex. "He'd share when you caught him. Jimmie wasn't cheap."

Nathan was pulled away by Ray, who asked, "Can you call that liquor store around the corner you're such a good customer of? Tell them don't close, we'll be there in a minute. Need more kegs."

Nathan looked at him incredulously. "For what? I bought four."

Ray said, "Been gone. So's your bar."

"My bar!" His pride and joy, a very well-stocked bar, was gone. "The whole thing?"

Ray said, "Almost. Just a little green stuff left. Some kind of minty stuff. Think it's a liqueur."

Nathan asked, "Need money?"

Ray laughed. "Nah! We took up a collection, me, Avi and Dave. Be right back."

His first Irish wake was obviously a success. Jeez, these guys can drink, he thought.

Later, much, much later, and after another beer run, he went towards the kitchen to get himself a beer. He heard a loud slap and turned toward the noise.

There sat Lou, a red mark on his face and a young lady walking quickly away from him. He saw Nathan and waved him over. "Young Nate," he said, "great wake."

Nathan sat beside him and said, "Yeah, it is that."

Lou said, "Enjoying your first wake?"

Nathan thought a moment and said, "Yeah. Yeah, I am. Different than I thought it'd be. Everybody's partying, having a good time. Thought it'd be more somber. You know, everybody crying over Jimmie."

Lou said, "Not the way he would've wanted it at all. He enjoyed life. Should've known him when he was younger. Full of the devil." Lou burped and grinned.

Nathan said, "What I've been hearing. Everything from a saint to a common hood to an IRA terrorist."

Lou said, "Some of what you heard was true. He was a fair man. Give you the shirt off his back if he liked you. Common hood? No way was Jimmie common. He did stuff, sure, but he never cheated on his taxes or ran around on his wife. Never held a gun to anybody's head that I know of. He may have shared in somebody else's haul. To my knowledge he never stole anything. Well, maybe when he was young, but hunger will make you do things."

Nathan clinked glasses with him and said, "Must have been something, IRA and all?"

Lou looked at Nathan dead serious and said, "I wouldn't know and neither would Jimmie. Fact is, I came over on an educational visa and never left. Got caught smuggling Cuban cigars across from Canada.

"Jimmie's brothers were in the IRA, Jimmie wasn't. His brothers were caught, a couple hanged and one shot to death. Jimmie was young at the time. Mother and the local priest sent him to Canada and he snuck across the border into America." He laughed and said, "Nathan, if Jimmie was anything, he was a real man and don't you forget it."

The wake was starting to clear early in the morning. Terri and Nathan were cleaning up, although he felt like hell. As he was loading up a trash bag from the front room, a voice from behind said, "Nice place, Nathan." He turned and it was Sal the bookie from the bar. Sal was dressed in a suit. It was unusual for Sal. He normally wore slacks, a pullover shirt and carpet slippers. At least he did when he came to the bar to collect or pay those few winners from his book.

"Thanks Sal, glad you could come. I know you and Jimmie were close."

"That we were," Sal mumbled in a hoarse voice. "Want you to meet my nephew. He helps me with the book sometimes. Paulie, this is Nathan, he's at Jimmie's a lot and bets occasionally."

Nathan nodded to a very thin young man with crossed eyes. He was the exact opposite of Sal. "How ya' doin', Nathan?"

Nathan said, "Good, Paulie. Nice meetin' ya'." Somebody yelled for Sal and he left them. "Jimmie always spoke well of your uncle," Nathan lied.

Paulie said, "Unk liked doin' bidness wid' Jimmie. Very profitable. 'Specially for him and Greer."

Nathan let his comment pass, but thought it odd. Jimmie wasn't a gambler. He went back to cleaning while Paulie followed Sal.

CHAPTER THIRTY

Nathan had a strange call on his answer machine a few months later. The call was from the home where Jimmie's wife and daughter were. Terri had dealt with the lady from the home about the funeral arrangements, so he couldn't imagine why they were calling him. The person from the home asked him to return her call and left no further message. He decided to do it the next day. Surely, she wasn't there on Sunday afternoon anyway.

Busy the next day, he forgot all about returning the call to the home. He had auditors in. Actually, he had the auditors' exit interview and had been arguing with them over accounting classification issues. Just trying to polish the apple a little. The site was the darling of Wall Street, having posted their seventh straight quarterly profit, but every operating statement could use as much polish as possible.

Later in the day, he was tired of the auditors and decided to leave work. He called Terri. "Want to get together tonight?"

"Yeah. Be late though. I'll be here till eight."

"How about I meet you at the bar? Dealing with the auditors is causing a major thirst."

Terri said, "You got it, big fellow."

***

He knocked off early after losing the argument with the auditors and went to Jimmie's and shot the bull with Lou. The bar was surprisingly busy for five o'clock. Lou could still spend time with him, though. The new management believed nobody should ever wait for a drink and always had a full complement of bartenders.

Lou was working with two other people behind the bar. One of his fellow bartenders was a good-looking redhead named Sally, mid-thirties with a winning chest and personality.

Nathan had checked her out in the odd moment. "Lou, how's Sally working out?" he asked, motioning toward her. She was stretching to reach a bottle on the top bar shelf. She was drawing the attention of every male, and some females, in the general vicinity.

"Nate my boy, what you're really asking is, have I nailed her yet?" He grinned, "The answer is I won't tell. If you're asking about her abilities as a bartender, and I've read you wrong and indeed slighted you, the answer is good. And I apologize."

Nathan said, "So you haven't nailed her yet?" They both started laughing.

Lou said, "Glad to see you haven't changed. Are you sure you're not Irish? Maybe the name got fucked coming through Ellis? A lot of names did, you know."

"That's probably it. Meldonegal or some such shit," he said. "What do you think?"

Lou didn't answer initially, as both watched Sally climb down the short push ladder the staff used to get to the top bar rack. "Must be it. Is that just a perfectly lovely ass or not?"

"Does this remind me of things?" said Terri, coming up behind Nathan. She gave him a kiss and tousled his rapidly thinning hair.

"Yeah, what?" He pulled up a stool closer to him for her to sit. "Thought you had to work late."

She stuck her tongue out at him. "The secrets told in here never stay secret. I remember how mad you used to get. Now what were you boys whispering about?"

"What's the old saying?" said Lou. "If more than one person knows it, it ain't a secret."

Unfortunately Sally chose that moment to get back on the ladder. Terri, seeing her, said, "Oh," and hit Nathan in the ribs.

"Another old saying. No matter what happens, someone will take it too seriously," said Lou.

"I love old sayings," said Nathan. "How about never lick a steak knife?"

"Never heard that one," said Terri. "How about gossip is the most powerful force in the universe?"

Lou asked, "How about never ask a woman if she's pregnant unless you see a baby coming out?"

Nathan said, "Or a reason why we have daylight savings time?"

"Doesn't make any sense, Nathan," said Terri.

Nathan, feigning a hurt expression asked, "Like a fuckin' stitch in time saves nine makes sense?"

"Actually, it does make sense," said Lou, watching Sally climb the ladder again. "Reminds me. You guys missed somethin' funny as hell last night. This beautiful, smartly dressed woman was sittin' at the bar. A redhead she was. Been beltin' 'em back all afternoon. Guy sittin' next to her for about an hour finally says to her, 'Hello there, gorgeous. How are you?'

"She turned around, faced him, looked him straight in the eye and said, 'Listen! I'll screw anybody, anytime, anywhere, your place, my place, front door, back door. It doesn't matter. I've been doing it since I got out of college. I just flat-ass love it.'

"I'm as close as we are now serving the guy a beer. Eyes wide with interest, he says to her, 'No kidding? I'm a lawyer too! What firm are you with?' Thought I was gonna' die laughing."

***

It was Tuesday morning by the time Nathan saw the note he'd made to call Ms. Lewis. "Shit. Forgot all about it." It'd be nice to know how Betty and Dotty were doing, he thought, and called the home. "Ms. Lewis, this is Nathan Melton. I apologize for being so late returning your call. Been on the road. How is Mrs. Collins?"

"She's fine. It's her bill I'm concerned with, Mr. Melton."

Nathan said, "I thought that was all covered."

She said, "So did I. It hasn't been paid. Not for the last two months. I assume there is some kind of mix-up. I was given your number in New York to call if there was a problem."

Nathan said, "I'm sure there's some kind of mix-up, but I didn't have anything to do with setting it up."

"Mr. Melton, unfortunately you're the only person connected with Mr. Collins I can get in contact with. The address where we've been sending the bills is now sending our correspondence back, unopened. When I called the attorney handling the account, I was told nobody had ever heard of him."

Nathan said, "Ms. Lewis, let me call the person who set this up and I'll get right back to you."

"Please do."

He excitedly called Terri. "The guy handling Betty and Dotty is screwin' up at the home. They tried to call this guy and nothin'. People where he works say they never heard of him. Would you straighten him out?"

Terri asked, "What are you talkin' about?"

Nathan said, "Mrs. Collins and Jimmie's daughter. Nobody is payin' their bills."

Terri said, "What does that have to do with me?"

Nathan said, "Nothing really. Other than you know who to call."

There was a moment's silence, and then she said, "I thought you knew. Jimmie never met with my guy. He said you were handling it."

Nathan said, "Jimmie told me he was using your guy. Said it was all set up."

"Let me get back to you. The last time I talked to Jack Williams, my guy, he told me he never heard from Jimmie."

Terri called Nathan back an hour later. "Sorry it took me so long. Not my guy. He said Jimmie broke three appointments. The last time he talked to him, Jimmie told him he had someone else."

"Shit! That's bad. Jimmie told me Fat Sal was lookin' for a guy. Then he said your guy was handlin' it. We need to find out who's supposed to be doin' it and find out why they aren't."

Terri asked, "You going to talk to Sal? Cause my guy knows nothin'."

"If I can find out how to get hold of him. God only knows," he said. "I'll call the home and get 'em current. I'll call Lou and find out how to get hold of Sal."

Calling the home, Nathan said, "Ms. Lewis, sorry to be so much trouble. I'm still trying to find out who is supposed to be doing it. The guy I thought was doing it, isn't. Until then, what would it take to bring the account current?"

"Right now, Mr. Melton, they are $6,746.89 behind. On an ongoing basis, rent is $3,000, food another $300, medication $430 and nursing care $800 a month roughly. That number depends on the amount of home care required each month."

"I'll send you a check to cover what's owed and one for the next month. Say, $10,000? Please get back to me if you receive anything from the person who's supposed to be paying. Do you need me to FedEx the check or is regular mail okay?"

"Please FedEx it." It seemed Jimmie had a poor track record with the home already.

"Ms. Lewis, would you please give me the name you have for the person handling the account?" She gave it and he wrote it down. Don Greer.

He called and asked Terri. "Don Greer mean anything to you?"

"Never heard of the name. Give me the info and I'll check it out."

Nathan gave it to her and then called Lou to see if he could help locate Fat Sal. "Sure, Nathan," said Lou over the phone, "he's right here. Hang on."

Sal said, "Hello Nathan, what can I do for you? Looking for some action?"

"No, Sal. Got a call from the nursing home in Florida. The guy you set Jimmie up with hasn't paid the bills for the past two months."

Sal hesitated, "What are you talkin' about, Nathan? I didn't set Jimmie up with anybody," said Sal. "He told me you were takin' care of it. The fuck you tryin' to pull?"

Nathan said, "I got a call from the home. Must be some kind a' confusion. Sorry for the call."

"Should be," said Sal. "Say, you ain't tryin' to hustle Jimmie's money are ya'?"

"Go fuck yourself, Sal."

He called Terri. "I don't know what's going on, but Sal says he had nothing to do with it. He all but accused me of stealin' Jimmie's money."

"That's absurd," said Terri.

Nathan said, "Came out awfully fast too. I remember his nephew said somethin' weird at the wake."

"Weird how?"

"Somethin' like Sal was still makin' money off of Jimmie. As a matter of fact, his nephew mentioned the attorney by name. Greer."

"His nephew? That skinny, cross-eyed kid?"

"Yeah. You don't think they're playin' games with Jimmie's money do you?"

Terri said, "Duh! A dishonest bookie? Never happen. Let's get the rest of the group together and see if anybody knows anything."

"Yeah," Nathan said. "Set it up."

***

Terri called and got them all together at the bar that night. At the meeting, Terri said, "The people at the home said this guy never worked at the law firm he gave. I called. It's a firm in Miami. Told me they never heard of him. Also, there wasn't a trust document filed, at least not one that I can find. Should've been over three and a half million with the bar, his savings and apartment in that account. Plus whatever else Jimmie had. I checked the American Bar Association and the Florida Professional Licensing Association. No listing. All I can think to do is ask around."

"The bad thing is, if somebody is rippin' Jimmie off, they're not gonna' say so." Ray said.

"Thought of that," said Nathan. "I don't know any other way to do it. Costin' me over three grand a month. I can't see a huge investigation or anything. It has to be Fat Sal."

"Who?" Marie asked.

"He's the fat bookie always wears house slippers, honey," said Dave. "Nathan, you shouldn't have to pay the whole thing. We can all pitch in on that. The thing is, either this Sal, or someone else, is ripping Jimmie off. In my book, it's a low person who would take advantage of a dying man."

"Got that right," said Avi. "I'd like a piece of him."

"Rip the motherfucker's heart out," said Ray.

Marie asked, "Maybe I'm missing something, but how do you know it's Sal, Nathan?"

"At the funeral Sal's nephew made a comment about his uncle and Don Greer makin' money off of Jimmie."

Marie said, "He actually said that? Maybe Jimmie was betting. Greer is a fairly common name."

"Too weird, Marie," said Nathan. "Jimmie told me Sal was lookin' for a guy."

"Jimmie had us all looking," said Marie.

Nathan said, "What he said when I asked him was he thought I was handling it. Then he accused me of stealin' Jimmie's money."

Ray said, "Gotta' be Sal."

"I agree. Can't really go to the cops," said Julie.

Avi added, "Present company excepted," he nodded to Stuart and Ken. "We may have to take matters into our own hands." That quieted everyone as they all thought about what they'd do to Sal.

At this point, Nathan was thinking along the lines of putting his foot up the person's ass and wondered would the guy call a proctologist or a podiatrist?

"It's true, going to the police would be no good," said Ken. "The money overseas is a problem."

Nathan said, "Got a funny feeling about Sal. He was really quick to say no," said Nathan. "Compared with what his nephew said."

"Just playing devil's advocate," said Marie.

Avi said, "What about no record of Greer as an attorney?"

Marie answered, "Just in Florida. Need to do a bigger search."

Julie said, "But the guy supposedly worked for a firm in Florida."

Avi said, "Figure Greer is an alias. Can you guys check him out? Maybe do something with his credit, Marie? And you Ray, ask some of your connections." Both nodded.

"Hell, we know it's him," said Ray.

"We find something we can hit him with. Proof. Maybe he'll change his tune," Nathan said.

"The guy's a fucking bookie, Nathan. He's going to lie no matter what kind of proof you got," said Ken.

"Not him. Greer. Find him and confront him," said Nathan.

"Maybe, but before we do anything I want to be positive it's not just a screw-up," said Marie. "Dig further into this Greer guy and see what my people find. They're trained for this."

"You guys do that and I'll go to Florida and talk to the people at the home," said Nathan. "The key is getting the money back for Betty and Dottie. If it is Sal, we have to come up with a way to get him to give it back."

CHAPTER THIRTY-ONE

Nathan was heading to Florida, not really knowing what the hell he was doing, but he was going to solve this little mystery. As a connoisseur of English murder mysteries, he felt more than adequately equipped.

He'd called the night before and Susan Lewis, the home director, promised him the opportunity of speaking with any of the staff he wanted. She doubted the family would be much help, but spoke to the doctor and got clearance for him to question them.

He found the center with no trouble. He entered the activities center and asked directions at a large reception area. The receptionist was kind enough to escort him to the administrative offices. He was met by Susan Lewis in the office foyer.

Susan was attractive, mid-to-late thirties, average height with beautiful, long red hair. His first thoughts were, with all the amenities and Susan thrown in, he might move here himself.

"Thank you for helping us out in this situation, Mr. Melton." She motioned him toward a loveseat in the foyer.

"Quite welcome. I'd do anything for my friend Jimmie. He was a good friend," said Nathan.

"I've racked my brain and can come up with nothing. Of course, he worked more closely with Shirley Abbot, our Fiscal Officer. We've talked and we're both stymied. Would you like for me to call her down?"

"Please. That would be very kind of you." Master Stroke. Nathan, the super detective on the case, thank you.

She called and spent a short time on the phone. Whoever she was talking to must've been waiting for her call, as it seemed to be picked up quickly. She told him a little more about the facility while they waited for Shirley Abbot.

Within minutes, a large, well-dressed black woman joined them. "Let me introduce Shirley." Shirley and Nathan shook hands.

Shirley sat next to him and said, "Susan and I compared notes and could come up with nothing yesterday. Overnight, I remembered Mr. Collins saying his representative was down here. I took that to mean Florida and in the vicinity of Crestview. I hope that helps? Of course, the address we had was a Miami firm. I never met this Mr. Greer," she paused and consulted her notes, "but the people at the firm say he never worked there. They never heard of him." She laid her notes on her ample lap and said, "The account was set up for monthly billing. After receiving nothing from Mr. Greer, I called. This is normal for new accounts. We like to make sure everything is running smoothly. That's when I was told there was no such person at the firm. This was shortly after the second billing had gone out. I alerted Susan that there might be a problem."

"Everything helps. Thank you. The one thing we, his friends, are worried about is fraud," Nathan said.

"We discussed the same thing," said Susan, looking at Shirley. "I called most of the law firms in the area. I was hoping a mistake had been made. Then I called the Florida Board and they had no record of Greer being currently licensed. They even checked for similarities in the name and came up with nothing. They also went through back records, but found nothing at all for that name. As a favor, they checked nationally and no one is currently licensed under the name."

"Wow, figure the name isn't that irregular."

"We thought the same, Mr. Melton," said Shirley. "There were similarities, but no match. Not in the surrounding areas or even the Southeast."

"The trust is sizable. More than adequate to care for Betty and Dotty," Nathan said.

They talked for another fifteen minutes or so, but nothing really productive came out of it. Then he told them that he vaguely remembered Jimmie saying something about meeting with the attorney down here on his last trip.

This sparked something with Susan, who asked Shirley to get the visitor's log. She explained to Nathan that the center was required to maintain a log of all patient visitors.

Shirley returned shortly with the logs for Jimmie's last visit. The listing showed Jimmie and two unnamed guests. Susan said, "My apologies, Mr. Melton. Our policy is that the principal guest signs for the visiting party. We'll change the policy immediately to insist all guests sign in."

"Maybe it's time I spoke with Mrs. Collins," said Nathan.

***

Susan led him up to the Collins' apartment and gave him a brief tour of the facility on the way. They seemed to go out of their way to keep the residents busy.

Nathan asked, "Is this natural, Susan? To keep the residents so entertained?"

"Yes. We don't want them hiding out in their rooms. We'd rather they be active. Actually helps us keep track of them."

Susan let them into the apartment and Betty Collins greeted them. It was spacious and well furnished with a beautiful view of the golf course. He'd never met Mrs. Collins before.

Nathan said, "How are you, Mrs. Collins? I was a friend of Jimmie's."

"Jimmie talked about you a lot. He liked you. And it's Betty. Not Mrs. Collins."

"It's nice finally meeting you. Jimmie talked about you constantly."

"Jimmie had a scrapbook of some of your adventures on Wall Street. Come in."

Susan, sitting in on the interview as policy, sat with Nathan on a brightly colored yellow sofa. They chit chatted a moment and then Nathan, using a cover story, explained why he was there and what he wanted. Betty was hard pressed to remember names. No way could she remember conversations with her late husband from a couple of months ago. "Jimmie had so many friends it was hard to keep track. Maybe Sal Russo would know."

Nathan said, "Sal's in prison now, Betty. I'd have to contact him by mail or through his attorney."

She sobbed and said, "Poor Sal. I know he'd help. Why do you need to contact anyone? Dotty and I are fine."

Nathan started to speak and Susan shook her head. He then said, to not worry her, "Just a minor business matter pertaining to the bar. Some kind of insurance thing. Nothing really to concern yourself about. We jus' want to find out who Jimmie's lawyer is so he can straighten out the matter for the new owners."

He was ready to give up, having exhausted all conversation, when Dotty came into the room. She'd just awakened and was rubbing her eyes. Dotty was fully grown. About medium height, she had to weigh well over two hundred pounds. Although Nathan knew she was severely retarded, she didn't actually look it.

Nathan was introduced to Dotty, who was in a shy mood. She turned her head and wouldn't speak, sitting on the arm of her mom's chair.

Nathan motioned to Susan that they should leave, and as they were saying their goodbyes, Dotty spoke. "I heard you from bed. It was Uncle Sally. He came over with Dad and another man. The other man takes care of us. Daddy said so."

Nathan looked at her, amazed she'd talked. "Thank you, Dotty. Was it thin Uncle Sal or fat Uncle Sal?"

"Momma says you should never call people fat. It makes them cry." Dotty turned her head back toward her mother for verification. Betty nodded.

"You're right, Dotty," said Nathan. "I'm sorry. Your mom's right. How about short Uncle Sal or tall Uncle Sal?"

She giggled, "It was short Uncle Sal, silly. Tall Uncle Sally is in jail."

"Thank you, Dotty. You're a very smart little girl," Nathan said and she beamed.

"You're welcome, Mister. I can't talk to you because you are a stranger and want to get in my pants. Why, Mister? Why do you want to get in my pants? You got your own."

Nathan smiled. "I'm a friend of your daddy. I'm not a stranger."

"My daddy is dead."

Nathan asked, "Dotty, do you remember what the other man looked like? The man your dad said was to take care of you?"

"He was just a man. Maybe he was tall. Not as tall as you or my Dad. He didn't talk." Dotty was tired of the conversation and asked her mom for a cookie.

Betty said, "You know, come to think of it, I remember the man vaguely. Don't think it was one of my better days when they came down. I remember he had this odd colored black hair. Odd because it was too black. And his name may have been Gray, or Green or something beginning with a G."

"Greer, Momma," said Dotty.

Nathan said, "You've both been very helpful. Thank you." Dotty beamed.

When Nathan left he was really down. Susan noticed it and said, "It's sad, isn't it?"

***

Nathan managed to get in the car before he started crying. He hurried to the airport hoping to make the late flight. He was cutting it close. He turned in the rental car and ended up chugging to the gate. He called Terri on his cell as soon as the pilot made the announcement. "Productive trip. You guys get anything on Sal? 'Cause he's right in the middle of it."

"Marie got a look at his bank statement. In his line of work there are always large deposits going back and forth. Nothing really outstanding."

He told Terri what he'd found out. "Son-of-a-bitch. We just make him talk and find out who the guy is in Florida. Get back the money," she said.

"Sounds pretty easy," he said. "And if Sal tells us to go fuck ourselves? What do we do then?"

Terri said, "You beat him up."

"It's nice to see you've put a lot of thought into this. You remember Sal is with the Gambrellis? You don't just beat up one of those guys. Not often."

"Once they find out what he did, they won't care. Most of those guys liked Jimmie."

"Terri, they probably got a piece of it."

Terri thought and said, "Naw. A lot of them came to the service. They liked Jimmie. Sal Russo was his best friend. What about Petey? You think he'd be part of somebody robbing Jimmie?" Terri wasn't giving up. "Nathan, they wouldn't let anybody else do it."

Nathan answered, "No. But Sal and Petey are in prison, remember? Maybe it was set up after they went in. Reminds me, can you contact their attorney? Maybe they know somethin'."

"Yeah," she said. "I'll call Sal's wife and find out who it is."

"Get everybody together. We'll attack this as a group. I'm getting in late, but we'll meet with them tomorrow at the bar at, say seven? And don't say anything to Sal the Bookie."

CHAPTER THIRTY-TWO

Still a little tired from the trip, he left the office early the next day for the seven o'clock meeting. Nathan was convinced that Sal the Bookie either was a major part of it, or at the very least had something to do with it. He couldn't see him as the mastermind, but maybe he was selling old Sal short.

He took it easy on beer while waiting for the other members, who arrived in two beer's time. They moved to a couple of tables in the back for privacy. Everyone was anxious to know what he'd found. Terri hadn't let the cat out of the bag.

Nathan quickly went over what he had. He told them about his conversation with Jimmie, where he mentioned Sal Ricco, the Bookie. Jimmie had told him Sal knew a guy down there that he was going to meet. When Jimmie returned from Florida, he told Nathan it was taken care of. Nathan asked if it was Terri's guy. Jimmie obviously misunderstood him, Nathan thought, and said yes.

Then he hit them with the biggie, Dotty Collins. How she'd told him Uncle Sal, short Uncle Sal, not tall Uncle Sal, her Father and another man came one weekend. Her Father told her Uncle Sal and the other man would take care of them. Then the clincher for him. They both remembered the name Greer. He finished up with how Sal the Bookie acted when he talked to him on the phone. He looked around the tables for reactions, finishing with what Sal's nephew had said at the wake.

"We also checked the visitor logs. Unfortunately, they don't keep specific logs. During the period in question, it showed Jimmie with two visitors. Their names weren't listed, just other visitors. Plus, this ties in with what Paulie said at the wake, how his uncle was going to 'earn' off of it."

Marie added, "My people checked on bar admissions and came up with the same thing as the home in Florida did. The New York Bar shows a couple of Greers and we're checking them now. If it's an alias, we aren't going to have much luck."

Nathan said, "Ray, any idea on how we approach Fat Sal?"

"Two ways. You get a made member to approach his boss and ask for a sit-down. You have to convince his boss a wrong has been done. By a wrong, I don't mean in the normal sense, like a crime. I mean something has been done to a made member. Jimmie wasn't made, but he was an associate. That counts. Sal is also an associate. He ain't made, but he's an earner for one of the Capos. Guy named Dom I happen to know, not well, but on nodding terms. Dom's all right, but he ain't gonna' be happy losing an earner like Sal. Dom's got half a million on the street with Sal at three points.

Sal Russo could've done it, straightened it out, but he's in prison now, along with Petey and most of that crew. We can try, but I don't know how much influence Russo carries from the can."

Terri said, "Maybe here it would be good if Stuart and Ken left."

"No way," said Stuart, sitting beside Gail. "Maybe we can't do anything direct, but Jimmie was our friend too."

Ken nodded and said, "What's the second way, Ray? Number one seems out of the question."

"The second way is you get him by himself and beat the shit out of him till he talks. That's the best way. Of course, he has to disappear afterwards. Innocent or guilty, either way he has to go. You sure as shit don't want anyone to know you did it. Dom will be on you quick, losing an earner like Sal."

Marie said, "There has to be another way."

"None that I know," said Ray. "Gonna' have to force him to give the money back. He ain't gonna' volunteer it, that's for sure. Once you force him, you're gonna' haf' ta' deal with Dom. Believe me, he ain't gonna' be happy."

That brought a chill over the crowd. Terri brought them back. "Well, the way I see it, it's up to us to get Jimmie's money back. For the protection of everyone here, if you aren't willing to break some laws to avenge Jimmie, you need to leave." Nobody moved. "I'm serious. If you're the least bit squeamish you need to back away."

Dave asked, "Are you saying murder, Terri?"

"Not if we can help it. We're talking serious here. You heard Ray. If you aren't willing to maybe break some laws, leave now." Again, nobody moved. "Okay. We'll take door number two, Monty." The crowd cracked up.

Dave brought them back to reality. "Everybody needs to really consider what we're doing. I mean, we are regular people. What do we know about this kind of thing?"

Nathan said, "That's the problem. We're regular people. Out of our element and these guys play for keeps."

Julie said, "We have to do something. Jimmie was our friend."

Ray said, "Need to kill the rat bastard."

Nathan said, "I'm not going to kill anybody. Neither are you guys. Think about it. Which one of you could actually pull a trigger? Kill this fat bastard for taking Jimmie's money?"

Dave said, "Nobody's talkin' about killin' anybody, Nathan."

"You didn't hear what Ray said?" He looked around and nobody said anything. Most were looking at the floor. "Ray, you sell cars. Gail, you're a model. Marie, you run a fucking collection agency for godsakes. Dave, please. I just can't see it. Terri, you're the nicest person anybody's ever met. You cry in movies. Julie, you won't watch the friggin' news because of the violence. And me, I got a three-legged dog that I paid over five grand to fix because I couldn't put him to sleep. And he wasn't even my dog."

"And he bites you regularly," said Lou.

Finally, Gail said, "I don't think I could. But we've got to do something."

Ray said, "That's true. We're all smart people. Certainly smarter than friggin' Sal the Bookie. Has to be another way."

Dave said, "I think Avi should be appointed our leader. I may be out of line," he looked at Avi who nodded, "Avi has done this sort of thing in the past. Israeli intelligence and all."

No one said anything and Avi took it as acceptance of him as the leader. Avi said, "First thing we need to do is find out all we can about Sal. Ray, I'm going to need your help here."

Ray said, "Easiest thing would be to use Gail or Julie or one of the girls to lure him."

"Hold on," said Avi. "Julie isn't getting involved in anything."

Julie said, angry, "You hold on, Avi. I'll take the same risks as everyone else." He started to speak and she continued. "The exact same." She was flexing newfound power since agreeing to see Avi again.

Ray said, "We use one of the girls to either dope his drink here and catch him coming out or have him come to her apartment." Ray continued, "one of the things is, you don't want to be seen much with him just before. But what are you going to do afterwards? If he don't disappear, then we do."

Everybody was thinking it, but Lou asked it. "What exactly are we going to do to Sal? Avi, you're the leader."

Avi was quiet and didn't answer at first, as if deep in thought. Everybody leaned forward for his answer. "Well, we are going to have to do something." Whoopee! They all knew that.

"Well, it can't be murder. I mean shit, guys, Ken and I are cops," pleaded Stuart. "Got to be another way. I don't know how Ken feels, but I'll go along up to a point. I don't mind bending a little, but I can't be a part of breaking the law. You guys can't either. You aren't the kind of people to do something like that. Besides, as a cop and your friend, I won't let you."

"S'pose we can do it in a way that he won't know it's us?" Nathan asked.

"How?" asked Ray. "What are you gonna' do, Nathan? Hypnotize him? You got a shiny watch?" Ray paused. "We got to do him to protect ourselves. We've already done one down in Costa Rica. I listened to all that stuff about justifiable and everything. I thought we were gonna' sing Kum-bi-ya. Who's gonna' do it?"

Terri said, "That lady in Costa Rica had a heart attack. We felt so bad we sent money to her family. Not the same, Ray."

Nathan asked, "Who wants to do it?" There was complete silence. "Didn't think so. Maybe we all need to think about that and discuss it tomorrow. We need to come up with an alternative." Stuart nodded.

"Agreed?" Avi asked the group. They all nodded affirmatively.

Gail had been sitting with her back to the wall, facing the open bar area. She suddenly got up and moved toward the door. They stared at her to see where she was going and saw the reason she'd rushed away. Sal had come in the door. Stuart got up to go after her, but Nathan pulled him back down.

They stared at Sal in his splendor. At least he was wearing shoes tonight and not bedroom slippers. Sort of shoes; they were Hush Puppies. No socks. Nicely cut slacks and an Italian knit shirt hanging over the pants. It must be a big night for Sal. He had on his wig. Partially straight. Jet black. A color black that doesn't grow on humans. And Gail was talking to him. They were laughing. Then they sat at the bar together. Still laughing, it appeared that Sal was buying Gail a drink.

"She's going to blow the whole thing," said Stuart.

Ray said, "Looks like she's going to blow Sal."

Avi said to all of them in disgust, "Just the kind of crap you get letting amateurs play spy."

"Hold on, Avi," said Dave. "She may get something valuable. You can't condemn her yet. Not till we hear what's going on."

"Yeah, but she's being seen with him," said Avi.

"So is everybody in the bar," said Julie.

***

They sat sneaking glances over in the direction of Gail and Sal. After thirty minutes, Sal left and Gail remained sitting at the bar.

"Now what's she doing?" Avi was pissed.

Terri said, "Making it look good. A real amateur would've rushed over and told us what happened."

Gail had another drink at the bar and then got up and followed Marie, who'd gone to the bathroom. Gail came out first and left the bar. Stuart trailed behind her.

Marie came out and walked over to them. "She got all kinds of information from him. She's going to have dinner with him tomorrow. She wants to talk to him. Gail wants to make sure he did it. She'll meet us here after dinner, about eleven."

***

They filed out of the bar. Avi and Julie were getting a taxi. Ray, Dave, Ken and Lou and Marie crossed the street to take the subway. Terri and Nathan started their walk. They were both quiet. He said, "That Gail is somethin', huh?"

"Yeah. She's never been a big talker. Always been more of a doer. We talked about it earlier," said Terri. "She was afraid unless somebody pushed, we'd all end up not doing anything for Jimmie. Form committees and stuff. Just talk."

Nathan said, "Definitely reminded me of that Monty Python movie 'Life of Brian.' Remember? The Jews had all those committees battlin' each other." He laughed, "We probably needed a push. Frankly, I don't have a warm and cozy feeling about our 'fearless leader' Avi."

"He's some kind of spy or somethin'. At least that's what he told Dave."

Nathan said, "I thought if you were a spy you weren't supposed to tell anybody."

"What, that's like some kind of procedure?" He grinned and she said, "Screw it. Somebody has to lead. We follow if we want to." He didn't say anything so she added, "leave it alone, Nathan." He started to speak and she added, "Leave it alone. I know you, Nathan. Just leave it alone."

Nathan said, "I was thinking about what Ray said. I admit, I hadn't really thought about how. Had you?"

Terri said, "Not really. I just never thought that far ahead. Could you do it?"

"Maybe. I don't know. I think I could if it were him or me. I just have to picture Betty and Dotty."

They walked a bit and Terri said, "I guess I could too. Maybe. If we can't come up with something, some trick, and you have to do it, I'd have to help you and I'm not sure I could."

"Thanks. You don't have to help. I'd like to kind of keep you out of it. As much as possible, anyway."

She looked at him and smiled. "Thank you for the sentiment, but you know how clumsy you are. If I don't help you or take part, I'll end up all night at the emergency room waiting for them to take a bullet out of your foot." It was funny, but he didn't laugh. She was telling him she loved him. Or she was telling him he was one clumsy fucker, one or the other.

CHAPTER THIRTY-THREE

The next morning Nathan called his brother. After a couple of minutes of "how's the golf game, getting any, where you going on vacation," and other idle chitchat, Nathan asked him to get him a clean gun.

"A what?"

"Something small and throwaway. Lynn, send it express," said Nathan.

Lynn started laughing and said, "What the hell you need it for?"

"Protection."

Lynn asked, "You think you're going to get robbed in the next two days? Send it express?"

Nathan said, "Just send it to me, Lynn."

"Okay, okay. Calm down. I'll send it. Something with stopping power, like a Glock or somethin'?"

"No. Make it a .22 caliber. With a silencer, if possible." Nathan was reading a Tom Clancy novel. "Make it a revolver."

"Sounds like a professional hit. If it were anybody else, I'd swear that's what it was. Are you sure? Never mind. You'll have it tomorrow. A silencer, subsonic cartridges, the works. Have to be an automatic, can't silence a pistol. Remember, for your own protection, to pick up the casings after you're done. Automatic spits 'em out. Your office?"

"Subsonic cartridges?" said Nathan. "What the hell is that?"

Lynn said, "You said you wanted a silencer right? Not worth a shit with regular cartridges. Won't work."

"Yeah. Please. And Lynn, thanks." Let it suffice to say that software is a tough business.

Lynn said, "Nathan, be careful, okay? You sure you don't want something larger? You got to be in a fucker's ear to do anything with a .22. Liable to get hit with a ricochet off the skull as anything."

"The .22 is good. I'm always careful. You know that."

Lynn said, "Right," laughing.

***

Jimmie's friends met that night in the bar. Terri and Nathan got there after seven and almost everyone was there. Ken and Stuart called Lou earlier in the day and said they'd go along with anything but the big "M."

It felt odd in the bar that night, almost eerie. It was almost like no one wanted to talk about it so they kept their distance. They all had their own little corners of the bar. Ray playing darts with a group of people no one knew. Dave and Marie sitting in the back talking to another couple. Julie and Avi in deep conversation on the other side of the bar. None of the principals wanted to be in a position to talk.

About ten-thirty Gail came in and walked straight to the back of the bar, motioning for them to follow. They pulled out chairs and Gail had the floor.

"You won't believe this son-of-a-bitch. Bragged about it. Told me how stupid Jimmie was putting all that money in a friend's hands. He didn't go into specifics, but he's involved. Didn't give me any names. He did it, though. He had a helper, but he did it. Told me so. Fucker bragged about it."

"He actually said he did it?" asked Julie.

Gail said, "Not in so many words, but he did it all right. He did everything but say he did it."

Everybody was mad and trying to talk at once. The table was buzzing.

Ray said, talking over everyone else, "Okay, we know what we got to do. We make him tell. Back to my question from the other night. Who and how?"

Gail said, "He's meeting me at my apartment tomorrow night. I told him we had to be very discreet. Mitch can't find out." Mitch was supposedly the guy who had paid for the apartment, Gail's ruse for so many years.

Terri asked, "Is Stuart comfortable with that?"

Gail said, "He doesn't know." Looking at the expectant faces gathered around her, she added, "And he won't be told." No one commented. "Sal will be there around nine for dinner."

"Okay," said Ray. "That's when. Now who and how?"

Avi asked, "Anybody?" Everyone looked away.

"I can't believe you bunch of chicken shits," said Gail.

It was silent for a full minute. As Nathan suspected, his friends weren't capable of murder. After asking his brother to send the gun, he'd come to the realization that he wasn't either.

Nathan said, "S'pose we dress up so he can't recognize us? Tell him we've been following him and know he has Jimmie's money. Just like it's a robbery. We pretend to rough Gail up so he doesn't suspect her."

"Never work," said Dave.

Nathan said, "You got anything better, Dave?"

Dave said, "Suppose he recognizes someone?"

"We just won't screw it up," said Nathan.

"Nathan, if we do, then Dom is after us. Too risky. Has to be a better plan."

Nathan said, "Okay, I'm listening." It was completely quiet, then Nathan said, "If it doesn't work, then I'll do it."

Avi asked, "How?"

"Shoot him," Nathan said.

"You gotta' gun?" Terri asked, staring at him in shock. He didn't answer her.

"What about noise? Gun inside will be loud as hell," said Dave.

"Got a silencer." Everybody was looking at Nathan in a new light. Especially Terri. "Make it look like a professional hit. Little .22. All to the head."

"Doesn't matter," said Avi. "Maybe Nathan's plan will work. What about noise, Gail? Liable to get loud, us making him talk."

"My apartment is the only one on the floor. There is an attic between my floor and the floor beneath. Store a bunch of stuff in it. Well cluttered, well insulated," said Gail. "If it's noisy during the interrogation, shouldn't matter."

"Okay. After he tells us, we hold him until we get the money back. As soon as he walks in the door, we'll grab him from behind. Be wearing masks. Scare the shit out of him."

Avi said, "We'll have some kind of tarp down for the blood." Someone in the group gasped. "Just in case we have to smack him around some. Gail, does your building have a freight elevator?"

Gail said, "Yes. Nobody works the front from eleven to five the next morning. Everything is keyed. There is a camera on the door. Don't worry about it."

Avi said, "What do you mean don't worry about it? It'll have us coming in and leaving the building."

"No, it won't," said Gail. "I'll take care of it."

"I love you to death, Gail," Nathan said. "You are a very resourceful lady. If you say you're going to do something, you do it. Please don't take this wrong. How are you going to take care of it?"

"Turn it off. I own the building." Nathan wasn't the only one seen in a new light. "All that stuff is in my office up in the penthouse. I'll just turn it off. As a matter of fact, I'll turn it off early tomorrow evening. Then there will be no record of you guys coming in. Why don't you come in like workmen making a delivery? Later, with masks, he won't recognize you guys. I'll leave word with Ed the doorman that I'm expecting a shipment. Come just before seven. I'll come a little after and give Ed the night off. I do that a lot since I have all the equipment in my apartment. When there's no doorman on, tenants buzz people in who don't live there."

"Wow," said Ray. "This fuckin' Mitch bought you the whole building?" Ray gaped at Gail, who ignored him.

"Who's going to be with me?" Nathan said.

Ray volunteered and was shot down by Gail. "I don't care what kind of disguise you put on, he'll know who you are. You're closer to him than the rest of us."

"I'll go," said Avi and Lou in unison.

"Me too," said Terri and Julie in unison.

"We don't need any women," said Avi.

"Bullshit," said Gail. "I'm the star of the show and I say they go."

"Ray, you and Lou be the outside guys," said Avi.

"I want Lou inside," said Nathan.

"Can't. Sal will recognize his voice."

"No offense, Dave, Lou's done this type of thing before," said Nathan, nodding to Dave, who grinned. Truth be known, Dave didn't want any part of the inside.

Lou said, "Besides, we can do Irish accents like we're terrorists. We'll be the IRA. Story is we were planning on stealing Jimmie's money and he beat us to the punch. We know he has Jimmie's money."

"Fine," said Avi, miffed. "Dave and Ray outside."

***

The next morning Nathan's package arrived from his brother Lynn. Nice automatic with a screw-on silencer. Also, he'd sent a box of surgical gloves. Nathan smiled. His brother had always thought he was dumb as dirt and looked out for him. There was a little note enclosed telling him there was no such thing as a totally quiet silencer. He said it would make a noise like a skinny girl farting.

***

Nathan called Terri and they had lunch together at a little Italian restaurant on 53rd. Good place, good food, and an unpronounceable name.

"Nervous about tonight? I sure as hell am," he said.

"Yeah," she said. "I'm nervous. Did you ever just want to go away? Go to an island or something and just kind of hide? No worries, no problems."

Nathan said, "You mean on vacation? Or forever?"

"I don't know whether I could stand you forever. I'm sure I could stand you for a long time though. No worries. Just think about what you are going to do that day."

"Maybe after this is all over. Maybe because of all this, who knows? I wouldn't mind going to an island with you. Eating coconuts and stuff," said Nathan. "Or we could go instead of doing this?"

"We couldn't stand ourselves if we just walked away," Terri said.

"Shit! New Yorkers are famous for walking away. Turning a blind eye. Not getting involved," he said. "Not the ones I know. They don't turn away for shit."

She smiled. "You think you know New Yorkers, huh?"

"Damn straight. Nosiest bunch of people in the world. Butt into everything. Rude, don't get me started."

She was laughing hard. "Yeah. Can't line up either." He laughed and she continued, "You do know New Yorkers. You going to be okay?"

"Maybe," he said. "Don't know. Kind of new to me."

She said, "Want me to do it? I've thought about it and I think I can. I'll be there anyway."

"You'd never let me forget it." He laughed. "I'll be all right. Besides, the plan's gonna' work. I just said I'd do it to keep everything movin'."

Terri asked, "What about if it doesn't?"

"It's gonna' work." Looking around at the other diners staring, he said, "I'm sorry, Terri. Just nerves. Used to get this way before a football game. I'd pee fifty times in a two-hour stretch before a game started."

Terri said, "I always wondered about that. What do players do during a game? If they are on the field?"

"You just pee."

She asked, "On the field? You can't pull it out. You're joking?"

"Pee where you're standing. Don't pull it out. Hands are so wrapped you'd hurt yourself trying to pull it out. If it's cold, it feels good. If it's hot, you catch a rash. Like a fat boy's rash."

She made a face and said, "What about the other?"

"Same."

"Wish I hadn't asked now. Glamorous football players," she laughed. "You guys must smell. I'll never be able to watch now without wondering who's peeing."

Walking back to the office after lunch, Nathan kissed Terri and said, "You know you don't have to be there tonight?"

"Still can't believe you volunteered," she said.

"They wouldn't have listened to me about trying to scare him. I'm going to do it and it'll work." He snorted. "Fuck, we're all regular people who met in a bar. We're not killers."

She smiled, "We owe a friend a great debt."

CHAPTER THIRTY-FOUR

That evening they met at the bar. Nathan had a dolly with some computer boxes he'd gotten from work for props. He, Lou and Avi had jeans and tan work shirts, going for the workmen look. Avi brought wool ski masks for later in dealing with Sal. He said psychologically the masks would put Sal at a disadvantage.

"Avi, you got to do something with the curls. Just doesn't look right," said Ray.

"Plenty of orthodox workmen," said Avi.

"Wear a cap," Lou said.

Marie, very nervous that Dave was involved, asked, "Can we have a prayer?"

"We're kind of in a hurry," Lou said. "How about after?"

"Defeats the purpose. It's nice afterwards, but you really should do it before something dangerous," said Marie.

Ray said, to hurry matters along, "Okay. Nathan, why don't you lead us."

Nathan said, "Huh?" Ray nodded toward Marie, who was tearing up. "Oh yeah." Falling back on his one and only prayer, Nathan began, "Now I lay me down to sleep…"

Julie laughed and Terri hit him in the ribs, saying, "Something a little more appropriate," as Lou snickered.

"Appropriate? Let's see," he said. "Bow your heads please." He looked around to make sure every head was down. With a smile on his face, he continued, "Uh, the man sayeth to me and I sayeth back to him and to the congregation. Woe is he who tries to score when the congregation sayeth 'push 'em back, push 'em back, way back.' Be true to your school.

Let your banner fly. For we rejoice when the righteous scores. Righteous
are we. And the scorer shall lie in splendor with a cheerleader in the
back of a station wagon. Amen."

Julie, Ray, Avi and Lou said in unison, "Amen."

Nathan received a massive pinch from Terri as Marie started crying
loudly and Lou said, "C'mon."

***

All nervous, they made the delivery just before seven. The plan
was that Lou would interrogate Sal. He was the best at sounding Irish
naturally. Julie and Terri would be there as gang members, filling in
where necessary. In the apartment, the plan was for Avi to hide inside
a coat closet and catch Sal from behind. Nathan would be just around
the corner and come at Sal from the front. Lou and Julie would follow
Sal and Gail inside the apartment from a hiding spot on the stairwell
landing. Lou had previously undone the bulb.

Gail would meet Sal outside the apartment "by chance." She would
act like she was coming into her building after running out to pick up
an ingredient for her cooking. Terri, with her mask on, would grab Gail
to help with the 'she wasn't in on it' appearance. Julie would be a last
resort back-up. She would be positioned at the front door to keep Sal
from leaving if he got away from the others. She would be armed with
a baseball bat.

They would let Sal see Gail being roughed up. That way Sal wouldn't
have an adrenaline rush from being duped by Gail and fight. They
wanted to give him one thing to worry about. Them. Not Gail.

Dave and Ray would watch from the outside to make sure Sal showed
up alone. Dave would call and let them know when Sal arrived. If he
wasn't alone, they'd clear out and wait for another time. Gail, whether
or not Sal was alone, had a previously prepared, partially cooked dinner
ready.

Then, hopefully, it would be a simple 'scare the shit out of Sal until
he told them the truth.'

***

Waiting for Sal to show up at nine took forever. From eight on they
watched the bank of cameras trained on the outside of the building. At
a half past, Gail went down to wait with Dave, and Lou and Julie went
to the stairwell.

As soon as Gail saw Sal arrive, she would go outside and do her
"store" acting bit, coming back in with him. That way the apartment
would be dark inside when they came in.

As the time came for everyone to take their place, nerves hit Nathan. "I hope the shit he's alone," Nathan said to Avi and Terri. "I don't think my nerves could take much more of this. Surely not another night."

Terri asked, jokingly, "You don't have to pee?"

"Yeah. Now I do. Thanks, Terri." All he needed was to think about it.

"You'll be all right, Nathan," said Avi.

Avi's cell rang and he answered. Nathan had gotten his wish. Avi repeated what Dave told him. "They're coming up and Sal is alone. Dave will wait a few minutes and come up. Ray will stay down there watching." Avi quickly opened the door and alerted Lou and Julie.

"Fuck!" They both looked at Nathan. "Gotta' pee."

Terri patted his arm and said, "Too late. Hold it. You aren't playing ball now and I hate the smell of urine. Be a big boy."

"We'll see who's a big boy the next time we have monkey sex," Nathan said.

Avi and Nathan put their masks on and Avi took his spot in the closet. There was a foyer leading from the front door to the formal living room. Nathan took his spot around the corner, Terri behind him.

The mask was hot, his adrenaline was up, or both. Nathan was sweating like a pig. Maybe Sal would think he was a robber with the flu or something.

They heard voices and then a key opening the door. Gail saying, "Come on in, honey. I'll get a light."

Gail and Sal moved down the dark foyer. Gail's hand came around the corner reaching for the light switch as Avi came out of the closet and Lou came through the door behind Sal.

Avi and Lou grabbed Sal from behind. Nathan rushed around the corner and collided with Gail, knocking her down. He then grabbed Sal in a reverse full nelson hold. He found out why nobody uses that move. Sal bit him and he head butted Sal. Sal was out cold.

Avi and Nathan held Sal up while Lou spread a tarp over the floor.

Julie asked, "Jeez, what stinks?"

"It's Sal. He shit his pants," said Lou.

They laid Sal on the tarp then dragged him into Gail's big walk-in closet. Lou and Avi stayed with him while Nathan looked for something to put on his cheek where Sal bit him. He saw Terri with an ice compress on Gail's forehead, bruised from him running over her. They both glared at him until they saw he was bleeding. Terri cleaned the wound while Nathan prayed Sal didn't have HIV.

Terri stopped his bleeding and Nathan went to check on Avi and Lou. Everything was cool. Sal was out cold. Julie was standing guard, bat in hand.

"Wake him," said Lou to Julie.

Julie disappeared in the foyer bathroom and came out with a wet cloth. She leaned over and started lightly tapping him to wake him. Nothing. She put the cloth on his forehead and squeezed it. Water ran over Sal's face, but he was still out. Nathan leaned over and tapped him a bit harder, still pissed about being bit. Nothing.

"Help me get his pants off and then hold ice right over his eyes," said Lou to Julie.

"Uh uh," she said. "He shit his pants. Sure you want to take them off?"

"Only way we're going to get rid of the smell," said Lou.

This wasn't in the script, but they all helped with Sal's pants and underwear, throwing them in the garbage.

"Still bad," Lou said.

Coming from the kitchen with ice, Terri held her nose. "Wash him," said Terri to Nathan.

"You wash him," Nathan said. "I'm not touching Mr. Shitty Pants."

"Fuck it, we'll just smell him then," said Lou. Lou had an old straight razor and started stropping it to sharpen it. Nathan looked at him and Lou said, "I'm supposed to scare him right?"

Terri straightened her mask and put the ice on Sal. Sal came to almost instantly. Lou let him take in the situation as he was awakening. Sal could see Gail tied up and gagged.

Lou then put the razor against Sal's penis. "Feel this, you miserable bastard?" Sal nodded. "You're going to tell us what you did with Collins' money." Sal grinned. "Did I say something funny?" Lou grabbed Gail by the hair and held the razor to her throat. "We were planning on stealing that idiot's money, but you beat us to it. You think this stupid bitch knows anything?" Lou asked, looking at Nathan.

"Must, she's with this bozo," Nathan answered, using his best Irish accent. It came out more Italian.

"Hold him, Charley," Lou said to Nathan. "I'm going to find out quick. You don't fuck with the IRA, boyo."

Nathan, figuring out he was Charley, held Sal down. Sal couldn't actually see Lou pretending to hit Gail. He was smacking a flour sack Terri had brought in earlier.

Sounded realistic to Sal, who said, "She ain't got nuttin' to do with it. Let her go." Nathan was proud of old Sal taking up for Gail. Then Sal shit again and Nathan lost his newfound respect.

Lou said, "Tell me, fat man, or we'll cut her throat." Sal said nothing. "Did I tell you this is the IRA you're fuckin' with, fats? Tell me?"

"Tell him to quit shittin', too," Nathan said.

Gail screamed and Lou held her head up so Sal could see the ketchup on her neck. Nathan hoped he couldn't smell the ketchup because he sure could.

Sal started squirming and screamed. Lou slapped him and he stopped. Sal said, "You're gonna' kill me anyway. Why should I tell you?"

"Think about it, dumb ass," said Avi in the absolute worst Irish accent known to man. "Why would we wear masks if we were going to kill you?" Nathan could think of a bunch of reasons and pulled his mask up over his nose to cut down the stench.

"You killed the girl," said Sal.

"She's not dead. Didn't cut deep enough," said Lou. "Say somethin', bitch." Sal couldn't see Gail.

Gail screamed, "Tell 'em, Sal. These people are maniacs. They'll kill us if you don't." Smack into the flour sack went Lou's hand. "Oh," she moaned.

"If I tell you, you'll let us go?" Sal was begging. Who could blame him?

"Once we get the money." Lou was doing his nails on the other side of Sal. Everybody was comfortable, but Avi and Nathan who were holding Sal down.

Sal told them plenty. As a matter of fact, once he started he was hard to stop. He and the attorney planned to steal the money from the beginning. The attorney was supposed to pay the monthly bills at the home. He and Sal would each take three million, assuming the balance would cover any long-term expenses for Jimmie's family.

Lou asked, "Is that all of it?" Sal nodded.

"Where do we find this attorney so we can get the money?"

Sal said, "No. I'll get it from him. Sorry bastard wasn't holdin' up his end."

Lou said, "No way, Sal. We'll get it. Give us his address and I'll leave you and the girl with Charley and Eddie. Once we have the money, you and the girl will be released."

Sal croaked, "It's Greenblatt. That's his real name. Office in the Twin Towers."

Avi looked at Sal. "If you're lying it won't go easy. You'll die slow." Lou rubbed the razor against Sal's penis, drawing a thin line of blood. Lou then showed the razor to Sal, blood dripping from it.

Dave walked in from outside, saw what was going on and ran for the bathroom. Sal and Nathan passed out. Sal shit again.

***

Nathan instantly came to when a cold compress was placed across his face. He raised his head, taking in what was happening. "What's goin' on?" Nathan asked Gail, the first person he saw.

"Sal's dead."

Nathan screamed, "I told you to do it my way!"

"Sal had a heart attack. Same time you passed out, hero," said Gail. "We tried to resuscitate him, but it was no good. Went fast."

Dave, back from his trip to the bathroom, went through Sal's pants for his car keys and wallet. Sal had $4,500 in his wallet. Dave placed the money on a coffee table and went downstairs to take Sal's car keys to Ray, who would search the car for valuables.

Avi and Lou rolled Sal up in the tarp. Gail unlocked the freight elevator and they carried a very heavy Sal down to it slowly.

Dave met them at the elevator downstairs and told them he and Ray found betting slips and $155,000 in Sal's car. They kept the money and left the slips in the car so the cops would know Sal was up to no good.

Ray backed Sal's car up to the loading dock. They unwrapped Sal and put him naked into the back seat.

Avi said, "Lou's handiwork changes our story somewhat. Dave, put about $40 in his wallet and leave it on the driver's side floor. With his dick all cut up, we can hope the cop's think it was a jealous lover or something. We'll just leave him in long term parking at the Newark Airport."

Nathan said, "Two in a row for heart attacks! We gotta' find someone in better shape to play with."

Nathan sat in the front with Ray. Avi and Lou got in Dave's car and they followed Ray in Sal's car to the airport.

CHAPTER THIRTY-FIVE

The next evening, everyone met in Nathan's conference room after hours for privacy. Julie took notes during the Sal episode, so she held the floor.

"We now have a name and where the lawyer works. And he is a lawyer. I looked him up in the ABA. David Greenblatt. Alias Donald Greer. Sal knew him for ten years. Originally from the city, his practice is mostly workers comp, auto injuries, that type.

"He was, at one time, a client of Sal's and owed him a considerable amount of money. When Jimmie mentioned his problem to Sal, the first guy Sal thought of was Greenblatt. Sal said they planned to skim Jimmie's money. Sal figured the mother and daughter would never use up the seven million. They'd pay the bills and keep the rest.

"Anyway, he hadn't talked to Greenblatt in awhile or gotten his piece of the pie. He was surprised to find out Greenblatt hadn't paid the Crestwood bills. Apparently, this guy had bigger plans than Sal. We called the number Sal gave us for his office and he wasn't in, according to his secretary. Must be doin' well. Dude's office is in Tower Two at the World Trade Center."

Marie said, "You guys did an amazing job to get all that. Where do we go from here?"

Terri said, "We obviously have to take this to the next step and get a fix on when he'll be in his office."

Julie looked up. "Secretary said she expects him day after tomorrow,"

Terri said. "I looked in the phone book for a home listing. Must be a zillion of them."

Marie said, "That would most likely be my area. I volunteer to start the search. I have a couple of people who are excellent on skips. Hopefully he's coming back like the secretary said. We'll have something in a matter of minutes on a local address, especially if his office is leased in his name. Got to be careful, though. With the kind of money he has, he can get lost quick if he wants to and knows how to do it. We gotta' watch we don't spook him."

"We took almost $160,000 off Sal. That gives us operating expenses," said Dave.

Nathan said, "I think we need somebody in charge. To make sure everything is funneled correctly. Unless somebody else wants it," he added, "I volunteer Terri as treasurer. She'll pay for the Collins' and handle the operating fund." There was a chorus of yeses from the crowd.

Avi said, "I assume we'll all be involved when we find this Greenblatt?" All nodded. "Hopefully we'll get lucky and this guy will return to his office. Marie will get his home address. That done, we'll do some surveillance and when he comes back, we just bust in on him. We'll use the same plan Nathan came up with originally." He did his Irish voice and said, "Nobody fucks with the IRA." Everyone laughed. They were ready to get it done.

***

Nothing came from Sal's death. It was a one-paragraph item in a couple of papers the next day. Thankfully there are a lot of murders in New York and Northern New Jersey. It was really hard to make the news for a run-of-the-mill bookie who had a heart attack, which is the way the paper said he died.

The group kind of thought the Mafia would have looked around some. Apparently, good old Sal was not very well liked or missed. Everybody seemed to have bought the robbery story. Nobody seemed to care about what Sal was doing at the Newark Airport. It was his own money lost, not Dom's, so it didn't cause a big stir with the Gambrelli's. His Capo was pissed, but got over it.

Nathan spoke with Sal's replacement the next night when he came to the bar to introduce himself and take bets. "What the hell happened to old Sal?"

"Sal was fuckin' around and got caught," said John Morganti, Sal's replacement. "Broad's husband offed him."

Morganti was a muscular, bald guy just under six feet. He was taller than most of the New York Mafia guys, who ran kind of short, but made up for it by being fat and hairy. Not being a flashy dresser, he preferred casual clothes and not a lot of jewelry. Maybe he was going incognito?

Lou said, "Who woulda thought old Sal was fuckin' somebody's wife?"

Morganti said, "Husband nailed him good."

Lou asked, "Wow, what happened to him?"

"Dude cut his pecker damn near off," said Morganti.

"How you know it was over a girl? Could've been fuckin' around with some guy's boyfriend," Nathan said.

Morganti looked at him. Like he was sizing Nathan up. Then he burst out laughing. "Get the fuck outta' here, Nathan. Sal wasn't no fag. You don't know how it goes in New York, Nathan. Just remembered you ain't from around here. That's a definite sign it was somebody's wife. Believe me, Sal wasn't no fag. He would've never worked for Dom if he was a fag."

"Oh," Nathan said. He almost asked if Dom checked for stuff like that. And how did he check for stuff like that? Did he wave "it" in front of new recruits? Dom didn't appear that irresistible with his low-to-the-ground fat ass. Nathan figured he'd leave well enough alone.

***

That evening, a quick meeting was held. Marie announced that she'd had no luck finding Greenblatt's home address. They were working on pinning down the name on the office lease. It wasn't under Greenblatt or Greer.

Avi said, "We gotta' find this guy. Finish the job."

Nathan said, "And the job is gettin' the money back."

Ray said, "Guy's gotta' be punished doesn't he, Nathan? Can't just get the money and let 'em go."

Dave said, "Nathan's got a point. Get the money back and it's over with."

Gail said, "It would be a travesty if we just let the guy go. We owe Jimmie that much. I think we have to punish him."

Julie said, "Us punish him?"

"Somebody's got to. Can't call the cops." Ray was adamant.

Avi asked, "Anybody else? Okay. We do it."

"Do what, Avi?" asked Terri.

"Take care of him."

"Bullshit. We just get the money back. Not up to us to punish anybody," Marie said.

"We owe it to Jimmie," said Avi.

"I'm in to get his money back," said Ken. "What you guys do, I don't want to know."

Ray said, "Fuck, we got to do somethin'."

"No, we don't," said Terri. "We get Jimmie's money back. Jimmie wouldn't want us to kill somebody for him. Jimmie wasn't that way and you know it. We get his money back. Maybe do something dirty to the guy. But we sure as hell aren't executioners."

Avi said, "We have to find the guy first, so it's all conjecture here. We'll decide when we find the guy."

"We take care a' him then," said Ray. "I already decided. This time, I'll do him. I want this one."

***

Terri asked Nathan later, "What the hell are we going to do? When we get to the end and they want to kill this guy?"

Nathan said, "God, I don't know. Ray says he wants him. Sal didn't bother me. Was a heart attack. I doubt this Greenblatt asshole will be so obliging."

"That's not the problem. We gotta keep them from doing anything. Save them from themselves," said Terri.

Nathan asked, "This isn't fun anymore."

She asked, "Paying back these guys for Jimmie is supposed to be fun?"

"No," Nathan said. "Life in general is supposed to be fun. I'm not weird or anything, not a serial killer. Life is supposed to be what you make it. It's always been fun for me 'cause I've always made it that way. This has ceased to be fun, arguing with Avi and these guys."

CHAPTER THIRTY-SIX

Then the whole world wasn't fun anymore. The planes hit the Twin Towers. Nathan was in his office when his secretary came in. She told him a plane hit one of the towers and it was on TV. He rushed to the conference room where the TV was already on and the room was crowded. He arrived just as the second plane hit.

"What the hell's going on?" Harvey demanded. "It's not cloudy or anything. Don't these pilots know where they're going?"

One of the programmers said, "Weird stuff coming in off the net. Saying it might be sabotage."

Another programmer said, "So much trash on the net you can't believe anything. Got to be an accident. Those poor people."

They sat mesmerized, watching the TV as did most of America that morning. How could something like this happen? Reports started coming in pointing toward terrorists. It was all so unbelievable. How could anyone consciously do something like this? Take the lives of innocents? Then the reports became clearer. Osama bin Laden was suspected. He had a huge terrorist organization spread over the world.

What kind of man could he be? To try to further a cause, under the mask of religion, by killing innocent people? And the ugly parallels. On one side you had terrorist pilots willing to die to kill people. On the other you had truly brave fire fighters and policemen rushing into those buildings, willing to die to save the same people the terrorists were trying to kill. What courage that had to take.

Nathan had always considered himself a fairly macho individual. He was strong from years of lifting weights and participating in football. Yet he didn't think he could have rushed into those burning and tumbling buildings to save lives. He'd like to think he would, but he wasn't sure he'd have had the courage exhibited that day.

***

Later that morning, moved by the horrible tragedy as well as the heroics, several employees asked permission to go down and try to help. He gladly granted their wishes. The rest decided to wait until tomorrow to go, figuring it would be too chaotic today. It seemed, by the shots they were seeing on TV, that they really didn't need more people down there at the moment.

The next day Nathan went with a large group down to the site early in the morning. They waited with a mob of hopeful volunteers for several hours. The people running the rescue mission were taking people with specific skills: carpenters, equipment operators and healthcare people. Nathan's group didn't have any special skills and just wanted to be laborers, but they had all they needed and told them to check back in the afternoon.

New York had changed. The streets were different. People were friendlier, helpful. Total strangers spoke to each other. It seemed the mood of the country had changed too. Everyone was proud to be an American again. It was then that Nathan noticed a change in himself. He was proud to be a New Yorker.

Growing up in the South, he'd always made fun of New York. Maybe it was envy, the Yankees winning everything all the time. Whatever, he continued to make fun of them even after his move. Living in New York for two years hadn't changed him. If anything, it made his prejudices worse. When people asked him where he was from, or lived, he always told them Atlanta, just living in New York temporarily. Not anymore. Rudy was his mayor and he was proud of it!

***

Early the next day, he got a call from Lou. It seemed "old buddy" Paulie, Fat Sal Ricco's nephew, was in the bar and crying in his beer. With his uncle dead, Paulie was out on his ass as far as a job was concerned.

Paulie was never part of the mob officially. His uncle paid him to help out, but that was it. After Sal's death, nobody wanted him.

Lou commiserated with Paulie, told him he'd try to help him. Then he said he had a legal matter to take care of and maybe he could use the lawyer that helped Jimmie. Paulie laughed and told him the guy was a crook, but Lou persisted. Paulie gave him a home address on Madison and 53rd, half a block from Nathan's office. Lou told Paulie he had to run to the restroom and did, stopping to call Nathan.

***

Nathan almost ran, and got to the bar ahead of everybody else. Lou was working behind the bar and was trying to get a last minute replacement. The minute he saw Nathan he broke out in a big grin and came from behind the bar to hug him.

Helen, Lou's boss, yelled as she came through the door, "What did you guys hit? The lotto?"

"Close," Nathan said. "Big stock deal."

"Helen, can you cover for me for a while?" asked Lou.

"Sure," she said. "Take the day. You look like you've got celebrating to do."

Ray walked in and the hugging started all over again.

Helen said, "Damn, Nathan. You give everybody else the tip but me?"

"I didn't know you then, sweetie, or you'd of had it."

With the address, Marie ran down Greenblatt's phone number under another alias, Swanson. She called repeatedly, but there was no answer. Avi faked a FedEx delivery to the address, but no one came to the door.

Ray had slipped by before going to the bar and paid for some information. The doorman told him that he thought Mr. Swanson had left town the day before and that his office, located in Tower Two of the World Trade Center, was destroyed. The doorman told him Swanson missed the destruction by meeting a client in New Jersey that morning. Mr. Swanson's secretary died in the attack.

"One less place to look," said Ken. "We got to get in that apartment as soon as possible."

"We're going to have to break in," Lou said.

"No, I can finesse it. I'll use my badge and get us in on police business," said Ken. "Stuart and I will approach the Super and get him to let us in. Ray, Avi and Nathan can come and help after we get in. I'll call you on my cell. Lou, you'll be at the door inside and Dave will watch on the floor. We don't know what this guy looks like so you guys grab anybody coming to the door. Dave, if this guy comes to the floor and gets spooked, you'll have to stop him from leaving the floor. Anybody comes to the floor, you call Lou on his cell. Have all but the last number dialed."

"Ken, want to wait till we get his ID from DMV?" asked Stuart.

"Better go ahead and hit it," said Ken. "Guy may be already gone. If we wait, he will increase his lead on us."

They hit his apartment. They wanted to thoroughly search the place, but leave no signs of anyone being there in case Greenblatt was just out for the day.

It was a small, two-bedroom apartment facing Madison. Ken assigned everyone a particular area of the home. He assigned Ray the kitchen and Nathan the small office next to the kitchen. He told Ray to be sure to check the packages of food.

"What exactly are we looking for?" asked Ray.

"Barring suitcases of money, look for bank accounts or numbers, like for an overseas account. Nathan, you got the stuff for the computer, right?"

"Yeah." He had a software program one of his guys gave him to defeat Greenblatt's password and a zip drive to copy his hard drive. Computer guys are handy.

It didn't take long to search the office. There were no files and his desk was one of those Office Depot cheapies, one drawer and that was it. He did have a couple of floppies and Nathan copied them and went in to help Ray.

Ray was busy going through Greenblatt's pantry, so Nathan rummaged through Greenblatt's refrigerator and found two half-gallons of ice cream.

"You saved me some?" He pulled them out to see what flavors there were.

Ray said, "After all the shit I took about that friggin' ice cream last time, there was no way I was going to mess with it."

Nathan dug into a drawer and found two spoons and went over next to Ray. Offering him a spoon, he sat down beside him.

Ray dipped his spoon in and took a bite, then asked, "What flavor did you get?"

"Pistachio."

Ray said, "Trade?"

"Hell no. Mine's almost full."

The other guys got a little mad when they found them eating ice cream. Not that they'd done any better. The last hope was Greenblatt's computer, because they found absolutely nothing in the apartment. Stuart gave the doorman $100 to keep his mouth shut and call if Grennblatt returned. As of now, they were dead in the water.

But not for long. Nathan turned the zip drive over to Terri, Julie, and Marie. They had the job of going through Greenblatt's computer files.

Julie found an odd number and word in one of the files. She checked it with friends and discovered it was an account number and password. Another set of numbers led her to the bank, located in Brussels.

She got together with Terri and they did an account check and discovered a little over three million dollars in the account. Not all of Jimmie's money, but a hell of a start. They had to get it out of the account before Greenblatt did something with it.

They couldn't direct it to an account in the U.S. without someone having some heavy questions to answer, as well as paying taxes on the money. They decided to establish another account with the same bank and switch it, using a different password. They then ran it through ten more banks before feeling comfortable enough to switch it to a bank in Mexico.

CHAPTER THIRTY-SEVEN

Marie had big news three days later. She'd located Greenblatt. Through Stuart, they even had a picture of him. Sort of a picture. His driver's license. The picture was grainy, but he'd recently renewed his license, so it was current at least.

Ken ran a check on his credit cards. He discovered they'd been used to purchase airline tickets to Cozumel, Mexico, and then at a hotel outside of San Miguel. The group was ecstatic. Almost like making it to the Super Bowl. But they weren't finished yet. They didn't know for sure it was him and they still had to get the rest of the money.

"Jeez Ken, black and white?" asked Ray.

"Guy's white and his hair's black. Could be color for all you know. What do you want from me, Ray?"

"Color would be nice," said Ray.

"Well, you ain't got it, Ray," said Ken, shaking his head. "What you got, Ray, is where the fuckin' guy is and a picture."

Asked Ray, "How do we know it's him and he's still there? Cozumel? Where the fuck is it?"

"In Mexico, Ray," Nathan said. Hell, he knew that much and wanted to show off. "Big tourist area. I was on a cruise ship that visited there one time. But I didn't get off the boat."

Ray asked, "Why not?"

Warming to the subject, Nathan said, grinning, "I was tryin' to wine and dine this aging gymnast. Should have gotten off," said Nathan, shaking his head.

"You said tryin?" asked Lou.

"She was lesbian."

Lou said, "Yeah?"

Nathan, still grinning said, "Yeah, had to a' been. Wouldn't go to bed with me." For this Nathan got a shot in the ribs from Terri.

"All men are the same," said Gail.

"God, that's depressing," said Julie.

"I'm sure this is our guy," said Marie.

Avi asked, "How sure?"

"Ninety-five percent sure. Ken's info confirms his credit card number. Either him, or somebody traveling on his card. Two men with him," Marie looked down to consult her notes. "Manny Estes and Louie Prontas. They flew out of here with him. Same connections and this guy paid for their tickets."

"Probably hired muscle," said Ken. "If he's traveling with the money, he'd want some kind of protection."

Dave asked, "Why do you think he's got the money with him?"

Stuart said, "We know it's not at his apartment. Not in his office, or if it was, it's gone. Fuckin' bin Laden took care of that. If it's gone, there would be no reason to run, no money. Muscle means he's probably protectin' somethin'."

Dave mused, "Could just be protecting him."

"Could be, but I doubt it," said Stuart. "I'll bet he was spooked by Sal's death. Maybe figured he was next? With Sal gone, he didn't have to split the money with anyone, if he was ever planning to. Didn't know if Sal told anyone, so he ran to make sure of it. Didn't cover his tracks. He may think whoever is after him isn't that smart. He's got the money. I'd be willing to bet on it."

Ray said, "Are all of us going down or should just a couple go to check out if this guy is the right guy?"

"We all don't need to go," said Marie.

"Okay, fine," said Ray. "How about Avi, Nathan, Lou, Ken, Stuart and me?"

Ken said, "I can't go. Divorce starts next week."

Stuart said, "I'll go. You got two bodyguards to deal with."

"If Stuart's going, so am I," said Gail.

Avi said, "Need someone here to cover. Ken's out. Dave will be muscle if we need it. Terri, Julie and Marie can do the computer stuff." To Julie, he said, "That okay, honey?"

Julie looked at Terri, who nodded. "You guys get an account number, we can do the transfer."

Terri added, "Or try to get you out of a Mexican jail." She stood, walked over in front of Ray, got in his face and said, "Anything goes wrong, Ray, I'll have your nuts in a vise."

Gail asked, "What's our plan?"

"Make it up as we go along," Nathan said.

Avi said, "That's just what we don't want to do. We need something concrete. Have some kind of focus. Who's gonna' do what. Can't just barge in. Spook him, we may not get another chance."

"How we going to do that, Avi? We don't even know what's going on." Nathan was a little resentful.

Avi said, "I'll do the planning on the way."

Ken said, "I'll be here if needed."

Terri asked, "What about the divorce?"

Ken said, "How long can it last? Fuckin' marriage wasn't that long."

***

Nathan took a taxi to the airport the next day after spending the night with Terri. He'd gotten the "all clear" from Marie that the three men were still checked into the hotel. He met Gail and Stuart and they had a couple of parting drinks before their flight was announced. They were soon joined by Avi and Lou and they headed to the gate, running into Ray.

Ray said, "Sorry. Got held up by the Purple Robe people, that religious group that's battling the Moonies for control of the airports."

"Bunch of beggars," said Stuart.

"Good-lookin' beggars," said Nathan.

"Bald-headed girls turn you on?" Gail laughed. "You got a problem, Nathan!"

"I talked to one of 'em about their religion," said Ray. "They're the Baba Rum Raisins. The girls that ask for money in the purple robes are called the Raisinettes. Religion's kind a' like the Muslim's. They go on Hajj except they go to the Mississippi River."

Stuart asked, "They're like a water religion?"

Ray said, "Naw. Guy that started 'em, Shay Baba, or somethin' like that, was buried in St. Paul. When the Mississippi flooded in the 90s, he and half the cemetery was washed away. To make it easy for 'em, they can just go to any spot on the Mississippi and pay homage."

Ray looked around, scratched his head and said, "This new Newark airport is alright. The old one, you had to keep your tetanus shots up to date."

Nathan slowed, letting the others pass him heading to the gate. Walking beside Ray, he asked, "You bring the special surprise?" Ray gave him a thumbs-up signal.

***

The flight into Cozumel was uneventful. Or as uneventful as it could be, being one of those places where you couldn't go to straight from anywhere. They had connections in Atlanta, then Miami.

Flying in was beautiful. It was the largest island in Mexico, about twelve miles long and ten wide. The island was surrounded by some of the whitest beaches on Earth.

To make things easy, they checked into the same place as Greenblatt and his boys, the Coral Princess Hotel. The hotel was a high rise facing the ocean and Ray and Nathan decided to bunk together.

Naturally, after tipping the bellboy, Ray headed for the closest bar while Nathan chose a quick shower.

After he finished showering, and while changing, he fiddled with the TV and found a ball game. He watched until he finished dressing and met Ray in the bar.

"What's up, Champ?" Ray said as Nathan entered, pointing to a cold Mick Light in front of an empty stool.

"Thanks for the beer." Nathan turned to the bartender, who was wearing a large nametag. He was watching a Spanish Soap Opera. "Julio," he said, reading the man's nametag, "any chance we can get a ball game on the TV?"

"Not on at this moment, Senor."

Nathan asked, "When your show's over, turn it on 53."

"Si." He never even turned. Must be a good one, thought Nathan.

Ray asked, "Who's playing?"

"Braves and Yanks in that inter-league shit."

Ray yelled, "Turn the fucking TV on 53, Julio. And right damned quick."

Some people don't care who spits in their drink, Nathan thought, as Julio angrily changed the TV. They watched the game, had some more beer, and were eventually joined by the others.

"Anybody come up with anything?" asked Gail.

Nathan beat Avi to the punch. "We find out what rooms they're in and watch them. When the room's unguarded, Ray and I go in. You guys watch for us."

"That's it? That's your plan," said Avi.

"It's the KISS method. We'll revise it as needed. What's wrong with that?" Nathan asked.

"Other than it won't work, you mean?" he replied.

Nathan said, "You got something better?" A surprise to him, no one came to his support.

"Yeah, maybe use Gail as a decoy," Avi said.

"That's great, if we were going to be here a while," said Lou. "You don't think they'll notice us after a week or so?"

"I think it would happen sooner than that," Avi countered.

Ray said. "Let's get the lay of the land. We assess their weakness and then react. Do it on the run like Nathan said." Ray was baiting Avi and he got a bite. Avi was ready to get in Ray's face.

Lou stopped them by saying, "Ray's right, we just got here. Let's see what's going on first."

"I want to check out the muscle. See how good they are," said Stuart.

A little miffed at Avi, Nathan went to his room after dinner. He was tired and hurt that no one, other than Ray, saw the merit of his approach at getting the money back.

***

Nathan heard a loud thump and came slowly out of a deep slumber. "Hold on." Sleeping in the nude, he threw on a shirt, figuring it was Ray, and opened the door.

Thankfully it was a long shirt, as Gail was first through the door. "Hello, Nathan. What are you doing? Whoops, help him, Stuart." Stuart steadied Nathan, who was trying to quickly pull on a pair of boxers.

He pushed his foot through the pee hole and almost fell. Why is it, he wondered, that when you're hurrying, your foot always goes into the pee hole?

Gail said, "Nice seeing you, literally. No wonder Terri's so protective of you."

"What are you guys doin'? I was sound asleep. Thought Ray forgot his key or somethin'." Nathan gave up and stood with one leg through the pee hole of his boxers, pulling his shirt down in front. He tried hard not to look odd as he stood, both feet together.

Gail said, "We came up to see if you were mad. You are, aren't you?"

Feigning indifference, he said, "About what?"

"We didn't support you against Avi," she said.

"Oh, about the plan. I didn't notice and it doesn't matter."

"Avi is a little pushy sometimes," said Stuart.

"Like being a little pregnant, isn't it?" Nathan said, "It really doesn't matter. Be Ray and me that does it. We'll do what we want anyway."

Gail said, "Now there's a team player. Glad we came up and checked on you, 'Mr. I'm Not Mad.'"

"Shit, it's not rocket science, is it? We need to get in the room. They need to be out of the room," Nathan said.

Stuart said, "Think, Nathan. If you had a bunch of money in a room would you ever leave it unguarded? You can bet one or both of the muscle lives in there. Bet they're armed to the teeth, too."

"So, we get rid of them," Nathan said.

Gail went to the heart of the problem, "How?"

"Me and Ray got a surprise for 'em."

Stuart asked, "Care to share it with us?"

Nathan said, "When we get the kinks out, I'll let you in on it."

***

Ray came in an hour later. "About time, roomy," said Nathan. "Stuart and Gail were sniffin' around about our special surprise. I didn't tell 'em."

Ray asked, "How'd they know we had one?"

"Wild guess."

Ray said, "Oh."

"I appreciate you takin' up for me downstairs."

Ray smiled, "Friggin' Avi. All talk. Course, it would be nice if you had a plan."

"Got one. It's secret."

Ray laughed, "You don't, do you?"

Nathan shrugged, "No."

***

The next morning, Ray and Nathan approached the desk clerk. They slipped her a twenty, showed her a picture and asked about three men traveling together.

"Si, Senors. They have two adjoining suites, one man in one and two men in the other," said the clerk. "Tony Estaban, Larry Pronto and Donald Greer, all Americano. I checked them in."

Ray asked, "Which room is the one man in?"

"The man that paid took both keys."

"Did they put anything in the hotel safe?" asked Ray, giving her another $20.

"Nothing, Senor. They had very little luggage, but went shopping immediately. Lot of shopping."

Nathan said. "See that your memory becomes not so good." She smiled as he gave her $100.

Ray and Nathan enjoyed playing detective. They were arguing over who was Kojak and who was the curly-haired guy when the rest of the group trudged into the hotel coffee shop.

CHAPTER THIRTY-EIGHT

For their industriousness, Ray and Nathan were given the first watch and found great spots in the lobby. The rest of the group headed for scuba diving. Neither Nathan nor Ray particularly cared about the sun, so they didn't mind the inside watch. Besides, the bar was open.

They were still in the bar, alternating between watching the elevators and the news coverage of the terrorist attacks. Of course, they were drinking beer when Avi and Lou came running in.

Avi asked, "Thought you guys were watching."

"We are," said Ray, thinking heroes didn't have to take any shit. "What does it look like we're doing?"

Avi said, "You fat tub of shit, Lou and I passed Greenblatt sitting at the pool bar."

"There's no need for name-calling," said Lou, stepping between them as Ray climbed off his stool.   Nathan said, "We've been watching the elevators and he didn't come through the lobby. If he's at the pool, there is another exit."

Leaving the bar, they checked the hotel for additional exits. They found out you could take the elevator to the basement, which had an exit door as well as an opening to the pool.

Ray and Nathan were fired for the day. Avi would cover the lobby, Lou the basement. They would stay in touch by cell.

Ray started to argue about being fired, but Nathan motioned to Ray and they headed to the elevator. "The bodyguards are either upstairs or they went out with Greenblatt," he said. "Here's the plan. We go to the floor and pull the fire alarm. If they're in, they'll come running out. When they do, we'll see 'em and phone Gail and Stuart and tell them to watch them while we hit the room. Bam, it's all over. We get the money and run. Sound like a plan, Stan?"

"Course it do, cause you da' man," Ray said, high-fiving his partner. They were much better at high-fiving now. They generally did it without falling. "Then we'll be heroes again and won't have to listen to that friggin' Avi anymore."

Nathan said, "Okay, when they run out and the coast is clear, you go inside and I'll be behind you. If somebody's in there, I'll get the drop on them while they're dealing with you."

Ray said, "Why do I have to go first?"

Nathan explained, "It's my idea. If it'd been yours, I would've gone first."

Ray looked a little dubious and said, "What if there's more than one guy?"

"Then we fight like hell. We'll still have the element of surprise because I'll delay coming in."

Ray said, "But I'll be getting the piss beat out of me."

"It's my plan, Ray." Nathan was hoping there was just one. Ray thought for a second and started shaking his head no when Nathan said, "If we have to go again, I'll go first." This was more to Ray's liking. "Fuck, you should want me to go second. Remember the guy in Costa Rica? I have more stopping power. The guy will be on you."

Ray thought for a second and said, "Nope. If we have to go again, you go first."

Nathan pushed him toward the elevator, just a little pissed. As they walked down the hall after getting off the elevator, Nathan pulled the fire alarm.

He and Ray stood nonchalantly by the coke machines while everyone ran out of their rooms. They watched the two rooms. Shortly, a heavy-set, darkly tanned big man came out in the hall followed by an even bigger man with a shaved head. They looked up and down the hall for a minute, then went back inside and closed the door.

"Did you see those guys?" Ray said, "We should have brought machine guns and a friggin' tank with us. What kind of assholes are gonna' risk getting burned to death to save some other asshole's money?"

"Well-paid assholes," Nathan said. "Think we should go tell them downstairs?"

Ray said, "Just that we saw the guys and can identify them. Describe them and all. We won't tell them about pulling the fire alarm."

Nathan said, "Deal."

They got downstairs and everybody was bitching about some idiot pulling the alarm. Not just the rest of the group, but everybody in the hotel. There was a lobby full of mad people.

Nathan and Ray agreed that whoever did it was an idiot and gave them the two guy's descriptions. They told them they happened to be on Greenblatt's floor when the alarm went off. They were heading for the stairs when the two goons came out in the hall, then went back in.

"Well, means we're gonna' have to do something else," said Stuart. "Were these guys armed?"

"Yeah," Nathan said. "They weren't pointing or anything, but they had those shoulder holster jobs on. Why?"

"Just an idea. I'm going to catch a taxi and go by the local cop palace. See what's shakin'," Stuart said. "Be back in a few."

***

After Stuart returned, they decided to hit the room that night. Greenblatt left the hotel in a taxi and Stuart and Gail followed him. They'd call when he was on the way back. Stuart worked his magic and called the police and alerted them to the fact that two heavily-armed desperados were holed up in the hotel. He thought they were planning on robbing the place.

It worked like a charm. As soon as the police hauled the two goons away, it was show time for Ray and Nathan. Avi and Lou were to act as lookouts.

"Let's get in and out. Grab it and haul ass," said Nathan.

"You're going in first this time. Your turn," said Ray. "Remember?"

Nathan said, "My turn? You never went. It's your turn."

"You're scared, Nathan. If you're scared, I'll go first," said Ray. "Just admit you're scared."

"Fuck you and your 'ifs.' If your aunt would've had balls, she'd have been your uncle."

"My aunt did have balls," Ray said, walking down the hall to the room.

Ray unlocked the door with his pick and Nathan stepped inside. No one was there and they headed in opposite directions, searching quickly. Ten minutes into the search, Nathan found it. Three briefcases full of money hid in the acoustical ceiling above a pullout panel in the suite foyer. "Ray, come here."

Ray hustled in just as Nathan's cell rang. They looked at each other. "Could be trouble," Nathan said and both started walking toward the door.

Ray whispered, "Probably just the other guys checkin'. See if we got in okay."

"Door, Ray," Nathan whispered, moving into the coat closet and hitting the light switch as the door opened.

The big bald guy came rushing through the door. He spotted Ray with the help of the hallway light and ran for him, catching Ray in a headlock. Nathan stepped in after the bald guy hit Ray and whacked him in the forehead with one of the briefcases. It apparently was a cheap one, as money flew across the room. Both the bald guy and Ray were in a heap on the floor when Nathan turned on the light and closed the door. Nathan figured he'd hit the bald guy harder than the bald guy hit Ray, as Ray came around first.

Nathan had the bald guy hog-tied with his belt and strips of linen. He placed a gag in the guy's mouth in case his first reaction was to scream.

Ray went to get some water to revive the smarmy bastard. He returned and dumped the water on Baldy, who immediately came around, spitting water. Ray didn't help matters as he kicked the bald guy after regaining his senses.

Nathan had the silenced Glock 17 the bald guy had been carrying pointed right between his eyes. "Mister, you're fucked. I will remove the gag in a moment. If you try to yell or alert anyone, I'll kill you. Do you understand me? Please nod if you do." He nodded. "Do you believe I'll kill you if you scream?" He nodded again. "Good. Take the gag off, Ray." Baldy stared over at Ray.

"Damn, Nathan, supposed to use a fake name like with Sal."

"I don't remember what they were. And besides, you never came inside. You didn't even have a fake name, Ray."

"Oh!"

Baldy started begging as soon as the gag came off. "I didn't have anything to do with it. I'm just hired help. If he stole your money, it's him. You got to believe me."

"Oh, I believe you all right," said Ray. "Big guy like you cryin'. What's the matter with you? We just want our money back."

"How'd you get away from the police so quick?" Nathan asked Baldy.

"Gave 'em $100. They said it was a fine. Let us keep our guns. My partner had to go in and sign some forms."

"Hold the gun on him, Ray, while I pick up the money and call Lou."

As he dialed Lou, Ray was playing with the gun, twirling it like a cowboy, and asked, "Is this thing on safety?" Baldy, still tied but figuring Ray didn't know what he was doing, rushed Ray with a bunny-hop step. Ray tried to quit twirling and point the gun as Baldy crashed into him. Both went down as the gun went off.

Nathan didn't know what to do, so he jumped on Baldy's back and started choking him to get him off Ray. For all he knew, Ray was hit and Baldy had the gun.

On the floor, they rolled over, Baldy now on top of Nathan, Ray on top of Baldy. On the bottom, Nathan used his legs and the wall for leverage, kicking off and rolling at the same time. Now he was on top and Ray on the bottom, Baldy in between them.

Nathan had Baldy in a chokehold and stood up, trying to pry him off Ray. Up came Baldy but Ray came up with him. Nathan tried whirling Baldy so he could hit him somewhere other than the top of his head. As he twirled him, Baldy and Ray traded positions. Ray now had his back to Nathan.

Nathan looked into Baldy's face and saw a neat hole right between Baldy's eyes. "Ray, are you hurt?" Nathan asked, looking directly into the back of Ray's head.

"I'm okay. Getting tired though. I got him."

Nathan asked, "Who has the gun, Ray?"

"Me. He tried to get it from me."

Nathan raised his hand to Baldy's neck and felt for a pulse, Ray still between Nathan and Baldy. Nathan was able to reach over Ray.

"This fucker's dead, Ray. You shot him between the eyes."

Ray let go of Baldy and he fell to the floor. "Gun just went off. I didn't shoot him. Let me go, Nathan."

Nathan released the bear hug he had on Ray. "You'd need more than Johnny Cochran to get off on that one brother, gun still in your hands. Hell of a shot though, right between the eyes. Probably killed him instantly."

Ray was stunned. Both stared at Baldy lying on the floor. "I didn't mean to do it," said Ray.

Nathan said, looking at Baldy, "We have no more questions for this witness, Your Honor."

Ray shrugged. "Guess the safety was off."

"Duh! You think so?" Nathan couldn't believe this shit. "Thankfully the damn thing had a silencer. Still pretty loud though." Ray nodded. "We got to get his ass out of here. Any ideas?"

Ray asked, "Me?"

Nathan said, exasperated, "You shot him. You should have to think of how we get rid of the body."

Ray said, "Okay, okay. It was an accident. He rushed me. It was his fault as much as mine. What am I supposed to do?" He stared at Nathan, "Train him for a house pet? Damn, more whinin' out of you than my first wife." Nathan stared at him and he looked away and said, "If he hadn't of rushed me and got shot, we'd probably still be fightin' him.

Big guy like that." He looked at Nathan and shrugged. "Sorry, Nathan. You just agitate me sometimes. Okay? Sorry. What do you want me to do?"

"Go to the freight elevator and see if anybody's using it." Nathan scratched his head, thinking.

Ray started laughing and said, "Good thing nobody saw us through the window. Must have looked like we were dancin'"

"Or killin' some guy," Nathan said and Ray left to check on the elevator. Now Nathan had to come up with what to do next. Why was it always him? He could be a great follower. He didn't always have to be in charge.

Ray was back moments later. "Room service guys are using it. They say they use it all night. Guests aren't supposed to use the freight elevator, anyway."

"Guests aren't supposed to shoot other guests either, are they?" He shook his head and began pacing. "Fuck! That was the easy solution. Knew it was going to be harder." Nathan looked out of the window a few feet away. "Hey, these guys have a shitty view. All they got is that alley and the jungle. Our room fronts the ocean. Wonder if this is cheaper?" Bingo! "Got your screwdrivers?"

Ray said, "Yeah. Always got my tool set. That's what I used on the door. You know that."

"Give me a Philips head." Ray handed it to Nathan, who started unscrewing the bolts put in to keep the window from being opened.

"What the fuck? You cold? Want to let in some heat from outside?"

Nathan said, "No. We're going to drop this fucker in the dumpster under us. Help me get him up."

Ray was astonished. "Four floors?"

"Yes," said Nathan. "Fifty-foot drop. Should go right to the bottom of the trash with his weight."

And he would've if the dumpster lid had been opened. *Crash* went Baldy on the steel dumpster doors. Head first. They couldn't believe no one heard the bang. Sounded like a bus hitting a semi head on.

They had to go down, pick him up and toss him in the side. He was considerably more compact after hitting the dumpster and fit nicely.

Ray asked, "What do we do now?" They were back up in the room.

"Screw the window shut. Pick up the money. Grab the briefcase and get the hell out of here." He shrugged, "Thank God they have adjoining rooms. You plant the stuff in the other room while I tidy up. Other guy can't be that far behind."

Nathan tried to wipe up the bloodstain on the carpet from Baldy. It was big, and it wasn't coming up, so he moved the room desk over on top of it. Felt like Martha Stewart. Of course the desk was now in the middle of the room, but it couldn't be helped.

Ray returned and they both got on their knees to pick up the money.

Ray said, "We just got to make it through the night. I planted the cocaine. Hopefully, after we tip them off, the cops will keep Greenblatt busy for awhile. Remind me to tell Willie Cheech thanks when we get back. I want to get out of here in the morning. Early."

Nathan said, "If we can't get out in the mornin', then we get another hotel."

Ray asked, "What are you going to tell the people at the front desk? I don't like my room anymore? Too much noise with the banging on the dumpster and shooting and all?"

Nathan looked at Ray and thought, who's the Chatty Cathy now? Nathan said, "Somebody is gonna' find Stumpy at some point in time. We got to get out of here."

Ray said, "You call him Stumpy?" They both started laughing.

"Yeah. At this point, Baldy is a shadow of his former self. Stumpy fits. It's like those guys doin' personals ads in the New Yorker. Tall, thin, like long walks on the beach. Girl shows up and the guy looks like you. Of course, so does she." Nathan added, "No offense, Ray."

"None taken, Nathan," nodded Ray.

They were still laughing, sitting on the floor picking up money when the cell rang and the door burst open. The big, dark guy came rushing in. He tripped over Nathan, almost got his balance, then tripped over Ray and went right out the window. Seconds later they heard a big bam!

Nathan said, "Jeez, are we surrounded?" They looked at each other then both ran to the window and looked out. The big dark guy was in the dumpster and not moving. All you could see were the soles of his shoes peeking out of the trash.

Nathan had to catch his breath. "I thought I told you to close the window and screw it back in?"

Ray looked at him. "Good thing I didn't." He looked out the window again, turned and said, "Weren't you supposed to close the dumpster?"

Nathan nodded, "Lucky it was still open. Saves us a trip, huh?""

Ray said, "You can just barely see his feet sticking out of the garbage from up here. Probably can't see it from down there."

"He's not moving," said Nathan, staring down at the dumpster. "Must've knocked himself out."

"Or broke his fuckin' neck," said Ray. "Hope so. Son-of-a-bitch scarin' people like that."

Nathan said, "Give me the fuckin' screw driver."

They finally picked up all the money. Nathan said to Ray, "They no longer have us outnumbered. My partner 'Deadeye' and me against Greenblatt? I like our odds."

Ray said, "Want me to go close the dumpster?"

Nathan said, "Fuck it. Call the cops and tell them there's dope in Greenblatt's room. He's a big Americano dope dealer. Killed his partners and put them in the dumpster." Wiping his brow, he said, "We may jus' get out of this yet, Pardner."

They went down to the front desk after Ray made the call and asked the desk clerk to put the three briefcases in the hotel safe. Had to be better places, but they couldn't think of any.

After the briefcases were checked, Nathan asked Ray, "What do you want to do now?"

They both turned toward the sirens pulling up out front. Ray said, "Drink. Need a drink."

CHAPTER THIRTY-NINE

They walked into the bar and Avi and Lou were sitting at a table. Lou jumped up and said, "Where have you guys been?"

Nathan said, "The fuck you mean, where we been? We been doing what we're here to do. Where the fuck have you guys been?"

"We called when we saw the first guy coming in," said Avi. "The cell wasn't answered. Figured you guys had high-tailed it."

"Asshole," said Ray. "You called as the fucking guy was coming in the door. Same thing with the second guy."

Avi asked, "What second guy?" and Ray went after him. Lou got in between them.

They calmed down and Lou let them go. Nathan was drinking Lou's beer while the short fracas was going on.

"You were still there when the second guy came in?" asked Lou incredulously. He grabbed his beer from Nathan and took a long slug from it. "Fuck," he said, wiping his mouth on his sleeve. "Just kissed Nathan. Damn!"

Ray said, "Who called the second time?"

Nathan looked at his cell and scrolled down calls received. "Jus' my office."

"We got the money," Nathan said. He drank from Avi's beer. "Where are Stuart and Gail?"

"They followed Greenblatt to an Italian restaurant. Supposed to be authentic," said Avi.

"Thank you, Mr. Food," said Ray. Avi moved toward Ray again, but Lou had stayed between them, not trusting either.

Avi asked, "So what happened upstairs?"

"Ray shot the first guy and we threw the second out the window." Nathan figured he didn't need to tell them the part about Ray playing with the gun. Or the guy tripping over them and falling out the window.

"What?" asked Lou. "Is that what all the sirens are about? You guys are a crime wave."

Ray said, "No. It's a big drug bust. That is, as soon as Greenblatt finishes eating."

Avi asked, "What?"

"It's a long story," said Ray. "It was our plan. Why don't you guys call Stuart and Gail and tell them to come home. Fuckin' date's over."

Avi asked, "Where's the money?"

"Hotel safe," Nathan said. "You'll need to sit up tonight and make sure none of the clerks steal it. Lou, after you call Stuart and Gail, you need to book us some flights to get out of here tomorrow. Pronto! Then figure out how we're going to get this cash back into the U.S. for Betty and Dotty. Me and my little buddy are going to sit here and get very drunk." Avi started to say something, but thought better of it.

But Nathan and Ray didn't. Get drunk that is. A couple of beers and they were incredibly tired. The adrenaline rush was over. They went up to the room and left everybody celebrating.

"Ray, you going to be all right?" He didn't answer. He was sitting on the bed staring at the floor. "We got back Jimmie's money," Nathan said.

"Yeah, you're right. Just makes you feel odd. Ending somebody's life."

"Couldn't have made you feel too odd. You took to it like a duck to water." Ray smiled. That was the intended reaction. "You were so fucking quick I didn't have time to react," said Nathan. "Scared the hell out of me."

"Yeah," he said. There was a little pride showing in his eyes.

"Jimmie would've been proud. You know, he told me something the night before he died. He was talkin' about dyin' and said he really didn't care. Said he was tired."

"Tired of living?" Ray asked.

"No. That's what I asked him. He said he was just tired. He'd lived enough. Just wasn't worth the hassle anymore. Livin'…Said it was time for him to go. Just wanted to get it over with. It was sad. He told me that life was too short to be a sad person. Got to enjoy it. Said he'd enjoyed his." Nathan looked at Ray. He was no longer looking at the floor, but at him. "I think he'd be happy now. Don't you?"

Ray smiled. He jumped up and hugged Nathan. They were dancing around the room and hugging. "I don't care about the rest of it, whether we're caught or not. It's fuckin' over," Ray said.

Nathan knew exactly how he felt. Something hanging over your head so long, finally over. You're scared and finally get through it. Like a weight lifted.

They took turns showering, hit the mini-bar, got dressed and headed back downstairs. He and Ray hustled to the bar. It was empty. They decided to order drinks and beers. "Put it on my room tab please. Lou O'Shea, 749."

Ray started laughing. "You've been doing that since we've been here, haven't you?"

Nathan said, "Maybe."

"Any on mine?"

Nathan smiled. "You know I wouldn't screw my little buddy."

The waitress came and they greedily drank the beer down. They ordered another and clinked glasses with the drinks. Nathan motioned to the waitress to put the drinks on his tab.

"Mr. Magnanimous," said Ray.

"Somethin' I was wonderin', Ray. How did you get the cocaine past airport security?"

"I keistered it."

"What?"

Ray said, "I put it in a baggie, put Vaseline on the baggie and jammed...."

Nathan said, "No, no ,no ,no no. Don't wanna' know."

***

The next morning on the way to the airport they stopped at the largest bank in town, Citibank. Nathan opened an account with $3,716,428 and set it up where Crestwood could bill the bank directly. When the bank paid the bill, the bank would automatically add $2,000 a month for incidental expenses for Betty and Dotty. He picked up account signature cards for Terri before leaving the bank.

One more stop in town, the post office, where he mailed the cards and account information to Terri. He didn't want to have anything on him if checked at Customs.

***

The flight home was even longer, with four connections before landing in New York. The six rushed ahead of their fellow passengers to get through passport control and Customs.

Gail, Stuart and Nathan planned to share a cab home. A quick trip, thought Nathan, until he looked at his watch. Maybe not so quick this time of day. Forty-five minute cab ride max and home. Seemed like forever since he'd been there. Home, brush teeth, shave the stubble, shower and drop in bed. Call Terri and unpack tomorrow, Nathan thought.

After a long but thankfully uneventful flight, what they didn't want to see were the long lines at Customs. Flight must have come in just ahead of them, someone pointed out.

Nathan got in the passport control line. Although long, the lines were moving quickly. At least he was ahead of the others.

Finally, his turn! The good-looking babe with the three screaming brats moved and he gave his passport to the agent.

The agent punched his passport number into the computer and started fidgeting. "Date of birth, please."

He gave it to the agent, thinking he'd never asked that before. Must have been the new security after the World Trade Center attack. "Wait a second. Isn't it in my passport?"

The clerk ignored him. "Purpose for your visit to Mexico?"

"Vacation." Out of the corner of his eye, he saw two men approaching. Customs Agents.

They stopped at his line and one said to him, "Please come this way, Sir." The other had positioned himself behind Nathan, blocking him in line.

He followed them meekly, hoping Avi and Ray saw him and could do something to get away. He didn't know what, but something. He was thinking, I'm done. Fucking murder. Those frigging guys going out the window like mountain goats in Cozumel. Someone must have seen it. Facing prison or worse at his age. Whatever. They had Jimmie's money. He'd do it again.

He followed the lead agent. Maybe the rest of them could slip out of a door or something, he hoped.

Nathan was led to a door that opened into a large room full of agents. They passed through to a smaller room with only a card table and four aluminum chairs. Oh, it's just to play bridge! Got to keep your sense of humor, Nathan said to himself. He was told to sit. Both men stayed in the room with him, but neither spoke. One sat beside him. One stood by the door. They were obviously waiting for a superior. Mother Superior, he chuckled to himself. What's with me? Must be nerves, he thought. He wondered what the interrogation would involve. He looked up. No dangling single bulb. I'm nervous, he realized.

After fifteen minutes of sitting, he asked, "What are we waiting for? I'm tired and I want to go home." Neither of the agents responded.

Okay, he thought. It's like that, huh? He drummed his fingers for a while then whistled tunelessly to fuck with them. Give them a little Chinese water torture.

Two hours later, three men entered the room, all in suits. Dark fucking suits! One approached him while the two original Customs Agents tried to squeeze out of the small room like something from the Three Stooges. But he didn't laugh.

"Nathan Melton?" one of the men asked him.

Wouldn't it be a trip if he weren't, he thought "Yes," he answered. He would have loved to "just say no" like the drug slogan.

The man read him his rights after telling him he was under arrest. I'll play along, he thought. He tried to think what an innocent person would say in this situation. Would they be afraid to be indignant? Or does being indignant mean you're covering up?

All he could come up with was, "First, I need to see some ID so I'll know whom to sue. Then I'd like to read your warrant." He thought that was pretty good for being under pressure. Maybe with more time he could've done better. All considered, it was pretty good.

The first suit handed him his ID while the other two started fishing in their coats for theirs. Nathan looked the ID over. It just said Robert Adams, United States Attorney, Southern District, New York. The other two showed IDs from the Securities and Exchange Commission.

What was going on? He passed them back their IDs. Still silent, one of them handed him the warrant. He started reading the legal mumbo jumbo, but tired of that quickly. Nathan skipped down, looking for the murder charge. He found the charges section and typed neatly were two SEC charges for securities violations.

He could have kissed them. Given tongue and swapped spit. Tooty-fruity SEC charge, not murder. Probably give him quiet time. Couldn't watch "Frazier" for a week or something, he mused, for the moment, at least, relieved.

CHAPTER FORTY

It took Nathan a couple of days to decide he may have been just a shade too happy about the SEC violations. The euphoria of not being arrested for murder, no matter how unintentional or accidental, wore away quickly. All it took was the drive to the Federal Courthouse in Manhattan and being locked up. He had to spend the night in a wing of the Manhattan City Jail where Federal prisoners were kept. Needless to say, it sucked.

Terri arranged for an attorney. The attorney got him bail the next day. At the arraignment Nathan arbitrarily pled not guilty.

In the discovery process, Nathan and his attorney learned that the SEC had received a tip. His attorney was able to discover who had provided the tip. It was one of the venture capital firms, incensed over the profit that Nathan made on his stock. They felt the profit should've rightfully been theirs.

Never mind the fact the greedy bastards had already made a ton of money on the deal. Having cashed in over a year ago they were long out of the picture, and the profits.

His attorney argued that he had brokers buying in a blind trust as the price fluctuated. Didn't wash. It was true, but didn't wash.

The last quarter was what did him in. Concerned he wouldn't be able to get enough stock, Nathan bought too much. His bad luck!

After a lengthy negotiation with the U.S. Attorney's office, he settled and pled guilty to insider trading. He agreed to a twelve-to-eighteen month sentence at a Federal Prison Camp and to a fine of five million dollars. According to his attorney, the judge would probably be lenient if the fine were paid beforehand, so he paid it. Still left him with a lot of money. His attorney said that he'd get the low end of the sentence and he might shave something off the 12 months being a first-time offender.

While out on bond Nathan continued working, selling some of his stock as share prices slowly went up, cresting at $88 a share. He negotiated a nice severance package and left the company in the good hands of Harvey. His staff told him they would do another startup when he got out. They were all rich, him more so after the severance package, which covered the fine.

His staff had been forced to help the government in their case against Nathan so they wouldn't be charged with the same offense. They felt bad, of course, about cooperating with the prosecution, but he told them not to worry about it. Wasn't America great?

During the all-too-quick six months out on bond, he enjoyed himself while selling his condo and getting the rest of his affairs in order.

The guys threw him a going away party at the bar his last night and there was a huge turnout. He was heartened at the many wellwishers who partied with him the day before he was to be sentenced. The open bar probably didn't hurt either.

Ken asked, "What did you do, Nathan?"

"Officers of the company have to show how many shares they own of the company on a quarterly statement to the SEC and the public. I sold some of mine and bought others without telling."

"So," said Ken. "As long as you end up with what you're supposed to have, what's the difference?"

Nathan said, "Sometimes I ended up with more."

"So?" said Ken.

Nathan said, "So it's illegal. I'm looking at anything from probation to up to twelve months in prison."

"Doesn't sound right to me," said Gail.

Nathan said, "If you're looking for an argument from me, it ain't happening."

"You should haul ass, Nathan. You got the money," said Lou. He was right. Nathan should.

It went like that all night. Toward the end, Terri pulled him away and said a small group wished to have a drink with him in the back room. He followed and was mobbed by Ray, Lou, Avi, Julie, Dave, Marie, Stuart and Ken.

Avi called them to order as Nathan and Terri entered. "This is the first time we've been together since our quest began." Nodding at Nathan, he said, "Shame the reason, but I think it's time for congratulations." In front of each was a cognac snifter. "A toast," said Avi, as he raised his snifter. "To us, for doing the right thing in helping a very deserving man and his family." In unison, "To our friend Jimmie Collins." Laughter rang out in the back room.

***

Afterward, Nathan spent what would likely be his last night as a free man for a while with Terri. The woman he loved. Tears were shed and vows were made.

Before leaving, he said, "You know, Terri, I'm proud of myself, proud of you and the rest of the group. We did something right, something good. Not often you get a chance to do that. We helped our friend Jimmie."

The next morning he reported to court for sentencing. In a snit, the judge sentenced Nathan to thirty months and made the recommendation that he serve his time as far from home as possible, at the Federal Prison Camp in Jesup, Georgia. The judge also gave him three years "supervised release," which was basically parole, and suspended him from having any SEC involvement for five years. The judge also ordered him to sell all shares in the company. He almost laughed when the judge imposed that part of the sentence. That's what got him in trouble in the first place, selling his stock.

He'd probably have gotten the chair if he hadn't paid the fine, he thought. "So much for leniency," he said to his attorney, who replied they would appeal as the U.S. Marshall led him away.

Terri was sitting in the visitor's section of the courtroom and he smiled at her, mouthing the words" I love you."

She made a thumbs-up sign and said, "I love you, too."

Made in the USA